R.I.C.O.

R.I.C.O.

C.J. Hudson

www.urbanbooks.net

Urban Books, LLC
300 Farmingdale Road, NY-Route 109
Farmingdale, NY 11735

ISBN 13: 978-1-64556-372-3
ISBN 10: 1-64556-372-3

First Mass Market Printing October 2022
First Trade Paperback Printing April 2021
Printed in the United States of America

10 9 8 7 6 5 4 3 2 1

Distributed by Kensington Publishing Corp.
Submit Orders to:
Customer Service
400 Hahn Road
Westminster, MD 21157-4627
Phone: 1-800-733-3000
Fax: 1-800-659-2436

R.I.C.O.

by

C.J. Hudson

R.I.C.O.

The Racketeer Influenced and Corrupt Organizations Act is a United States federal law that provides for extended criminal penalties and a civil cause of action for acts performed as part of an ongoing criminal organization.

Chapter 1

Sunny wasn't a fool. She wasn't stupid by any stretch of the imagination. At 20 years old, she knew all too well what her father did for a living. The construction company he owned was a good front, but selling kilos of cocaine and bundles of heroin was how he'd amassed his immense wealth.

In her father's eyes, Sunny could do no wrong. She was the apple of his eye, and because of it, none of the young men in the neighborhood would come near her. They'd all heard the stories, some fabricated, some true, about how vicious he could be when it came to his first seed. He was very protective of her, which, to Sunny, turned out to be a blessing and a curse. It was a blessing because she didn't have to worry about anyone fucking with her. It was a curse because no one would fuck with her, especially the young men.

At an age when her hormones had taken over, and her body had matured faster than her father would like, Sunny desperately wanted some male attention. Her sexual urges were increasing by the day, and she didn't know how much longer she could ward them off. Luckily for her, one young man threw caution to the wind. His name was Jamaal. For three months, he'd noticed how other young men steered clear of her. He'd also taken notice of how her body had filled out, and he couldn't wait to rub his horny little mitts all over it. Because he was new to the area, he hadn't yet fully heard about Sunny's father's reputation. All he'd been told was not to fuck around with the young lady with the golden tanned skin. When he asked why, all he was told was, "because her daddy be on some other shit."

Jamaal shrugged it off, figuring that if he didn't mistreat the young lady, he would have nothing to fear from her father. It had been only two weeks since Sunny and Jamaal had started seeing each other, so he was more than surprised when she suggested that he come over to her house. Because he had a car, there would be no problem for him to get there. Like any other horny male trying to get a nut without getting his head blown off, Jamaal was leery of going to her house that time of day, but, as usual, lust won out over common sense.

Is the coast clear? he texted her as he parked ten houses down.

Nigga, the coast been clear. Bring yo' scary ass on.

Jamaal smiled as he subconsciously tugged at his crotch. He couldn't wait to dig into Sunny's juicy middle. Conquering her would cause his reputation in the streets to soar. He would be "the man." He thought about leaving his car where it was currently parked but decided to move closer to her house. That way, if her father came home suddenly, he could make a run for it. After slowly driving past her house, he hit a U-turn and parked a few houses down. For a few seconds, he just sat there, nodding his head to Lil Wayne's hit song "Lollipop." He smiled as he thought about the sexual positions he was going to put Sunny in. Jamaal was so turned on that when he got out of the car, his dick poked out like a javelin. As Sunny had told him to do, Jamaal went to the side door of the garage and let himself in. After taking a few steps inside of the garage, Jamaal froze. The young man nearly pissed himself when he looked up and found himself staring directly into the lens of a security camera. He was just about to turn around and haul ass when another door on the other side of the garage opened.

"Nigga, come on," Sunny told him, peeking out the door. Jamaal looked at the camera, then back at Sunny. "What?" she asked, following the trail of his eyes. "Nigga, I turned that shit off as soon as my father left. Bring yo' ass on in here."

His sense of fear now gone, Jamaal confidently strolled toward the door, giving the camera the finger on the way there.

"Don't get cocky, muthafucka," Sunny said.

Jamaal shrugged. "You said that the camera was off, right? Fuck it."

Once Jamaal was inside, Sunny led him to a large, black, leather sofa in the basement. His eyes were glued to her thick ass as she walked in front of him. If he didn't know any better, he would have sworn that it had gotten bigger since they'd met.

After taking a seat on the couch, Jamaal looked around and marveled at a few of the nice things they had. Hanging on the wall directly across from the sofa was a seventy-inch Sony big-screen television. Sitting on each side of it were two six-foot speakers. Jamaal could only imagine how loud it was down there when the volume was on full blast. He looked to his left and noticed a picture hanging on the wall. An older man, who Jamaal presumed to be Sunny's father, was smiling and had his arms wrapped tightly around an attractive female. Jamaal figured her to be Sunny's mother. Interested, he got up and walked over to it.

"Your parents?" he asked.

"Yes."

Something odd then occurred to Jamaal. "You know, sometimes you talk about your father, but you never talk about your mother. Why is that?"

Sunny glared at him for a few seconds before speaking. "Look, nigga, are you here to play Twenty Questions about my parents, or are you here to fuck?"

"Damn, ma, my bad," he said, sliding back down next to her.

Truth be told, he really didn't give a damn about her parents one way or the other. He was just nosy.

As soon as his ass hit the seat, Sunny was all over him. Placing her hand on his thigh, she leaned over and began kissing him passionately. After squeezing his thigh a few times, she let her hand slide up to his crotch. Although Sunny had never actually had sex before, she had played with a dildo once or twice, so she wasn't afraid of the pain that most times accompanied virgins. Jamaal was mildly shocked by her aggressiveness, but he quickly recovered and took charge.

As Sunny squeezed and massaged his dick through his sweatpants, Jamaal undid the drawstring. When they were loose enough, he pulled them down so that his dick would pop out. In his opinion, Sunny was acting like a real freak, so Jamaal decided to raise the stakes. He removed his lips from hers and whispered in her ear, "Hey, you wanna suck my dick?"

Sunny froze. She hadn't expected him to ask her to do that. She wasn't mad. She'd just never sucked a real live dick before. Practicing giving head on dildos was one thing but sucking on some real human meat was something different altogether. With her hand wrapped around his dick, she pulled back a little.

"You want me to do what?"

"I . . . uh . . . I mean . . . never mind," Jamaal said, thinking that he'd gone too far.

The last thing he wanted to do was piss her off and have to leave with blue balls. He leaned in to kiss her again but was stopped by her hand on his chest. She looked into his eyes and then down at his rock-hard dick. It looked so good to her.

It had never crossed her mind to give him a blow job, but now that she'd been presented with that option, she was seriously considering it. She stroked it a few times and felt it throb in her palm. Her pussy, already moist, became super wet. Sunny looked back up at him and smiled devilishly. Softly biting her bottom lip, she glanced at his pole one last time before lowering her head down to his crotch. She stopped just inches above his dick head. Lewd thoughts rushed through her head as she licked her lips.

If I'm gonna do this shit, I might as well go all the way, she reasoned.

"Oh my God, that feels so fuckin' good," Jamaal moaned as her lips wrapped tightly around his member. Just like she had on the dildo, young Sunny bobbed her head up and down. Her father would break her neck if he knew what his sweet, precious daughter was doing in his basement. Jamaal placed his hand on top of her head. He heard her gag as he pumped in and out of her mouth. Although Sunny was enjoying sucking dick, she was ready to be penetrated. She reached up and grabbed Jamaal's wrist to stop him from forcing her head up and down. She then got up from the couch and took off her shorts. Jamaal's smile widened when he saw her vagina.

"Got a condom?" she asked, eyebrows raised. As horny as she was, she wasn't about to have unprotected sex with him. Jamaal, on the other hand, wanted to feel every piece of her body. That was why he purposely didn't bring one. He was hoping that she would want him enough to forgo using one.

"Nah, I forgot to stop and get one," he lied. But Sunny was one step ahead of him. She reached down on the floor and picked up her shorts. Reaching into the right pocket, she pulled out a Trojan.

"Here, slick-ass nigga. Put it on."

Disappointment spread across Jamaal's face. He wanted nothing more than to feel Sunny's sweet walls. She crossed her arms and waited while he rolled it onto his dick. When he was done, she straddled him, reached down, and grabbed his meat. Just as she was getting ready to insert it into her young, virgin hole, she heard the front door open and close.

"Oh shit, my father's here," she half-yelled, half-whispered.

"What? What the fuck you mean your father's here? I thought you said that he wouldn't be back until like five o'clock."

Sunny looked at him as if he were crazy.

"Nigga, apparently, I was wrong. What, you gonna hang around here and ask him why he's home so soon, or are you gonna do the smart thing and get the fuck outta here?"

Jamaal didn't have to be told twice. As badly as he wanted to dig into Sunny's goodness, it wasn't worth dying for. As soon as he put on his clothes, he bolted out the same door he came in and headed for his car. He was so nervous, he nearly tripped over his own feet on the way there. Once inside his vehicle, Jamaal wasted little time gunning the engine and heading down the street.

"Fuck," he screamed at the top of his lungs. He was so close to getting that pussy, he could still smell it.

Meanwhile, Sunny, worried about how her father would react if he caught her in the house with the young man, grabbed her cell phone, and headed straight for a closet. She didn't go anywhere without her cell phone, so if her father saw it, it would be a dead giveaway. She hadn't seen her father go into this particular closet in nearly a year and prayed to God that there wasn't any reason for him to go in it today. No sooner had she gotten settled in it, she heard footsteps coming down the stairs. She did her best to keep extremely still, knowing that she would be in deep shit if he caught her. When Sunny heard her father talking, she realized that he wasn't alone.

A few minutes later, she heard her father go back upstairs. As soon as he was gone, the man who had come in with him pulled out his cell phone and made a call. Being the nosy teenager that she was, Sunny strained her ears, trying to hear what he was saying. She couldn't hear everything, but the little she did hear could have a catastrophic effect on her life, but the decision she had to make was an easy one.

Detective Anthony Warren sat in the passenger's seat of a black government-issued Crown Victoria munching on a slice of pizza. This was the day he'd been waiting for. He was about to make the biggest bust in his life, and his mood reflected his enthusiasm. His partner, however, Detective Harold Little, didn't share his conviction. In his opinion, the bust needed to be set up for several more weeks.

In his partner's zeal to become captain of the precinct, he was determined to bring down the biggest dope dealer in the city. The acting captain was only six months from retirement. The mayor would have to name a successor soon. Even though Detective Warren was younger than his coworkers, everyone in the department knew that he was the logical choice to be the next captain. Outside of the mayor, no one else knew that the only reason Warren was being fast-tracked was because of who his father was.

"What the fuck is your problem?" Warren asked, chomping down on another bite of pizza.

"I just don't know if this is the way to go about this, man. In my opinion—"

"I don't remember asking you for your fuckin' opinion," Warren spat, cutting his partner off.

Little's jaw clenched. Although the two of them worked together, he wasn't particularly fond of Warren. Actually, he couldn't stand him. "Well, I'm going to give it to you anyway. In my opinion, this bust feels like it's rushed."

"Rushed? What the fuck do you mean it feels rushed? Let me tell you something, Harold. This fuckin' scumbag has been selling poison to the neighborhood for the last ten-plus years. In two days, his ass is going *down*. It's time for his black-ass chickens to come home to roost."

Little glared at Warren. It was rumored around the precinct that he was a borderline racist. Now that Little thought about it, there were times when Warren would make sly comments about people of color. At the time, he took the comments in stride, feeling that his partner was just trying to lighten the mood. But now, he saw that he'd been terribly mistaken. His partner was, in fact, a prejudiced man.

Warren saw the fire in his partner's eyes and backed off. "Look, partner, I didn't mean it the way it sounded. I was just—"

"Don't worry about it. As soon as you finish your food, we'll put the final nail in this dude's coffin. You're right. It's time for his black-ass chickens to come home to roost," Little said sarcastically.

Chapter 2

Darnell McCord sat in his high-rise office, leaned back in his leather high-back chair, and with his eyes closed, his toes curled inside of his shoes, a low moan emitted from his throat as a brown-skinned honey took his manhood deep into her mouth. She was practically sucking the skin off his dick. He'd only planned on coming to the office to sign a few documents and go over some paperwork. Once he got there, however, a surprise awaited him. The wife of a man he'd recently fired was in his office. Her husband's source of income was all they had coming into their household. Losing his job would devastate their family. She'd tried to get him to go to his boss and beg for his job back, but he'd refused. His stubbornness had left her no choice but to take matters into her own hands. As soon as he left that morning to look for another job, she made her way over to the offices of McCord Construction.

"Your husband was caught sleeping on the job. That is something I am not going to tolerate," he'd told her.

"I understand, sir. But if you look at his work record, I'm sure that you can agree that he has been a model employee. He comes here every single day and works his ass off for you. How many workers do you have that have perfect attendance like my husband? Not many, I'm sure."

Darnell didn't have the heart to tell her that her husband had occasionally used some of his vacation days to take off from work. He knew from one of his many sources that whenever her husband did this, it was because he was posted up in a cheap motel fucking her sister. They would often meet at some time in the afternoon and screw the day away. Darnell really didn't give a shit as long as when he was at work, he did his job. But he wasn't going to pay his workers to sleep on his time.

"What's your name?" Darnell asked.

"Theresa."

"Look, Theresa, I'm sorry, but if I let your husband get away with sleeping on the job, everyone else is going to think that they can get away with that bullshit. It makes me look weak and soft as shit. Your husband is just going to have to learn a lesson from this. Have a nice day," he said, turning his back to her.

As he stared out of the window, he closed his eyes and fantasized. His dick grew hard as he thought about the voluptuous woman. He wasn't surprised at her actions, though. It wasn't the first time that a woman had visited him on behalf of her spouse, and more than likely, it wouldn't be the last. Darnell knew just how this would play out, so he waited patiently. It didn't take long for the woman to walk around his desk to try to negotiate.

"Please, Mr. McCord, are you sure that there's nothing I can do to change your mind? We have two kids and just bought a house. My husband really needs this job."

Darnell looked up at her. Her light brown eyes held the tears of a desperate woman at the end of her rope. And that was just the way he liked it. He leaned back in his chair and interlocked his fingers behind his head.

"You know, Lawrence is a good worker, so I guess I could be convinced to hire him back. But the question is, what are you willing to do to make that happen?"

Theresa looked down at Darnell's crotch and noticed that he had a raging hard-on. The fact that he wasn't even trying to conceal it told her exactly what he had on his mind.

"Anything," she said seductively as she slowly got down on her knees and reached for his zipper. As she unzipped his pants, Darnell could see her nipples hardening underneath her blouse. It was obvious that she was getting turned on too. Theresa then proceeded to open her mouth wide and wrap her thick lips around his meat. She started gently sucking the head, but she had engulfed the entire length of his shaft before long. With each suck, she convinced herself more and more that she was doing this for her family. McCord Construction paid their employees exceptionally well, around $60,000 a year, and there was no way she was going to let her husband fuck up making that kind of money just because she wasn't willing to suck his boss's dick. Hell, she'd sucked other dicks for free, so this decision was a no-brainer. Theresa gagged slightly as Darnell's meat grew in her mouth.

"Damn, bitch," he moaned in ecstasy as he pushed it down her throat. Truth be told, Theresa was enjoying herself. Darnell's penis was at least three inches longer than her husband's. Her pussy suddenly got moist. She yearned to feel him inside of her. Abruptly, she stopped blowing him and stood up. Darnell frowned, thinking that she was calling it quits.

"Hey, bitch, what the fuck do you think you're doing? Get back on your knees and finish the fucking job."

With a lustful look in her eyes, Theresa ignored Darnell's command. Instead, she just lifted her skirt and pulled her panties down. After taking them off, she threw them on the floor and walked over to the window. She leaned against the glass, placed both hands on it, and spread her legs.

"Fuck me, Mr. McCord. Please, come, fuck me," she purred.

Darnell looked at her plump ass and smiled. With his dick pointing straight out, he opened his desk drawer and took out a magnum-sized condom. After slipping it on, he took his pants off. Darnell gave her ass two hard slaps before placing the head of his dick just inside her moist lips.

"You want this dick, bitch?" he asked, taunting her.

"Oh my God, yes. I want it."

"How bad do you want it?"

"Oh God, I want it *really* bad," she answered honestly. Darnell gripped her hips and started pumping in and out. Theresa's pussy sounded like a soapy washcloth being squeezed as he fucked her.

"You know, slut pussy is the best pussy," he whispered in her ear. Thinking about her husband suddenly caused Darnell to get angry. He just couldn't understand how a sister this fine could fall for a white boy. The thought alone caused him to pound her walls with even more force.

"Say it, bitch. Say you're a slut!"

"Oh fuck, I'm a slut. I'm such a fuckin' slut," she yelled.

"Say you ain't no good, bitch! Say you ain't . . . no . . . mutha . . . fuckin' . . . good."

Each word Darnell spat coincided with a thrust of his dick deep inside Theresa's love cavity. Because he thought she was a sellout for marrying a white man, Darnell took great pleasure in humiliating her. In fact, it was turning him on.

"Say it, bitch!" he yelled, slamming into her. Darnell was fucking Theresa so hard, the windows threatened to shatter.

"Ooooh shit, I just ain't no fuckin' good!"

Hearing her bend to his will pushed Darnell over the climax threshold. His nut was fast approaching, so he had to act soon. Pulling her back from the window, he withdrew his dick, spun her around, and forced her back down on her knees.

"Open your mouth, bitch!"

Theresa opened her jaws wide and got ready to receive her naughty gift. Darnell grunted loudly and squirted load after load of come into her face and down her throat.

"Oh shit, baby, that was some of the best pussy I ever had."

"So, can my husband have his job back?" Theresa asked, wiping his seed from her face.

Because he felt like being an asshole, Darnell just stared at her, thus giving her the impression that she'd been played. After about ten seconds, though, he let her off the hook.

"I'll have my secretary call him. He can report to work tomorrow morning. Have a nice day," he said, dismissing her as he pulled his pants back up.

A sense of relief washed over Theresa. In her mind, she did what she felt she had to do. A broad smile was plastered on her face as she headed for the door. As she was walking down the hallway, she passed the secretary's desk. The lady sitting behind it looked up at her, shook her head, and smirked.

"Don't judge me, bitch. You don't know shit about me," she mumbled loud enough for the woman to hear. Her mission now complete, Theresa strolled through the exit with her head held high.

For the last five years, Larry had brought home a steady paycheck. Food was always on the table. The bills were always paid. His family never had to sit in the dark because the electricity was cut off. There was never a time when his family felt that he would let them down. Now, all because of a night of lust and a lack of sleep, he was unemployed. It scared him shitless to think that his wife would leave him because he no longer had a job.

Larry had been sitting at the bar for the past three hours, drowning his sorrows in a bottle of vodka. In his mind, he felt that he needed to be intoxicated in order to go home and reveal to his wife that he'd lost his job. He cringed as he remembered the look on her face when they'd moved into their new house. He also remembered how happy his kids were. The apartment they were living in was nice, but nothing compared to the three-bedroom, two-and-a-half-bathroom home they were now living in.

No fewer than five times in the last thirty minutes had Larry contemplated going to Mr. McCord's office and begging for his job back. But that thought had disappeared almost as soon as it had entered his brain. Larry was a proud man. The last thing he wanted to do was go back crawling on his hands and knees. For a split second, Larry foolishly thought about trying to blackmail his boss. Although he had no way of proving it, Larry had heard the rumors circulating throughout the construction site about his boss being a drug dealer. He quickly laughed that idea right out of his head. He wasn't about to snitch on a man as wealthy and connected as Mr. McCord, especially when he couldn't prove anything. Larry held up his empty glass and shook it, signaling to the bartender that he was ready for another drink.

"You sure, buddy?" the bartender asked.

"Yeah, I'm sure."

The bartender hesitated. He didn't want to be responsible for Larry leaving the bar pissy drunk and having a fatal accident on the way home. "I don't know, my friend. You've been putting them down pretty hard the last few hours. Maybe I should just call you an Uber so that you can go home and—"

"Look, man. I just lost my fucking job, and I have to figure a way to pay for the house I just bought. I don't need an Uber or a counseling session. What I need is another drink."

The bartender picked up the bottle of Ketel One and looked at it. He was still on the fence about whether he would serve Larry another drink.

"Look, man, this is my last one. After this one, I'm going to have to go home and face the music."

The bartender nodded slowly and reluctantly poured Larry another shot. He just had to hope and pray that he wasn't giving the man the last drink he would ever have in his life.

"Thanks," Larry said, as he quickly tossed the liquor to the back of his throat. After swallowing his drink, Larry smirked and shook his head. He couldn't believe how hard it was to find gainful employment. Had he found another job, he wouldn't have felt so bad. But he'd been pounding the pavement all day and hadn't come close to getting hired. After paying his tab, Larry took a deep breath and slid off the bar stool. He wobbled slightly as he headed for the exit.

The bartender watched him intently. He was impressed. He didn't think Larry would make it five feet before he keeled over, but much to his surprise, Larry was walking as straight as an arrow after his initial wobble. Just as he was about to walk through the exit, a large man wearing a

Cleveland Browns jacket made his way inside of the bar. He had an angry scowl on his face, and he was clenching and unclenching his fists. The look in his eyes was borderline maniacal. His head swiveled around and came to a stop at the far corner of the bar where a man and woman were making out. Seemingly in a fit of rage, the man in the Browns jacket stormed toward them. He was so focused on the couple that he bumped into Larry and nearly knocked him to the floor. The man was halfway to the couple when the woman noticed him. As soon as she did, she tried to push herself away from her cuddle buddy.

"Stop playing, baby," the man said, openly fondling the woman. "You know I like to feel on those big—" Before he could even finish the sentence, the man wearing the Browns jacket grabbed him by the back of his collar and yanked him to his feet. The shocked man never had time to react before a punch to the gut doubled him over.

"Mike! Stop!" the woman yelled. She slid out from the booth and tried to grab Mike's arm. Mike responded by roughly shoving her back down.

"Shut the fuck up! You wanna cozy up with another man's wife, huh?" he yelled, looking down at the man he'd just hit. "Well, you picked the wrong woman, pal."

Mike picked up the man and delivered another blow to his midsection. Every drop of air seemed to expel from the man's lungs as he fell back down. Now in the fetal position, the man desperately tried to catch his breath while holding his stomach.

"Stay . . . the . . . fuck . . . away . . . from my . . . wife!" Mike screamed. A kick to the ribs punctuated each word. Mike then grabbed his wife and dragged her toward the door. The other bar patrons froze. They were shocked that the bartender hadn't made a move to call the police. Right after Mike had dragged his wife from the bar, a few of the men went over to check on the man that he'd assaulted. One of the patrons, a woman who appeared to be in her mid-thirties, walked up to the bar and glared at the bartender.

"Didn't you see that? Didn't you see what that savage did to that poor woman? He just dragged her out of here like some kind of caveman."

The bartender's mouth fell open. He found it interesting that the woman was angry about the way the man had dragged his wife out of the bar but hadn't said a thing about how he'd beat the shit out of the man.

"Why didn't you call the damn police?"

The bartender leaned forward and got face-to-face with the woman. "First of all, it's kind of fucked up the way you're so concerned with a man pulling his cheating wife out of a bar, but not with what happened to that poor slob over there lying on the floor."

"Well, I—"

"And second of all, why didn't *you* call the police?"

The woman opened her mouth, but nothing came out. She was like so many other bystanders. Most people wanted the right thing to be done . . . as long as *they* didn't have to be the ones who did it.

"That's what the fuck I thought," the bartender said. "But to answer your question, I didn't call the police because the police was already here."

"Well, why didn't he stop that guy? Where the fuck is he?" she asked, looking around, confused.

"He just dragged his wife out of here." The bartender then walked away, leaving the woman standing there shocked.

"Well, damn," Larry mumbled to himself as he walked out of the bar. He knew that policemen generally got away with shit that regular citizens couldn't, but this seemed way over the top to him. The sad part about it, he thought, was that nothing would ever be done about it. Even if she went to file charges against her husband, the so-called blue wall of silence would, no doubt, protect him. Larry just shook his head in amazement as he pulled up next to the curb. He knew that he was slightly inebriated, so he didn't want to take the chance of pulling into the garage and tearing off his rearview mirror or accidentally sideswiping his wife's car.

"I should have known that this bitch was going to be here," he complained when he noticed Kelly's car parked in front of his. Kelly was his wife's best friend of twenty years. He and Kelly had never seen eye to eye, but he tolerated her snide remarks and condescending attitude because he loved his wife. Well, today, she was going to have to leave because he had some things that he needed to talk over with his wife. Larry was just about to unlock his door and walk into his house when his cell phone buzzed. He thought briefly about ignoring it, but something in the back of his mind told him to answer it. He looked at the screen and was pleasantly shocked when he saw the name McCord Construction appear on it.

"He . . . hello?"

"Yes, Mr. Burns? This is Eunice. Mr. McCord has instructed me to get in touch with you and inform you that he may be willing to give you your job back, with one stipulation, of course."

Larry nearly jumped ten feet in the air. Whatever stipulation his boss wanted to impose would be fine with him if he could get his job back.

"Yes, of course. Whatever he wants."

"Well, as punishment for sleeping on the job, he's cutting your pay by two dollars an hour." Larry's smile faded. He didn't like that one bit, but after some quick thinking, he decided that he would still be making more than the average construction worker even with the pay cut.

"Mr. Burns? Can you live with that?"

"Yes . . . Yes, I can."

"Good. Report to work tomorrow morning. And remember, this is the only second chance you're going to get."

Eunice hung up before Larry even had a chance to thank her, but that didn't bother him in the least. He was just happy to get his job back. He didn't know what had caused Mr. McCord to change his mind, and quite frankly, he didn't give a shit. He was so happy, he danced from the front of the yard to the back of the house. When he was done celebrating, Larry unlocked the back door and walked through it.

The door led to the kitchen, which was attached to the dining room. As Larry stepped into the kitchen, he heard his wife and Kelly giggling. Being the nosy fellow he was, he stopped to see what was causing their laughter. However, it was a decision that he would soon come to regret.

Standing there, frozen with shock, Larry listened to his wife reveal to her best friend how she went about getting her husband his job back. Every sordid detail that passed over her lips and into his unsuspecting ears was like sharp razors slicing and cutting their way through his heart. Larry trembled with rage. He had no idea how she'd found out that he'd lost his job, but right now, he wasn't concerned about that. He was so mad that he couldn't see straight. He balled up his fists so tightly that his knuckles turned white. He felt like such a fool. Here he was thinking that Mr. McCord was giving him his job back because maybe he'd realized that Larry was a valuable employee—when the truth of the matter was that he was being rehired because of his wife's bedroom skills.

Larry wanted nothing more but to go into the dining room and murder his wife and her bitch of a friend. In fact, he'd planned on doing just that until he heard his wife mention his daughter's name. The thought of his kids growing up with no parents gave him pause. He would have to find another way to get back at her. With a sinister smirk on his face, he left from the back of the house and texted her sister. Now, he was going to fuck her every chance he got. After making plans to hook up with her, Larry got back into his car and pulled off.

"If it weren't for my kids, I woulda killed that bitch," he mumbled to himself. He thought about the irony in the fact that a policeman could beat the shit out of his wife's lover in a public place and not have to suffer any consequences, but had *he* done that, he would surely have been arrested.

Maybe I need a career change, he thought, an idea forming in his head.

Chapter 3

Two days . . . All he had to do was wait two days. However, because of his desire to be a super cop, Warren decided that it would look better if he took down Darnell McCord alone. No one, not even his partner, had a clue of what he'd planned to do. To speed up the process, he called Darnell and told him that he was out of product. The way he saw it, he was an inch taller than Darnell and at least twenty pounds heavier, so when he flashed his badge and told Darnell that he was under arrest for drug trafficking, he could overpower him, if need be. At least, that's what he thought. Warren pulled in front of McCord's house and waited for him to arrive.

Fifteen minutes later, Darnell pulled into his driveway. Two black SUVs pulled up to the curb shortly after. Warren watched as Darnell's goons got out and looked around. One of them, a thick-bodied, dark-skinned brute by the name of Turiq, walked over to Darnell's truck and opened the door. Darnell stepped out of the Escalade, looking like new money. Fresh Tims pushed against the pavement. His True Religion jeans and Polo shirt were clean and pressed. A twenty-four-inch, platinum chain hung around his neck. Attached to it was a cross adorned with one hundred tiny diamonds. Although he was in his mid-thirties, Darnell was still young at heart. He leaned over and whispered something into Turiq's ear.

Turiq nodded his approval, walked over to his truck, and hopped in. Less than ten seconds later, both SUVs were pulling away. After they were gone, Darnell made his way over to Warren.

"Yo, what's good? Let's go into the house and handle this business, my dude."

Warren could feel the excitement as he followed Darnell into his house. This was it. He was about to make the arrest of the year. He grabbed a duffle bag from the backseat and followed Darnell into his house. The two men went into Darnell's basement.

"Have a seat. I'll be right back."

Warren plopped down on the couch as Darnell made his way up the stairs. Warren listened closely. As soon as he was convinced that Darnell was out of earshot, he pulled out his cell phone and made a call.

"Hey, partner. Listen, I'm over at McCord's house now. I'm about to make the bust."

"What? What the hell do you mean you're about to make the bust? That isn't supposed to go down yet. Why in the fuck are you always trying to play super cop?"

"Look, I know when it's supposed to go down. But an opportunity presented itself, and I had to take it. I know what the fuck I'm doing. Just get ready to say hello to your new captain. McCord's coming. I have to go."

Warren quickly went to the recorder function of his cell phone and pressed *record*. Since he wasn't wearing a wire, it was the only thing he could do to get something on tape. He prayed to God that the prosecutor would be able to use it. Darnell came down the steps carrying a black duffle bag. As the two men exchanged bags, Darnell's cell phone went off. He looked at the message for a few seconds and smirked.

"Everything okay?"

"Yep. It's all good," Darnell said as he placed the bag down at Warren's feet. Warren was still looking at his phone when he bent down to pick it up. The cop never saw it coming as Darnell kneed him in the nose.

Blood shot from his nostrils and splattered on the carpet. The pain was so intense that Warren nearly blacked out. Once his vision cleared, his eyes bulged at the sight of a .45-caliber pistol pointed at his head. "What the fuck, man?"

"That's what the fuck I'm wondering, muthafucka," Darnell yelled. "I let you into my inner circle, and you're a fuckin' cop?"

"Man, I don't know who told you that bullshit, but I am *not* the fucking police."

"Oh, so now you're gonna insult me by lying to my face?" Darnell asked as he cocked the hammer.

"Wait a minute, man! You've got this shit all wrong." Warren started to panic. He had no idea how Darnell had found out he was a cop, but if he didn't somehow convince him that he wasn't, it would most definitely be his last day on earth.

Darnell looked down at the man and shook his head. He knew for a fact that Warren was lying. "You're not a cop, huh?"

"Fuck, no!"

Darnell slowly placed the barrel of the gun to Warren's temple. "You sure?" he asked.

"You damn right, I'm sure."

Darnell took a step back and sighed. For ten hard seconds, he merely stared at Warren.

"Sunny, come out of that closet."

Slowly, the closet door opened, and his daughter stepped out. The sight of her nearly caused Warren to shit on himself. If he didn't know it a few seconds ago, he surely knew it now. He was fucked—Royally. Desperately, he tried to engage his brain and figure a way out of this mess.

"Darnell, man, I swear to God—"

"Muthafucka, shut yo' white ass up! I went against some of my closest associates and sold dope to yo' ass, and this is the thanks I get? This is the way you repay me, muthafucka? Sunny, play the fucking recording."

Sunny pulled out her cell phone and pressed the *play* function.

"Look, I know when it's supposed to go down. But an opportunity presented itself, and I had to take it. I know what the fuck I'm doing. Just get ready to say hello to your new captain. McCord's coming. I have to go."

Warren's pale skin turned ghostly white. Although he knew that it was a long shot, the only chance he had to make it out of this predicament alive was to go for his gun. As fast as he could, he reached behind his back and pulled out a .380 Smith & Wesson automatic. He was nowhere near fast enough. Before he could even get it pulled around, Darnell put a sizzling hot hollow point into his right knee. Warren screamed in pain. He was still clutching his gun, but that lasted all of five seconds as Darnell shot him in the shoulder. The bullet's impact caused Warren's back to slam against the floor, which, in turn, caused the gun to fly from his hand.

Darnell turned his head and looked at his daughter. There was a frozen look on her face. She was truly shocked by the violence that her father had just displayed.

"Sunny, you okay?"

Her father's voice snapped her back from the land of the shocked. However, she was still unable to talk. All she could do was silently nod.

"Thank you, baby," he said, hugging his daughter. Darnell then took out his cell phone and went to the camera mode. When he pulled up what he was searching for, he turned the camera to his daughter.

"Who the fuck is this nigga?" he asked, showing her a video of Jamaal walking through his garage. Sunny's mouth fell open. She was sure that she'd disabled the surveillance system.

"I asked you a question, Vanessa. Who the hell is this muthafucka?"

Sunny's mouth suddenly became very dry. She didn't know what to say or how to say it. She knew that her father wasn't an idiot. She didn't want to lie to him, but she didn't want to admit guilt either. In some ways, she felt she was in more trouble than Warren.

"He . . . He's just a friend, Daddy."

"So, what the fuck was he doing in my house?"

While waiting on her answer, Darnell casually strolled over to Warren, who was struggling to get to his gun. His hand had almost reached it when Darnell's Tims came crashing down on his hand. The sound of bones crunching resonated throughout the basement. Darnell then picked up

Warren's gun and shot him in the other knee with it. The pain was so intense that Warren could no longer scream. Darnell placed the police officer's gun on the table, walked back over to his daughter, and got in her personal space.

"Little girl, did you actually think that I would give you the ability to disable every alarm in the house? I should kick your fucking ass for even thinking that I'm that damn stupid. But you know what? You wanna be grown? I'm gonna give you some grown shit to do." Darnell grabbed his daughter's hand and led her over to the fallen officer.

"You see this muthafucka here? He came here today to bust my ass. He would like nothing more than to see me rot in jail for the rest of my life, but that shit ain't happening. This cracka is about to cash in a one-way ticket to hell, and you're gonna send him there."

A look of confusion overtook Sunny. She replayed her father's words in her young mind and figured she must have misunderstood. "I . . . I don't understand."

Darnell smiled at her. In his warped mind, there was only one way to punish her for trying to be grown. And that was to make her do something that no father should ever ask his daughter to do.

"Let me ask you a question, honey. Do you like all the nice things I buy for you? Do you like living in this nice house and riding around in the nice cars I own? What about all the designer clothes that I buy for you? Are you ready to give all of that up? You're 20, and I was thinking about buying you a car as a surprise birthday present."

Darnell then pointed at Warren, who was now drifting in and out of consciousness.

"This piece of shit right here was gonna take it all away from us. He was going to try to put me in jail for the rest of my life."

"But I still don't understand, Dad. Don't you have one of the best lawyers in the world? Whatever happens, can't he get you off?"

Darnell stroked her cheek softly. A slight smile creased his lips as he looked into her innocent eyes. She had no idea that her innocence was about to be taken from her forever.

"Baby, you have so much to learn. Just because you have a good lawyer doesn't mean you can get out of every situation. Sometimes, you have to take matters into your own hands. Now is one of those times."

He looked at the stunned expression on her face and wondered about what he was doing. Even though he'd built quite the empire over the years and was thoroughly enjoying his success, Darnell looked forward to the day he could retire from the game. He didn't want all his hard work to go by the wayside, so he decided years ago that Sunny would be the one to carry the torch. Gently, he placed his gun in her trembling hand.

"Shoot him," he said, staring down at the fallen cop.

"Wh . . . What?" she asked, thinking that she'd heard her father wrong.

"You heard what I said. *Shoot his ass.*"

Sunny stared into her father's eyes and saw a cold hardness that she'd never witnessed before. It frightened her. She glanced down at the bleeding policeman and pointed the gun at him. Her hand was shaking so badly that her father was afraid that she would drop the pistol.

"I'm sorry, Dad. I just can't."

Darnell smiled and nodded his head. He wasn't surprised that his little girl would hesitate to do such a heinous act. After all, he was the gangster of the family. She was just a 20-year-old trying to find her way. He did wonder, however, how much she knew about his drug dealings. He smiled at his daughter just before sneering down at the fallen officer. After staring down at him for a few seconds, Darnell turned his cold, hard eyes on his daughter.

"You say you can't, but I say you will." Darnell walked over to the recliner he usually sat in, stuck his hand into one of the cushions, and pulled out a .38 revolver. With a menacing look on his face, he walked back over to where his daughter was standing and pointed it at her head. Sunny's head snapped around. Her eyes grew twice their normal size as she stared into the barrel.

"Someone in here is gonna die today. You need to decide if it's gonna be him . . . or you."

"Da . . . Daddy . . . wh . . . wh . . . What are you saying?"

"I think I just said it. Five."

"Huh? Daddy, what are you doing?"

"You're a smart young woman. I'm sure you can figure it out. Four."

"Oh my God, Daddy, please, tell me!" Tears were now streaming down her face.

"Self-preservation is the first law of nature. Three."

"Daddy, please, you can't be serious!"

"Yes, sweetheart, I'm very serious. Please don't pretend like you don't know where we get all this money from."

When Sunny's eyes dropped, Darnell's suspicions were confirmed. His daughter knew exactly what he did to acquire his riches.

"And I'm pretty sure that you've heard of some of the unspeakable things that I've done to people who've crossed me. Am I right?"

"Yes, Daddy," Sunny said softly.

"So, you're okay with me selling drugs and killing people for us to maintain this lifestyle . . . as long as you don't have to get your hands dirty, right?"

Sunny slowly raised her head and looked into her father's eyes. She'd never really thought of it that way. Of course, she wanted to maintain her current lifestyle, but murder?

"That's what I thought. Two."

Darnell pulled the hammer back on the .38. "Decide, Sunny. It's either you or him. Who's gonna live?"

Sunny's hand trembled as she raised the gun and pointed it at Warren. She glanced at her father and gauged the seriousness in his eyes. Would he do it? Would he really shoot her? His own daughter? His own flesh and blood? Did she *want* to find out? She tried to read him, but it was no use. With fear in her heart, she lifted the gun and aimed it at the now-unconscious officer. She hesitated for a few seconds, and it seemed to make her father angry.

"Pull the fuckin' trigger," he screamed.

Sunny jumped as Darnell's voice boomed out. Out of fear of her father more than anything else, Sunny pulled the trigger. The bullet entered Warren's eye socket, causing his body to jump involuntarily. A pool of blood quickly spread beneath his head. Sunny's arm dropped to her side. She covered her face with one hand.

"Why, Daddy? Why did you make me do that?"

Darnell's cold eyes softened as he walked up to his daughter and wrapped his arms around her. He gently took the gun out of her hand and placed it on the table. He kissed her forehead and prepared himself to tell her the real reason he'd forced her to pull the trigger. Despite his grown-people-do-grown-up-things speech, Darnell had what he felt was a legitimate reason for her to kill Detective Warren. After allowing her to cry on his shoulder for a full minute, he placed his hands on her shoulders and looked into her eyes.

"Sunny, you're 20 years old, so I feel that it's time we talked. I was going to do this after your party, but what happened today has sped up my timetable." Darnell grabbed Sunny's hand and led her over to the couch. He was about to begin speaking but frowned when he noticed that she was staring at the dead officer.

"Hey. Look at *me*. Fuck that dead-ass cracka."

Sunny was shocked. She'd suspected that her father could be a hard man when provoked, but she'd never witnessed it firsthand.

"So . . . Sorry, Daddy," she said, flinching from the sound of his voice.

"Vanessa, for the last eleven years, I've always tried to be there for you and give you the very best that life has to offer. Am I doing it the right way? Some would say no, but I disagree. In my opinion, parents have to do what they think is in their child's best interest. Now, I'm sure that the asshole lying over there on the floor felt that he was doing what was best for his family. But there was just one problem with that. What he thought was best for his family could've potentially hurt mine. I wasn't about to let that shit happen."

Darnell paused for a few seconds to make sure that he still had her attention. Then he continued.

"My point is that self-preservation is the first law of nature. Never, and I mean never, love anyone more than you love yourself. If it ever comes down to it being them or you, you make damn sure that it's them. Now, you asked me why I made you do this. I didn't. You chose to do that."

"But—"

Darnell held up a finger to silence her. "I know what you're about to say. I said that I would shoot you if you didn't shoot him, right?"

Her tears drying, Sunny nodded her head.

"Well, first of all," he said as he picked up the revolver and showed it to her, "this gun doesn't have any bullets in it. I was never going to shoot you, baby. I'd never do anything to hurt you. I was just testing you."

"But why?" she asked, relieved now that her father told her that his threat was a hoax.

"Because I'm grooming you to take over for me one day."

Sunny's mouth fell open. All this time, she'd believed that her father had sent her to a private school when she was younger to get a better education so that she wouldn't have to live a life of crime like him. But, in reality, he wanted her to one day fill his shoes.

"But I thought you sent me to the private school to—"

"I sent you to the private school so I wouldn't have to blow up a damn public school because some wannabe thug nigga was fuckin' with my daughter. In the hood, there's always some hood nigga tryin'a make a name for himself. Sending you to a private school, I didn't have to worry about that so much."

Darnell's declaration of wanting Sunny to take over his drug empire had her head spinning. It was a lot for anyone, let alone a 20-year-old trying to find herself.

"Wow, this is a lot to think about," she said.

"No, it isn't. There's nothing to think about. The bottom line is this. Do you want to have a boss or be the boss?"

Sunny pondered her father's words as he took out his cell phone and walked to the other side of the room. She strained her ears, trying to hear what was being said, but he talked too low for her to do so. When he came back across the room, he had a half smile on his face.

"I've got some good news and some bad news. I'm pretty sure that this has been a traumatic experience for you, so I'm going to let you miss a couple of days of school."

"Fo' real, Daddy? Thanks."

"Don't get too damn happy. Remember, I said good news *and* bad news."

"Uh . . . Okay. What's the bad news?"

"The bad news is that I'm going to have new carpet put down and have this basement cleaned and the walls painted."

The fuck that got to do with me? Sunny wondered.

"And since I don't want you around while the work is being done, you're gonna stay at Turiq's."

Sunny's face instantly seized into a frown. The last place she wanted was to be cooped in a house with Tariq's bitch of a daughter Jazmine.

"What? Daddy, I don't wanna be stuck in a house wit' that bitch!"

"Hey, watch your damn mouth," Darnell scolded her. He wasn't naïve. He was well aware that his precious daughter used profanity and probably did much worse when she wasn't in his presence. But as long as he could see or hear her, she was going to show him the proper respect.

"Sorry, Daddy."

"All right. And that's just too damn bad that you don't wanna be in the same house with her. Consider it part of your punishment for sneaking that bastard into my house. The only reason I don't end his miserable-ass life is that you saved me hundreds of thousands of dollars in lawyer fees and buying off a fuckin' judge. Now, go pack."

"Yes, sir."

While Darnell was talking, Sunny was plotting. She was literally seconds from getting her cherry popped, and her father fucked it up. Still, she was grateful that her father was letting her off the hook.

"Thank you for letting Jamaal slide."

Darnell's eyes tightened. His lips curled into a wicked sneer. "I said I wasn't gonna kill him. I never said anything about letting him slide."

Sunny immediately began to worry. She didn't know what her father was going to do. But she knew that it wasn't going to be pretty.

Chapter 4

Jazmine checked the time on her cell phone and saw that she had about ten minutes until her father doubled back to check on her. It was something he'd done ever since he'd caught her sneaking out of the house to go to a party. He would leave, tell her that he would be gone a few hours, and then burst back into the house, trying to catch her up to no good. But there was one thing that her father hadn't counted on. His own predictability. As a matter of fact, Turiq had gotten so predictable, Jazmine could set her watch by it. Normally, she would sneak a young man into the house or just sit back and get faded, but tonight, she had different plans.

She'd been setting them up all day. Since eight a.m., Jazmine had pretended to be sick. Her father had just gotten over a cold, so she decided to use that to her advantage and act like he'd transferred it to her. It was an Oscar-worthy performance on her part, but she was careful not to overdo it. When she heard the door open and close, she knew that it was just a matter of time before she got out of the house to party. Hearing her father come up the steps, Jazmine quickly pulled the covers up to her shoulders and pretended to be asleep. She could hardly wait for him to check in on her and then leave. In no more than thirty minutes, she wanted to be in the middle of the floor, shaking her ass. She closed her eyes just as he opened her bedroom door. His footsteps were heavy as he walked over to her bed.

"Hey, Jazmine, wake up," he said in his heavy baritone voice.

"Yes, Dad?" she answered, feigning sleep.

"Get up and get dressed. Sunny's downstairs. She's staying with us for a couple of days."

The mere mention of Sunny's name caused Jazmine's eyes to pop wide open. The last person on this earth she wanted to be bothered with was Sunny's spoiled ass.

"What? Can't she go somewhere else? I don't feel like being bothered with her behind."

Turiq took a deep breath. He was hoping that his daughter wouldn't react like this, but he should've known better. The two girls had never gotten along. They were first introduced at a barbecue thrown by Turiq when he moved from Baltimore to Cleveland. An unforeseen circumstance had forced him to plant roots in Ohio. He'd heard about the kind of cake that Darnell was getting in Cleveland and wanted a piece of the action. Pointed in the right direction through one of his Columbus connections, Turiq moved swiftly to secure a meeting with the C-Town shot caller. At that meeting, Tariq was given a take-it-or-leave-it-offer of being called Darnell's second in command. Turiq wasn't particularly feeling the idea, but he wasn't stupid. He knew that in this game, your time could be up at any moment. Plus, with the amount of money he stood to make working with Darnell, he could afford to be patient. After agreeing to Darnell's terms, Turiq decided to throw a barbecue and invite his new boss and his daughter. He hoped that the two young divas hit it off and would become best of friends, but that plan backfired in a hurry. From the second they locked eyes, it was evident that they didn't care for each other.

Sunny never wanted to attend the barbecue in the first place. She'd stayed up all night messing around on her computer and talking to her friends, so all she wanted to do was sleep all day. Darnell knew she hadn't gotten much sleep, so he made her go as a consequence for not going to bed.

On the other hand, Jazmine wanted to go to the movies and was extremely pissed off when her father told her that she would have to do that shit some other time. As they were being introduced, Sunny and Jazmine sized each other up. The first one to speak was Sunny when she made an unflattering remark about Jazmine's forehead. The comment earned her a hard stare from Darnell. Jazmine responded by making a similarly mean remark about Sunny's short haircut. Tensions ran high between the two young ladies for the rest of the evening, neither willing to give the other the satisfaction of conversation. Since it was apparent that no bond was being formed, they were both instructed by their fathers to avoid each other, Jazmine, in particular.

Aligning himself with Darnell had provided Turiq with a significant influx of cash, and he wasn't going to let his hardheaded daughter fuck it up. The two young ladies hadn't been within ten feet of each other since that day, but they were suddenly about to be forced to cohabitate for the next two days. Turiq sat on his daughter's bed. He had a good thing going with Darnell. Not only had his income tripled since he came aboard, but he'd also convinced Darnell to let him invest in his construction company.

"Look, Jazmine. I know that you don't like that girl, but—"

"I can't stand her ass, Daddy," Jazmine said, cutting him off.

"First of all, little girl, watch your damn mouth. And second, why can't you stand her? Give me a reason."

Jazmine opened her mouth to speak, but she quickly closed it. Truth be told, she didn't have a legitimate reason for disliking Sunny. Nor did Sunny have a good reason for disliking her. The two girls just rubbed each other the wrong way.

"Uh-huh. That's what the fuck I thought. Your bratty ass don't have one. Now, get up, get dressed, and take your ass downstairs. And if Sunny tells me that you mistreated her while she was here, I'm pulling them damn keys."

Turiq's last statement snapped Jazmine to complete attention. Being able to drive her car meant everything to her. Now, she was *definitely* going to be on her best behavior.

"I guess the little tramp is going to be chillin' with me, huh?"

"Yep," Turiq said, smiling.

Jazmine frowned. That was the last thing she wanted to hear.

Unlike Sunny, Jazmine wasn't a virgin. She'd felt a dick sliding in and out of her before. And tomorrow, she'd planned on rendezvousing with a young man she was secretly seeing. Well, to the general public, he was a young man. But the fact that he was 24 years old explained why she was seeing him secretly. Jazmine knew that her father would skin her alive if he ever found out. She didn't want to even think about what he would do to Rick.

Like Turiq, Rick was a drug dealer. However, his product of choice to distribute was marijuana. Jazmine loved to smoke weed, making their union a match made in heaven. Neither one of them, however, was under the illusion that they were in a monogamous relationship. As a matter of fact, Jazmine had planned on sampling some new dick that she was expecting to come to her house before she went to the party. But thanks to Sunny's punk-ass father, her little plan was now shot to hell. After Turiq was gone, Jazmine reluctantly climbed out of bed and threw on a pair of Nike basketball shorts and a T-shirt. She grabbed her cell phone and her laptop and headed downstairs. When she got to the living room, she found Sunny sitting on the couch with her arms crossed. Her father was sitting next to her talking to her.

Yeah, you'd better talk to the bitch. I'd hate to have to check her ass in here, Jazmine thought. She smirked when she saw Darnell wag his finger at his daughter.

When Darnell saw Jazmine, he got up off the couch and walked over to her.

"How are you doing, young lady?"

"I'm fine, Uncle Darnell."

"How have you been?"

"He ain't none of your damn uncle," Sunny mumbled under her breath.

"Did you say something, young lady?"

"No, sir," Sunny answered her father.

Darnell and Turiq looked at each other and just shook their heads.

"These two . . ." Darnell said as he and Turiq headed out the door.

"We'll be back in a couple of hours. Try not to kill each other," Turiq said as he followed Darnell outside.

"This is some bullshit!" Jazmine yelled when she was sure that her father was far enough away that he couldn't hear her. "I had plans tonight. But now, I gotta stay here and babysit yo' ass!"

Sunny stopped scrolling Facebook and looked up. She stared at Jazmine for a few seconds before setting her cell phone down next to her.

"What the fuck you mean by that?"

"Just what I fuckin' said."

Sunny smiled. Three seconds later, she stood up, walked over to Jazmine, and got nose to nose with her. "Let me tell you something, bitch. *My* father is King Shit around here, *not* yours. So, don't get it twisted! You ain't babysitting no-damn-body."

"Whatever, bitch," Jazmine said to the back of Sunny's head as the young diva turned and walked back to the couch. Without saying a word, Jazmine picked up her laptop and left the room.

Five minutes later, she returned with not only her laptop but also a glass of vodka mixed with orange juice.

"Look," she said after taking a few sips, "I am about to have some company in about ten minutes, so I'm gonna need you to get ghost."

Sunny laughed out loud. "Yeah, right, bitch. Where the fuck am I supposed to go?"

"I don't know, and I don't give a fuck. I just need you to be the fuck away from here."

Sunny looked up from her phone and smiled. "How much you gon' pay me?"

"Excuse me?"

"You heard what the fuck I said. How much are you gonna pay me to disappear? Since you want to be a smart-mouthed bitch, I'm going to charge your ass."

"Uh, excuse me, but yo' ass is the one in here bragging about how your father is King Shit of Cleveland. You should have some money."

Sunny gave Jazmine a condescending smile before reaching into her overnight bag and pulling out a wad of cash. "Bitch, I have plenty of money. But since you're acting shitty, I want *your* money."

"I ain't giving you shit."

Sunny shrugged and dropped back down on the couch. "Oh, well. I guess three's fuckin' company then."

Jazmine walked toward the couch.

Not wanting to be at a disadvantage in case the situation went to shit, Sunny stood up. Once again, they were face-to-face.

"I should beat the brakes off your ass," Jazmine threatened.

"Bitch, I wish you would try it. I'll mop this muthafuckin' floor with your ass."

Jazmine weighed her options. She wanted to swing on the little princess in the worst way but concluded that Sunny wasn't worth her losing her car over. Shaking her head, she backed up.

"You're not as dumb as you look, bitch," Sunny taunted.

That did it.

Fuck that car. I'm fucking this bitch up.

Just before she could take a step forward, the doorbell rang. Sunny smiled. She had Jazmine by the balls, so to speak, and she knew it. Jazmine looked at the door and back at Sunny.

"How much, bitch?" she asked, finally relenting to Sunny's demands.

"Well, it was gonna be fifty. But since I gotta be a bitch, it's a hundred."

"A hundred? A hundred *dollars?*"

"Nah, bitch, a hundred pennies. Hell yeah, a hundred dollars."

The doorbell rang again.

"Time's a-wastin'. That nigga ain't gonna stand out there forever."

"How do you know it's a nigga?"

"Oh, my bad, bitch. I didn't know you swung *that* way."

"Oh, I see you got jokes, bitch. I'll be there in a second," she yelled when the doorbell rang again.

"Come on, now. Beat it, bitch."

"Not without my one hundred and fifty dollars. Every time you call me out of my name, the price goes up fifty dollars."

Jazmine ran up the stairs with a frown on her face, got the money, and came back down. She violently pushed the cash into Sunny's hand.

Sunny smiled as she went into the kitchen. "I'll be in the kitchen drinking up y'all shit."

"The kitchen? You ain't leaving the house?"

"Leave the house? You a funny bitch," Sunny said, as she grabbed her bag and made her way into the kitchen.

"Fuck," Jazmine mumbled as she stomped to the door. She took a deep breath and tried to calm down. With a sexy smile on her face, she opened the door.

"Damn, baby, I thought you was gon' leave a nigga hanging," her beau said, walking in. He frowned when he saw what she had on. "Hold up. Why you ain't dressed? You don't wanna go to the party?"

"Hell yeah, I wanna go. But I found out earlier that my dad won't be gone as long as I thought he would. So, if you want this pussy, you better bring yo' ass on."

Jazmine grabbed his hand and led him to a door that led to the basement. Before they hit the bottom step, they were all over each other.

Bobbing her head to Lauryn Hill's classic CD, *The Miseducation of Lauryn Hill,* Sunny rummaged through the cabinets until she found what she was looking for. There was barely enough liquor in the bottle for her to fix a decent drink, but it was all she could find. She didn't like orange juice, so she moved some things around in the refrigerator until she found a bottle of cranberry juice. As she mixed her drink, she snickered to herself as she thought about how she'd extorted cash from Jazmine.

"That'll teach that bitch to disrespect me," she uttered. As she sat there sipping her drink and listening to her music, a wicked thought popped into Sunny's head. For shits and giggles, she tiptoed into the living room to spy on Jazmine and whoever was desperate enough to give her the time of day. But when she got there, the room was empty. She crept to the stairs and was about to go up when she heard sounds coming from the basement. Sunny pulled out her cell phone and activated the video function. As quietly as she could, she opened the door to the basement and descended the stairs.

I'll teach this bitch to talk shit, she thought as she lifted her cell phone and got ready to record. Even though Jazmine had the lights dimmed, Sunny could still take a good video. She looked at the screen and damn near dropped her phone when she saw Jazmine sitting on a couch with her leg draped over Jamaal's shoulder. Jamaal was eating her out like she was a Thanksgiving Day feast.

"Jamaal? What the fuck you doing down here?"

Jamaal jumped and stumbled back. Because he'd never seen the two girls together, he had no idea that they knew each other.

"What the fuck, Sunny?" Jazmine yelled as she grabbed a couch pillow and tried to cover herself.

"You know what? Nigga, you ain't shit! Just earlier today, you were over my house trying to get in my pants, and now you're over here eating this slut out?"

"Hold up. Did you just say this nigga was over your house earlier? And just who the fuck are you calling a slut?"

"Yes," Sunny said, folding her arms." And I'm calling *you* a slut."

Jazmine gave Sunny the finger as she glared at Jamaal. She'd wanted him to come over earlier, but he'd lied to her and told her that he had an "errand" to run. Now, she knew the truth, and it bruised her ego. He didn't have shit to do. He just wanted to be with Sunny more than he wanted to be with her, and that shit hurt.

"You lying piece of shit. You told me that you had errands to run, but now I find out that you were over at this ho's house trying to get some pussy?"

Jamaal looked from Sunny to Jazmine. He was confused as hell. The way they talked about each other, he would swear that they were mortal enemies, but here Sunny was chilling in Jazmine's house.

"Wait, y'all know each other?"

"Don't worry about that, muthafucka," Jazmine screamed as she started pulling her shorts back on.

"What the fuck you doing?" Jamaal asked.

"Nigga, what the fuck it look like I'm doing? I'm getting dressed."

A scowl popped onto Jamaal's face. He didn't know what was up with these two broads, and he really didn't give a damn. All he knew was that he'd come there to fuck, and there was no way in hell he was leaving without getting some pussy. Because of Sunny's dad, he'd missed out on the kitty one time today. He wasn't about to let it happen to him again.

"Nah, fuck that shit. I ain't leaving out of here without smashing something." Jamaal took his sweatpants off. His rock-hard dick was pointing straight at Jazmine.

"Nigga, you better get the fuck out of here before I—"

Jazmine never had a chance to complete her sentence as Jamaal pushed her back down on the couch. Without a second thought, he pounced on her. He then placed his left forearm on her throat and pulled down her shorts with his right hand. Using his knees, he forced her legs open. After gripping his dick, he got ready to ram it inside of her. The tip had just begun to enter when Jamaal felt something cold and sharp press against the base of his penis.

"*Sssss*, shit," he grimaced as he started to feel pain.

"Nigga, if you don't raise the fuck up off of her, I'll castrate yo' bitch ass."

Jamaal slowly and carefully pushed himself off Jazmine.

As soon as her lungs refilled with air, she got up and punched him in the face. She then ran to the other side of the basement, reached behind a picture on the wall, and pulled out a gun. With tears in her eyes, she stormed back across the room and slammed it into the side of Jamaal's head. He crumbled to one knee. Blood trickled down the side of his face.

"Bitch-ass nigga, I oughta blow yo' muthafuckin' brains out," she screamed.

Fearing for his life, Jamaal slid back against the wall. Jazmine approached him with murder in her eyes.

Sunny didn't know if she had it in her to pull the trigger, but she'd learned earlier that day the stain taking a life could leave on your soul. She walked over to Jazmine, placed her hand on top of the gun, and pushed it down.

"Look at me, Jazmine," Sunny said softly.

But all Jazmine could see was the piece of shit in front of her. She continued to stare daggers at Jamaal, who looked like he was ready to piss on himself.

"Jazmine, look at me," she said louder.

Jazmine slowly turned her head toward Sunny. She wasn't a dummy, though. Out of the corner of her eye, she made sure to keep a close watch on Jamaal.

"Jazmine, you don't want to do this. Trust me, I know. Give me the gun."

Jazmine thought about it for a few ticks. Jamaal had come close to violating her in the worst way, and she wanted him to pay.

"Nah, his ass gotta pay for this shit," she said cocking the hammer.

Jamaal's dark skin turned purple. He said a silent prayer and begged the Almighty to rescue him from the predicament he now found himself in.

"Oh God, Jazmine, please don't shoot my ass! Let a nigga live!"

"Muthafucka, shut the fuck up," Sunny yelled. She held out her hand and waited for Jazmine to give her the gun.

Jazmine's finger trembled on the trigger as she turned back to look at Jamaal.

"You know what, muthafucka? Even after tonight, I was still going to give it to you because I wanted to fuck you. But you just had to try to take it, didn't you, nigga? Fuck killing you. I should shoot yo' fucking dick off," she told Jamaal, slowly lowering the gun until it was pointed at his groin area.

Jamaal's eyes got huge. They began to water. His mouth fell open. "Wait, don't shoot. Please, don't shoot," he begged.

"Yeah, that's right, muthafucka, beg," Jazmine commanded.

Sunny chuckled. She thought the situation was funny as hell.

"He ain't worth it, Jazmine. Give it here." Reluctantly, Jazmine placed the pistol in Sunny's hand.

"You okay?" she asked. Jazmine nodded slowly as she unsuccessfully tried to wipe away tears. At that moment, it didn't matter to Sunny that she and Jazmine had never gotten along. All she saw was a fellow female about to be abused, degraded, and molested by a sorry-ass man.

"Let's go, nigga." Sunny waved the gun toward the steps, letting Jamaal know that it was time for him to get the fuck out. As they walked up the stairs, Sunny made sure that she and Jazmine were five or six steps behind Jamaal just in case he got the dumb notion to try something slick. Every few seconds, he would turn around and glare at Jazmine. He wouldn't soon forget the knot that was forming on the side of his head.

"Nigga, take your bitch ass on up the stairs and stop looking at my girl!"

There it was. A bond that neither of their fathers had been able to create between the two young ladies was formed in the span of half an hour. All because of a thirsty, lust bucket, adolescent male who couldn't take no for an answer.

"And the next time you see us in the street, nigga, go the other muthafuckin' way. Now, get the fuck out of my house," Jazmine yelled. He was still halfway in and halfway out of the house when she slammed the door, hitting him in the back.

"Damn, I know that shit hurt," Sunny said as Jazmine continued to stare at the door. "You sure you're okay?" she asked.

"Yeah, I'm good. I just can't believe that nigga tried to pull some bullshit on us."

"Damn, girl, I thought you was about to body that nigga," Sunny said.

"I shoulda bodied his ass."

"No, you did the right thing."

Jazmine gave Sunny a strange look.

"Why are you looking at me like that?"

"You seem to know a lot about how it feels to kill somebody. Is there something about you that I need to know?"

"Uh, no," Sunny lied. The two of them hadn't bonded well enough for her to trust her with that kind of information.

"You sure about that? 'Cause down in the basement when I was thinking about blasting that fool, the look on your face made me think that you weren't new to that shit."

Jazmine was digging into her business, and Sunny didn't like it. She quickly changed the subject. "What time is it? Didn't your father say that they were going to be back in a couple of hours?"

"It hasn't been that long. We've got about an hour left. Come on."

"Where the fuck are we going?"

Jazmine didn't answer. Instead, she moved to the kitchen and poured herself a drink.

"I would offer you one, but you're underage."

"So are you."

"I'm 20."

"So am I, and the last time I checked, the legal age for drinking is twenty-one, so don't start that bullshit. We're the same damn age, so if you get a drink, I want one too."

"Fine, bi . . . uh, Sunny," Jazmine said, correcting herself. After fixing them both a drink, she placed the bottle under the sink and replaced the liquor that she'd poured out with water.

"You sneaky bitch," Sunny said, laughing.

Jazmine shrugged and put the bottle back into the cabinet. The two girls stared at each other as they stood there, sipping their drinks.

"So, are we just gonna stand here and stare at each other, or are we gonna squash this beef between us?" Sunny asked.

"I thought we just did," Jazmine responded.

Sunny had no idea how much Jazmine appreciated her stopping Jamaal from raping her. As soon as she placed the knife to his dick and forced him to get off her, Sunny, in her eyes, immediately became her best friend. Jazmine walked over to Sunny and held up her glass.

"To a new friendship?" she asked.

"I guess so, bitch," Sunny said, clicking her glass together with Jazmine's. After taking another sip, Sunny reached into her pocket and pulled out the money that she'd extorted from her new friend.

"Here, girl. The only reason I made you pay me was because you were acting like a supreme bitch."

"Yeah, I know. Sorry about that."

"No, you ain't. Stop lying." The two of them burst out laughing.

"By the way, my father is giving me a late birthday party next weekend. If you want to swing through, that's cool with me," Sunny said casually.

"What the hell is a late birthday party?"

"A damn party that he was supposed to give me for my birthday a few months ago but didn't."

"Oh. Yeah, I'm down. I'll be there." After finishing their drinks, the two young ladies spent the next hour getting to know each other.

"Damn, I thought they would have been back by now. I wonder where the fuck they at?"

"Girl, that ain't shit but a fuckin' setup. They left us together for this long on purpose."

"You think so?"

"I know so," Sunny said confidently. "They did this shit so we could get to know each other." Jazmine slowly nodded as she pondered Sunny's words. The more she thought about, the more sense it made.

"Oh shit," she said as she ran to the living room and came back with her computer.

"What's good?" Sunny asked as she watched Jazmine furiously tap on the keyboard.

The one thing that Turiq didn't know about his daughter was that she was a whiz with computers. He'd slipped up and let her overhear that he had cameras in the house. He wanted to monitor what she was up to at all times. Being as good with computers as she was, Jazmine easily found a way to hack the camera system. Now, whenever she wanted to engage in some foolishness when her father wasn't at home, she would simply go to her bedroom and cause the system to loop. That way, when Turiq checked his cameras, it would appear that Jazmine had never left her bedroom. After disengaging the loop, Jazmine grabbed Sunny by the wrist and took her upstairs to her bedroom.

"The fuck are you doing?" Sunny asked. Jazmine smiled devilishly as she showed Sunny her computer screen. Sunny's eyes roamed over the video of an empty house. There were four separate scenes.

"Jazmine, what the fuck am I supposed to be looking at?"

Instead of answering her, Jazmine clicked on the scene in the basement.

"This is a video of the basement about an hour ago."

"An hour ago?" Sunny asked, amazed. "That's impossible. An hour ago, we were down there about to fuck up a nigga," she laughed.

"I know. I hacked the server and looped the video. I also spliced the video to make it look like we came upstairs right after they left. As far as my father knows, we've been in my bedroom since he left."

"Damn, you a sneaky-ass ho, I see," she said.

Jazmine simply shrugged her shoulders. "With a father as protective as mine, it pays to know how to get around shit."

"I know the feeling. My father be on my ass too."

The two young ladies chatted and got to know each other. By the end of the night, they discovered that they had much more in common than they originally thought.

Chapter 5

Sporting a broad smile and a rock-hard dick, Pee Wee lay back on his king-size bed with his fingers locked behind his head. His freaky side piece Flora had just reminded him how good she could be in the bedroom when the mood struck her. Either he was too dumb to know or too sprung to care that the mood only seemed to strike her when he broke her off a piece of change. He was still turned on by their little role-playing episode of him being a pastor and her being a choir member in his congregation. Pee Wee was indeed a sick, twisted individual and would surely burn in hell for the blasphemy he and Flora had just committed. He looked puzzled when Flora came back into the room with a twisted expression on her face.

"The fuck wrong with you?" he asked her.

"This shit ain't right. You got me up in here screwing in my best friend's bed. Where they do that shit at?"

"Everywhere in America, so miss me with that bullshit."

"Man, this shit just ain't right."

Pee Wee frowned. Her complaining was beginning to make his dick deflate.

"You know, that's funny. I ain't hear none o' this shit when you asked me to pay your fuckin' car note last month."

"I—"

"I my ass," Pee Wee said angrily. "And I damn sure didn't have to hear your mouth when you texted me this morning and asked me to help you because you were behind on your fuckin' rent. Now, all of a sudden, after the fact, you want to start feeling bad? Fuck outta here."

"I'm just saying, Pee Wee, my girl is in Cincinnati taking care of her sick mother, and we're in here betraying her like this?"

Pee Wee stared at Flora for a few seconds before bursting into a fit of laughter.

"Taking care of her sick mother? I thought you bitches told each other everything," he said. "That bitch hasn't been to her mother's house since she got down there."

A perplexed look fell across Flora's face. "Wait, she ain't in Cincinnati?"

Pee Wee just shook his head. "Yes, she is. Pay fuckin' attention. She's down there, all right. But she ain't at her mama's house. That bitch is probably somewhere in a hotel with her legs cocked up in the air getting fucked by her ex."

"And just how do you know that?"

"Don't worry about all that. Let's just say that her mother is a greedy bitch who would sell her own soul for a few bucks."

Flora felt like a fool. She couldn't believe that her friend hadn't spilled the tea to her about what she was planning to do. Flora just shook her head. She and her mother didn't get along all that well, but she could never see her mother betraying her that way.

"Now, enough about that bitch. I'll take care of her when she gets back. It's time for you to show me what that mouth do."

Although Flora still felt bad about her actions, her son needed braces, and she needed to find a way to pay for them. And besides, it's not like she wasn't enjoying the sex. She looked on as Pee Wee stroked himself back to hardness. Licking her lips, she crawled into the bed and slithered between his legs. Pee Wee moaned as Flora pushed her thick lips over the head of his penis and down the shaft. He was just beginning to enjoy the blow job when his cell phone buzzed. He ignored it and started pumping in and out of Flora's mouth. It buzzed four more times before finally getting on his nerves enough to make him answer it.

"Whoever the fuck this is better have a damn good reason for disturbing me," he yelled into the phone.

"Li'l nigga, who the fuck you think you talking to?" Darnell shot back. The sound of Darnell's voice caused Pee Wee to sit up straight. His dick popped out of Flora's mouth so fast, it sprang up and slapped her in the bottom of her nose.

"Oh shit, I'm sorry, boss. I didn't know it was you." Pee Wee hadn't been expecting Darnell to call. After he, Turiq, and the rest of the crew followed him home, he'd been told that after checking on the corner dope boys they employed, he was free for the rest of the evening. The fact that it was Darnell calling him instead of Turiq made him nervous. Darnell never called anyone but Turiq.

"So, what's good, boss?" he asked nervously.

"Whatever the fuck you're doin', put that shit on hold. We got some shit we need to handle."

"Oh, cool. What's going on?"

"Li'l nigga, stop asking so many damn questions. Just be ready in ten minutes."

Darnell hung up without saying another word. Pee Wee, whose real name was Preston, thought it was disrespectful that Darnell always called him "li'l nigga" when he was a year and a half older than Darnell. But he had the good sense not to speak about it. Pee Wee had introduced Darnell to a few cats who needed a supplier, and as far as he knew, the operations had become more lucrative because of it. In his opinion, he was doing a hell of a job. But that's the problem with having an opinion.

Not everyone shares the same one that you have. As soon as Darnell had disconnected the call, Pee Wee jumped out of bed and started getting dressed.

"What the fuck? I thought you wanted to screw some more," Flora said.

"Some other time, baby. I got important shit to handle." Pee Wee continued to get dressed until he noticed that Flora wasn't doing the same.

"The fuck is you doing?" he asked.

"Nothing."

"I can see that. Put your fuckin' clothes on. I told you I had to go."

"I can't stay here till you get back?"

"What? Bitch, are you high? Hell no."

"Fine, then. I'll leave."

"I know you will."

"Well, can I at least have a few dollars so I can get something to eat tonight?"

Pee Wee sighed as he reached into his pocket and pulled out a crumpled twenty-dollar bill.

This bitch, he thought to himself.

"Here, and don't think yo' ass is foolin' me," he said, throwing the money at her.

"This all you gon' give me?" she asked, ignoring his last statement.

"You damn right! I just gave your ass bread to pay your damn rent! And like I said, you ain't foolin' me. Yo' ass ain't hungry. You just trying to cop some fuckin' weed."

Flora didn't even try to deny it. She couldn't. She loved weed more than a fish loved water and copping her a sack was precisely what she'd planned on doing with the money. After getting dressed, she quickly left. She hadn't gotten ten feet outside of Pee Wee's place before she was texting her cousin to tell him that she was on her way to pick up a dime bag. Five minutes after she left, Pee Wee came out of his front door and was surprised to see Darnell and Turiq standing outside of Darnell's SUV waiting on him. The large truck looked even more daunting, with the two gangsters standing beside it.

"What's good, boss, Turiq?" He spoke to both men.

"Where's your cell phone?" Darnell asked in a no-nonsense tone.

"Uh, right here," Pee Wee said, unclipping it from his waist.

"Let me see it."

Without questioning his boss, Pee Wee handed him the phone. He was shocked when Darnell dropped it on the ground and stomped on it. The plastic and electrical device were crushed under the pressure provided by Darnell's boot. Darnell then reached into his pocket and pulled out a brand-new iPhone X.

"Here, take this. It's your new phone. Everyone in the crew has one." Turiq then opened the back door to the truck and motioned for Pee Wee to get inside. Thoroughly confused now, Pee Wee did as he was told. When he climbed inside and saw who the occupant was sitting next to him, he nearly passed out. Wrapped in plastic from head to toe was the freshly deceased Anthony Warren. His pale white face had begun to turn an awful shade of blue. Pee Wee was in a state of shock. He only snapped out of it when Darnell and Turiq got in the front seat and slammed the doors.

"Oh shit!" he screamed. "What the fuck happened to Jeff?"

"First of all, his name isn't Jeff, dumb ass. It's Anthony Warren."

"As in *Detective* Anthony Warren," Turiq added.

"Det . . . De . . . Detective?"

"Yeah, muthafucka, *detective*. You brought a fuckin' cop into our organization, fool."

"Oh God, boss, I didn't know, man! I swear to God I didn't."

Darnell and Turiq looked at each other for a few seconds before turning around and focusing their evil eyes on Pee Wee. Pee Wee could feel the anger radiating off his boss. He'd fucked up, but he had no idea how. He'd done all the necessary research on the man who he thought was Jeffery Coles, but somewhere along the way, he'd made a major miscalculation.

"Do you know how much money this little fuckup of yours cost me?" Darnell asked, seething. "The dope this muthafucka was buying from me wasn't going back into the streets. It was going into a police evidence cage so that they could use it later to send us to fuckin' jail, you fuckin' moron."

Pee Wee opened his mouth to try to defend himself, but the .45 caliber Smith & Wesson handgun Turiq had pulled and was now pointing at him pushed the words back into his throat.

"Are you a cop, muthafucka?" Darnell asked in a low but deadly tone.

"What? Fuck. Nah, boss. I ain't no fuckin' po-po, man!"

Darnell shook his head. "I don't know if I believe you, playa."

"Boss, I swear to God, man. I'm official."

Darnell looked at his second in command. "Yo', 'Riq, you believe this nigga, man? You think he's telling the truth?"

Turiq cocked his head to the side as if he were pondering Darnell's question. He then cracked a tight-lipped smile and slowly shook his head.

"Nah, man. I don't believe this lying-ass nigga."

Darnell looked at Pee Wee and shrugged his shoulders. "See, now we got a fuckin' problem, man. My dude Turiq don't believe you, and he's normally a good judge of character, so if he thinks that you're full of shit, then chances are that you're full of shit."

Turiq cocked his pistol and aimed it square at Pee Wee's forehead.

"I'ma miss yo' ass, li'l nigga," Darnell said, an evil sneer plastered on his lips.

"Boss, man, I swear, I ain't no fuckin' cop!"

Turiq blew Pee Wee a kiss as he got ready to pull the trigger. It was something that Pee Wee had seen Turiq do many times before prior to ending an enemy's life. He closed his eyes and got ready to meet his incvitable fate.

"Yo', hold up, my Turiq. I believe him," Darnell said, having a sudden change of heart.

Turiq's face turned to a mask of disbelief. "What? You believe him? Man, this nigga's lyin', fam."

"Nah, he's tellin' the truth."

"But I'm sayin', I done blew him the kiss of death and everything," Turiq said, practically begging to kill Pee Wee's dumb ass.

"Put the gun away, my nigga. He's giving us the real."

Turiq frowned as he put his gun back on the seat. He hated stupid muthafuckas. Pee Wee, in his eyes, was a stupid muthafucka. He didn't deserve to walk among the land of the living.

Darnell took out his phone and dialed a number. "Yo', Lard. You and Duck come and get this piece of shit out of my whip."

After disconnecting the call, Darnell stared so hard at Pee Wee, the young man nearly wet his pants. He jumped when the door opened, and Lard reached his large hands inside the truck. With one quick and powerful jerk, Lard snatched Detective Warren's corpse out of it. Pee Wee's eyes trailed Lard and Duck as they carried the body to Pee Wee's car.

"Yo, man, why they takin' that dead muthafucka to my ride?"

"Because, li'l nigga, I brought it over here. Yo' ass is gonna transport it the rest of the way."

"Uh, okay, boss, but where is it goin'?"

"You'll find out when you get there. Now, get yo' stupid ass outta my whip before I change my mind and let Turiq push yo' shit in," Darnell spat.

Pee Wee quickly got out of Darnell's truck and headed toward his own car. It was a smoky-ray-colored BMW with tinted windows, a state-of-the-art sound system, and eight-inch televisions mounted in the headrests. Being a part of Darnell's crew was the way to go if you aspired to be caked up.

"Yo, Duck, hold up, man. Don't put that fuckin' dead-ass cracka in the front seat."

"Boss's orders, nigga. You got a problem with it, take it up with Darnell." After placing the body in the front seat, they both walked past Pee Wee and smirked.

"The fuck is so funny?" Pee Wee asked.

"Yo' dumb ass," Lard replied.

Pee Wee started to say something slick but wisely thought better of it. Lard wasn't the one to fuck with. He was a six foot three, 295-pound mountain of muscle who routinely broke bones and snapped necks at Darnell's command. He'd come to Darnell's attention one evening while Darnell was watching the news. He watched amused as Lard manhandled nearly an entire police precinct. The overmatched officers had tried everything from Tasers to nightsticks, but it was no use. The raging Lard threw them all around like rag dolls. It took three hollow-point bullets to subdue the big man finally. After recovering from the gunshot wounds, Lard was immediately transported to Cuyahoga County jail. Booked with felonious assault and resisting arrest, Lard faced a steep uphill battle to beat the rap. His job as a bouncer wouldn't come close to covering his legal fees.

That's where Darnell stepped in. Not only did he pay Lard's hospital bills, but he also provided him with a top-notch defense attorney. The powerful lawyer got the charges reduced to disorderly conduct. It didn't hurt that Darnell had greased a few palms to make it happen. When Lard walked out of the courtroom, Darnell and Turiq were the only people there to greet him. After taking him to dinner, Darnell offered Lard a position in the crew. He'd been with them ever since.

Pissed off and disgusted about having to ride in the car with a corpse, Pee Wee jumped in the car and slammed the door.

"Nigga, stop slamming my door," Duck said from the backseat.

"What? Nigga, this *my* damn car," Pee Wee corrected him.

"Oh yeah, that's right. This is yo' piece o' shit-ass whip."

"Man, fuck you," Pee Wee said, laughing.

Pee Wee and Duck were cool. They had always gotten along. But Pee Wee had gotten himself in a sticky situation, and there wasn't anything Duck could do to get him out of it.

"But on some G shit, my nigga, you really need to be more careful about who you bring into the fold, playa. Ya feel me?"

"I feel you, dawg. I'm just glad Darnell gave me a pass on this shit. That fuckin' lunatic-ass nigga Turiq acted like he really wanted to blast me over that shit."

"Man, you know how that trigger-happy-ass nigga get. But what I wanna know about though, dawg, is that fine-ass broad we spotted coming outta ya spot tonight. That bitch got that good-good or nah?"

"Nigga, you have no fuckin' idea. That bitch is a stone-cold freak," he said, reaching over the seat to give Duck dap.

"Real talk, nigga?"

"Real muthafuckin' talk, nigga."

"Damn, my nigga, you oughta let ya' boy hit that."

"Well, she is a freak. Maybe we can tag team on the bitch. We gotta keep that shit on the low, though. She's Paula's best friend."

"What? Yo' bitch, Paula?"

Pee Wee nodded.

"Man, you's about a foul-ass nigga, bro," Duck said, laughing. "But on some more G shit, you oughta see if Darnell wanna smash."

"What?"

"Yeah, I'm tellin' you, fam, you shoulda saw the way he was staring at shorty when she came out of ya' crib. That nigga was damn near droolin'."

Pee Wee thought about it and nodded his head in agreement. Not only would it satisfy his sick, perverted, voyeuristic way of thinking, but it would also put him back in his boss's good graces.

"You know what? I'm down wit' that shit, man. I'm gonna call that bitch tomorrow and hook that shit up."

Duck shook his head vigorously.

"Nah, man, you know Darnell ain't wit' that shit. We can probably run a train on that bitch, but the boss man probably wanna smash that shit solo."

"Yeah, you're probably right."

"Shit, nigga, I *know* I'm right. Give me her address, and I'll text it to him."

"Why? I can just text it to him myself."

"My dude, Darnell already pissed with you right about now. He don't wanna hear shit you got to say. It's best if this shit comes from me."

"Yeah, that makes sense. Boss man is pretty salty at a nigga."

"Here. Write her address down on this piece of paper, and I'll give it to him."

Pee Wee scribbled Flora's address down and handed it to Duck, who, in turn, stuffed it into his pocket.

"Now, I was thinking my nigga, after this, we should—"

"What?" Pee Wee asked when Duck abruptly stopped talking.

"Darnell just texted me and said that he needed to holla at me right quick. Here, blaze this up. I'll be back in a sec."

Duck tossed a half-smoked blunt over the seat and into Pee Wee's hands. As soon as Duck got out of the car, Pee Wee grabbed a lighter from his ashtray and fired up. He took a pull and blew the smoke in the direction of the slain police officer.

"You know how much trouble you got me in, muthafucka?" Pee Wee then hawked up some phlegm and spat on the body. While taking another puff, Pee Wee starting thinking.

Why in the fuck are we still sitting here? he wondered. He took the new cell phone that Darnell had given him and turned it on. The picture of a clown popped onto the screen, causing him to chuckle.

The fuck taking Duck so long?

Suddenly the smile slowly vanished from Pee Wee's face.

Darnell just texted me were the words that Duck had said to him. But Pee Wee knew for a fact that Duck didn't have texting service on his phone. He was notoriously cheap like that. A sinking feeling began to settle in the pit of Pee Wee's stomach. The cell phone vibrated twice in his hand. Frantically, Pee Wee reached for the door handle and tried to escape . . . but he was too late. A loud, thunderous boom shattered the windows and set off the alarms of some of the cars nearby as Pee Wee's BMW exploded. Darnell and Turiq smiled as they watched the fire consume the BMW.

"Let's get the fuck outta here, dawg," Darnell told Turiq.

Although the response time to the 911 calls was reasonably quick, there was still nothing anyone could do. The bodies were burned and charred beyond recognition.

Chapter 6

When Flora got home later that night, she saw an eviction notice taped to her door. Although Pee Wee had given her money to pay her rent, Flora, in true weed head fashion, had smoked it up. With an attitude, she snatched off the notice and balled it up.

The two-family house she lived in wasn't all that, but it was a place to lay her head. She often complained to the landlord about the noise coming from upstairs. At least three nights a week, her ears were assaulted by various women's cries of passion. By her account, she'd seen at least six different women follow Victor, the young man, upstairs. And those were only the ones she knew about. In true landlord fashion, Mr. Parker told her that as long as the other tenant was paying his rent, he was free to entertain his company as he saw fit. The statement wasn't entirely true. There *was* a noise provision in the contract, but as long as Victor continued to convince some of the freaks he came across to let the 65-year-old landlord sit in a corner, watch, and jack off from time to time, he would keep turning a deaf ear to her complaints. When Flora heard the door to the upstairs open, she quickly jammed the notice into her pocket.

"I don't know why you're trying to hide that notice. I already saw it earlier when I came home. I guess Mr. Parker ain't too happy about you not paying your rent."

"Nigga, fuck you and Mr. Parker. Hell, it's only a few days late anyway," she yelled at him.

"Now, is that any way to talk to your future husband?"

"Future husband? Nigga, you sound crazy as fuck."

"Damn, baby, why so mean? Whatever it is, I didn't do it to you."

Flora popped her lips and rolled her eyes. She wasn't mad at Victor, but she was taking her anger out on him. Shortly after leaving Pee Wee's house, Flora went over to her cousin's place to cop a twenty sack of weed. Much to her dismay, some of his higher-end customers had pretty much cleaned him out. All he had was a dime bag for himself, and since he didn't want to share with his cousin, he told her that he was totally out. Flora was extremely pissed off. Even though Mark's weed wasn't the best in the neighborhood, it did its job, nonetheless.

"What's really good, baby girl? Somebody stressing you out or somethin'?"

"Hell nah. Look, my bad. I didn't mean to bite yo' head off."

"It's all good, baby. Let me pour you a drink."

Flora cocked her head and sized up the tall, thin, young man. On a good day, Victor weighed a good 150 pounds. Flora reasoned that if he got too fresh, she could kick his ass with no problem.

"Yeah, a'ight. But don't get me up there and try some funny shit."

"Baby, how long have we known each other? Have I ever come at you on some slick shit?"

Flora thought about it and had to admit that Victor had indeed never come on to her.

"Nah, I guess not."

"Of course not. You're like a little sister to me," he said.

Little sister? The fuck is this nigga tryin'a say?

Victor turned and headed up the steps. A sinister smile was plastered on his face. He knew what effect the "little sister" comment would have on her.

"Now, yo' friend, Paula? That's one fine-ass woman. I could see myself rollin' around in the sack with her."

What's good wit' this nigga? I know he ain't sayin' I ain't worth fuckin'.

When they entered his place, Flora was surprised to see that it was above-average clean. The last dude she was dating was a complete slob. After getting her comfortable, Victor went to the kitchen and returned with two glasses, a carton of orange-mango juice, and a bottle of Absolut Vodka.

"Absolut? You ain't got no Cîroc?" she asked indignantly.

Victor kept his cool. He just smiled and shook his head. He was a master at the art of seduction, and a woman like Flora was mere putty in his hands.

"Sorry, ma, it's all I got right now."

"Okay," Flora said, shrugging her shoulders. Since she'd already gone through the trouble of walking up the stairs, she may as well have a drink or two. She watched Victor as he poured their drinks.

"Tell me when to stop," he said.

Flora waited until the glass was about halfway filled before stopping him. Since he offered the drink, she intended to take full advantage of his generosity.

"Yo, is this juice cool, or do you want something else?"

"Nah, that's cool. Can I use your bathroom?" she asked.

"Yeah, it's right down that hall," he pointed.

When Flora returned from relieving herself, Victor had poured both drinks. She grabbed the glass that sat on the table in front of him and switched it with the drink that he'd set down for her. Victor looked perplexed at first, but he burst into laughter when he realized what she was doing.

"Hey, a bitch gotta be careful nowadays," she said.

"It's all good," he said, still getting a kick out of her paranoia. Flora had no idea that *both* glasses were laced with crushed Ecstasy pills.

"So, why were you so upset earlier?" Victor asked. He really didn't give a shit. He was only stalling until the pill kicked in. However, the story of her cousin selling all his weed before breaking her off did amuse him.

"I'll be right back."

Flora watched as Victor got up and walked into his bedroom.

"Hey, don't bring yo' ass out here naked. I know that damn trick," she yelled. Flora had seen that one before. The brother of one of her high school friends pulled that trick when she was a teenager.

When Victor came back out, he wasn't naked, but he had changed clothes. Instead of the Cleveland Cavaliers jogging suit he had on, he now rocked a pair of black baggy shorts and a white wife beater. But what he was wearing was nowhere near as important to Flora as what he had in his hand. Pinched between Victor's fingers was a super thick blunt ready to be lit and smoked. Flora's eyes lit up. Although the drink Victor had fixed for her had her feeling nice, smoking a blunt was what she really wanted to do. And Victor knew it. He'd studied Flora. He'd watched her. Many times, when the two of them had passed each other, he'd smelled the strong odor of weed on her person. He knew that she was a weed head. So when Flora told him about how her cousin had played her when she'd went to cop a bag, a lightbulb went off in his head. Even though he'd made a few sly comments, Victor had never really come on to Flora. He'd heard about Pee Wee and knew about him being a part of Darnell's crew. Victor wasn't a punk, but he didn't want that smoke. But tonight was just one of those nights when his dick was hard, and for some reason, he couldn't get in touch with any of his jump-offs. Victor was just about to light up the blunt when he heard Flora's car pull up. He decided right then that he was gonna either get some pussy or get shot down and suffer the consequences.

"What you got there?" Flora asked, eyeing the blunt.

"Just a little something to put you in a better mood. I'm sorry that your cousin didn't come through, but, hey . . . if you're still in the mood to smoke—"

"Hell yeah, I'm in the mood to smoke. Fire that shit up, Vic!"

With his smile widening and his dick hardening, Victor slid back over to where he was seated, dropped back down, and pulled a lighter out of his pocket. Placing the blunt in his mouth, he flicked the lighter and lit the tip. Victor inhaled sharply and savored the moment as the potent smoke invaded his lungs. He held it for a good ten seconds before letting it slide out the side of his mouth. He smiled as he nodded his head.

"This some good shit," he said. Flora cleared her throat.

"You okay? You need a glass of water?"

"Oh, I see you got jokes. Set that blunt out and quit playing."

Victor laughed as he passed Flora the blunt. He was counting on her not being able to resist. All he had to do now was sit back and wait for the pill and weed to do their thing, and it would be a wrap. His dick hardened as he watched her lips curl around the brown paper.

"You want another drink?" he asked.

"Yeah, I can go for another one. Damn, is it me, or is it hot in here?" she asked, fanning herself. Victor smiled as he got up, grabbed the empty glasses, and left. When he came back, Flora's eyes were closed, and she was nodding her head to a beat inside of it.

"Here you go," Victor said, extending the drink toward her.

"Damn, nigga, what took you so––"

Flora's mouth got dry when she opened her eyes and took in the sight before her. This time, Victor was in his birthday suit. She swallowed the lump in her throat when she saw the size of his penis. She instantly became aware of what had been causing his female visitors to scream his name at the top of their lungs. To give his cock the full effect, Victor set the drinks down and stood straight up. Flora gazed at it for a few seconds before Victor grabbed her hand and led her to his bedroom. She wanted to resist, but the e-pill had her hot and horny. Five minutes later, like all the other women that had ended up in his bedroom, Victor had Flora screaming his name.

Thirty minutes later, Flora walked out of Victor's bedroom with a sore back, a sore vagina, and a broad smile on her face. Although she'd only been a couple of hours removed from sleeping with Pee Wee, the potent weed combined with the E-pill-laced drink and Victor's massive-sized penis had been too much for her to resist. Her legs nearly gave out as she made her way down the steps. The crisp air smacked her in the face when she opened the door leading from upstairs. Because she'd just been sweating, the air felt like miniature spears stabbing her in her cheeks. As quickly as she could, Flora pushed the door to her downstairs place open and darted inside. Had she taken a second to think, she would have remembered that she never got a chance to unlock the door before going upstairs with Victor.

A strange feeling settled in the pit of Flora's stomach as she made her way toward her living room. Flora froze when she turned the corner. Her heart stopped when she saw three men sitting on her sofa.

"Damn, bitch, whoever you were up there with tore that pussy out the frame," Duck said, laughing.

"Who the fuck is y'all? What y'all doin' in my place?"

As cool as a summer breeze, Darnell got up from the couch and walked over to her. Before she knew it, Flora felt herself falling to the floor, courtesy of a backhanded slap from him. While she was on the floor, he kneeled and got face-to-face with her. His eyes were cold and hard. His voice dripped with malice.

"If I don't ask you a question, you don't open your fuckin' mouth, you got that?" he asked in a sinister voice. Flora took one look into his eyes and immediately knew that he meant business.

She didn't know what the hell was going on, but from the looks of it, she'd walked into her own residence and stepped into a pile of shit. When she didn't answer fast enough, Darnell grabbed her under her chin and squeezed.

"I asked you a question. Have you fuckin' got that?"

Flora nodded silently as her entire body shook in fear.

"Good. Duck, go handle that."

Darnell waited until his minion was gone before turning his attention back to Flora. "Now, let's talk. A little over an hour ago, we saw you coming out of a house inhabited by an acquaintance of ours. His name was Pee Wee. Do you know him?"

Flora didn't know what to do. She didn't want to lie to the gangster but was afraid to tell him the truth. Darnell smiled at her just before slapping her back down to the floor.

"I see you don't hear too fuckin' well. Now, let's try this shit again. Do you know a muthafucka named Pee Wee?"

With tears cascading down her face, Flora nodded slowly.

"Now, we're getting some-damn-where." Darnell stared at her for another ten seconds before shaking his head. "Nah, sweetheart. You don't know him. You feel me? If anybody asks you about him, you weren't there, and you ain't seen that nigga in two weeks. You got that?"

Not wanting to get slapped a second time, Flora nodded her head in agreement before Darnell could even complete his sentence.

"Good." Darnell then reached into his pocket and pulled out a lump of folded bills. He peeled off five one hundred-dollar bills and handed them to her. Flora's hand trembled as she accepted the cash.

"That's real good."

Darnell nodded to Lard, and the two men headed for the door. Right before he left, he looked back at her sternly. He put his finger over his lips to remind her to keep her mouth closed. As soon as they were gone, Flora ran to the door and locked it. The visit by the goons had utterly blown her high. Suddenly, she jumped when she heard someone knocking at her door. Fear gripped her as she couldn't help but wonder if the thugs had come back to exterminate her. After a few minutes, she had finally gathered enough courage to get up and go to the door. Cautiously, she opened her front door and saw a piece of paper taped to it.

No matter where you go, I can still reach out and touch you, it said. Flora's entire body trembled in fear. She cautiously stuck her head out the door a little more, knowing that if they wanted to kill her, she would be dead already. It wasn't until her head swung to the right that she saw the horrific sight. Flora screamed at the top of her lungs when she saw Victor stretched out on the porch with three bullet holes in his chest. The message was loud and clear. If she wanted to keep her life, she would keep her mouth shut and accept the hush money.

Chapter 7

Detective Little sat at his desk, twirling a pen in his right hand. The task in front of him was to fill out paperwork for an armed robbery suspect. He'd arrested the man a few days earlier so that he could be processed. But an assignment that should've taken him no longer than forty-five minutes tops to complete was now approaching an hour. Every few minutes, he would glance down at his cell phone lying on his desk. It had been three hours since his fool of a partner, Detective Anthony Warren, had called him. He'd told him that he was going to try to take down one of the city's most notorious drug dealers by himself. It was a stupid move, and Little was praying that Warren hadn't signed his own death warrant.

On the one hand, Little understood why his partner was so anxious to take down Darnell McCord. For years, they'd been trying to put him behind bars, but the Cleveland kingpin had successfully beaten the rap on any and everything that they'd thrown at him. Not even the FBI had been able to make anything stick on him. The growing sense of frustration was being felt by law enforcement throughout the city. For all intents and purposes, Darnell McCord had become the modern-day Al Capone. He had become . . . Mr. Untouchable. Whichever law enforcement officer or precinct that was skilled or lucky enough to bring him and his crew down would be looked upon as legends. But when dealing with a criminal like McCord, you had to be patient. He was armed with a team of goons and killers and had one of the most powerful lawyers in the entire state of Ohio on retainer. When you went at him, you had to be sure. It had taken Detective Warren, working over two years as an undercover agent, to gain his trust. That's why Little couldn't understand why his partner wanted to rush things suddenly. When the bust went down, they would have over twenty FBI agents and uniformed officers at their disposal. All he had to do was wait.

Little knew it was a risky move, but he couldn't help it any longer. He snatched up his cell phone and dialed Warren's number. When the call went directly to voicemail, he hung up and tried again but got the same result. His throat became dry. His stomach began to feel queasy.

Something wasn't right. He could feel it in his gut. He slammed his phone back down on the desk so hard that it nearly cracked the screen.

A bead of sweat trickled down the side of his face. He went back and forth in his mind, debating whether to tell his captain what Warren was up to. He jumped when his cell phone buzzed. Without even looking at the caller ID, he snatched his phone off the desk and screamed into it.

"Jesus Christ, Warren, where the hell are you?"

"Uh, I don't know where the hell your partner is, but I do know where the fuck your wife is."

Little looked at his watch and cursed silently. He was so worried about Warren that he'd completely forgotten about the dinner date he had with his wife. He could almost feel her anger seeping through the phone.

"Oh my God, baby, I'm sorry. I completely——"

"Forgot, Harold?" she said, finishing his sentence for him. "Yeah, you seem to be doing a lot of that lately."

"Baby, I swear to God, I'm gonna make it up to you."

"Yeah, right. That's another load of bullshit you keep feeding me, but to be honest, Harold, I'm getting tired of swallowing it."

Little rubbed his face. His wife had a point, and he knew it. He hadn't done it intentionally, but over time, he'd started spending more and more time at the police station and less at home.

"Harold, does this have anything to do with Steven?" she asked.

Harold pulled the phone back from his face and looked at it. A touch of anger rose inside of him. When he didn't respond immediately, his wife knew that she'd touched a nerve.

"Look, I'm sorry, Harold, but I had to ask. I know that this isn't the ideal situation for us, but Steven is our child. It's our responsibility to take care of him."

"Don't you think I know that?" Harold said, a little louder than he intended to. "And what has Steven got to do with me forgetting a damned dinner date?" he said angrily. He didn't like what she was insinuating. He would never stay away from his son, regardless of his condition.

Steven's autism put a tremendous strain on the Littles' marriage. Not only were they burdened with caring for a child with a disability, but also the financial strain threatened to drive a tree-sized wedge between them. Medical bills were mounting up. With his wife Tracy being a stay-at-home mom, Harold's income was all they had to depend on. Harold had never thrown it in her face, but he was tempted to do just that after hearing her accusatory tone. He took a deep breath and was about to let her have it when she abruptly apologized.

"Harold, baby, I am sorry. I didn't mean to come at you the way I did. I just hate not being able to spend as much time with you as I would like. And I know you're not intentionally staying away from your son. I'm sorry I said that."

Harold smiled slightly as the anger drained from his face.

"I'm sorry too, baby. I'll be at the restaurant as soon as I can."

"Don't worry about it. My sister agreed to keep Steven for the night, so you just bring your fine, sexy ass home to me," she said in a voice that let the detective know that he was going to get lucky tonight.

"Yes, ma'am!" he said before ending the call.

Harold had no idea where his partner was. But the sexy tone his wife had just spoken to him in had caused him to stop giving a damn. Whatever mess Warren had gotten himself into had better be something he could dig himself out of. It had been almost two months since Tracy had given him some, and there was no way he was going to miss this opportunity. Faster than he'd moved in years, Harold put his paperwork away and moved toward the exit. He was just about to leave when he heard his captain call his name. With a rock-hard dick and his mind on his wife, Harold ignored his boss and kept it moving.

Darting from one lane to another and back, Harold drove down Saint Clair Avenue on a mission. He was about five minutes from hopping on the freeway when he cut his eyes down one of the side streets and spotted two fire trucks and a coroner's van.

"Fuck," he shouted as he slowed down and made an illegal U-turn. Harold had briefly thought about ignoring the situation and continuing on his merry way, but his conscience wouldn't allow him to. He had taken a sworn oath to protect. So no matter how much he wanted to get laid, he had a job to do. When he came to the side street, he made a right and cruised to a stop behind a parked SUV. He got out of his car and took his badge out. As he made his way through a sea of onlookers, he heard a familiar voice.

"Everyone, get back, please. This is police business. Move along, please."

Harold showed his badge and was waved through by one of the uniformed officers.

"Hey, Ted! Ted, what have we got?" Harold asked a fellow detective.

"We're still gathering information, but from the looks of it, two people were blown to bits while sitting in a car. Body parts are all over the place. The only thing we know for certain is that the car belongs to Preston 'Pee Wee' Wilson. Luckily for us, the blast blew the license plate clean off the car and over there by a tree. We were able to run the plate."

Howard raised an eyebrow. "Please, don't tell me that this is the same Pee Wee Wilson that runs with Darnell McCord."

"The one and only. Hey, I heard something about Warren being undercover regarding McCord," Ted whispered. "How's that going? Are we getting any closer to nailing that son of a bitch?" Before Harold could answer, an officer called out to them.

"Hey, Detectives, I think you guys should come over here and see this."

The officer's face was as white as a sheet. Howard knew that there was something terribly wrong. A bad feeling washed over him. With each step he took, the knot in his stomach got tighter and tighter. By the time he got halfway to the bushes, the officer who had called them over grabbed his stomach and was throwing up. Seeing this, Harold and Ted both picked up their pace. They needed to see what had caused the officer to lose his lunch. A collective gasp escaped both of their mouths when they looked down and saw a head lying in the bushes.

"Oh my God . . . It's Warren," Ted said in disbelief.

Chapter 8

Pier Ten was an upscale restaurant sitting on the edge of the water bank in downtown Cleveland. Some influential people often ate there. The food was excellent, the service was outstanding, and there was never a long wait to get served. The menu consisted mostly of seafood, but the place did offer a variety of premium steaks taken from the finest cuts of beef. They were also one of the few places in town that served lamb. Over the past five years, Pier Ten had twice been voted the classiest place to eat in Cleveland.

Most of the high-end customers didn't know that Pier Ten was once a meeting spot where some of Cleveland's dirtiest politicians would meet with figures of the underworld. It was at these meetings where back door deals were arranged. Hits on judges or witnesses who couldn't or wouldn't be bribed were made. It was the perfect place for them to conduct their business.

The nearest operating business was three miles away, so privacy was pretty much guaranteed.

That all changed when a judge's egotistical son got drunk and ran his mouth to a woman he was trying to screw. He wanted to impress her by bragging on his status and connection to prominent Cleveland figures. Unfortunately for him, it worked a little too well. After fucking the woman two or three times, he got bored with her and let her know that it was time to move on in no uncertain terms. Needless to say, the woman was pissed off. She'd foolishly thrown away her marriage on a weekend affair that was just that. By the time the woman had got done running her mouth, not only had the local police started sniffing around but also the FBI had put the place on their radar as well.

Louie Calhoun, the bar owner, felt that for the safety and freedom of all involved, it was best to close the place. It remained that way until a young businessman inquired about what it would take to purchase the property. At first, the owner refused to sell. He had no desire for his building to be taken over by an African American, or moulie, as he liked to call them. It wasn't until a few of the city's underworld figures put pressure on Louie that he caved. Louie did, however, voice his reluctance.

"If we start letting this moulie control real estate, we're all fucked. The way I understand it, he's already on his way to controlling the dope game."

"He'll control what we let him control," a broad-shouldered Italian named Pete said. "Now stop bitchin' and sell the fuckin' building."

The way they saw it, Louie could jack the price up 25 percent, and they could all stand to make a good piece of change. Even though Darnell knew that he was getting fucked on the price, he still agreed to buy it. Turiq never could understand why, and Darnell never felt the need to explain it to him. Once he purchased the place, Darnell didn't waste any time fixing it up. By the time he was done with it, it was one of the more elegant spots in the city.

Darnell was also smart enough to know that it would be extremely detrimental to put the place in his name. A few greased palms and well-placed bribes essentially ensured that the place was owned by a ghost. But today, the place was being used for more than an eatery. Some business had to be discussed—serious business.

Darnell walked into his conference room with Duck and Lard following closely behind. After taking his seat, he tossed a large manila envelope on the table. From the other end of the table, Turiq chuckled as he looked at his watch.

"I see you on Negro time, my nigga."

"Yeah, well, you know how it is. Did you tell these niggas what's going on?"

"Nah, I figured you'd want to relay that message."

"You figured right," Darnell said, his face turning deadly serious. Also seated at the table were four of Darnell's top street lieutenants.

The longest-tenured was Blue. He was a no-nonsense cat operating out of Cleveland's West Side. When it came to making that paper, Blue was all business. He kept his team in line and ruled with an iron fist. On more than one occasion, either Darnell or Turiq had to rein him in because he was too hard on his workers. At five foot seven, Blue had a serious Napoleon Complex. He would often stand on his toes in an effort to appear taller than he was. He was also hard on the eyes. With a scar running from the corner of his eye to his ear and an above-average-sized nose, Blue had to shell out a pretty fair amount of dough to get some of the finer women to keep time with him.

Trey was the total opposite of Blue. He too operated out of the West Side of Cleveland. Together, he and Blue supplied the area with 85 percent of its cocaine. Trey was six foot two, handsome, and a smooth talker. The ladies flocked to him in droves. A flashy cat, Trey loved to wear expensive jewelry and roll around in his gold Mercedes-Benz. Tariq had tried to get Darnell to make him tone it down, but Darnell refused. Darnell felt that since it was Trey's money, he could do with it whatever he pleased. Trey's problem was that he was careless. On more than one occasion, he'd gotten robbed by young women that he'd entertained at his house. He would do a few lines of coke with them, have sex with them, and then fall into a deep sleep.

Darnell suspected that Trey might have been dipping into the very product that he was supposed to be selling, but as long as his money never came up short, Darnell couldn't care less.

Sitting across from Trey was Damon. Damon was a greasy, low-life cat who'd been trying for years to get his weight up. Neither Darnell nor Turiq really cared all that much for Damon. In their eyes, he was a grimy muthafucka who would use his own mother as a stepping-stone in order to come up. He proved to be just as foul as they thought he was when he set up the previous lieutenant, Frank, to be robbed. Although Damon had been working for Frank for a year, he felt that he and Frank deserved a bigger piece of the pie than Darnell was giving them. Frank, on the other hand, felt that Darnell was more than fair.

Darnell hadn't had any problems with Frank, and he wasn't about to let Damon start any. In his mind, Damon had a lot of nerve even to be complaining. He was damn near starving when he first started working for Frank. Damon had been pushing prescription pills and Viagra when Frank offered him a chance to make some real bread. He saw the young man's hustling potential and envisioned him making a lot of money for the team. But just as it always does, greed reared its ugly head. Damon wanted more buck for his bang.

Soon after, his constant complaints got back to Duck and Pee Wee. Because the two capos didn't want their boss to be bothered with the ambitious street soldier, their solution to the growing problem was to simply have the young man killed. Frank begged them not to do it. He reasoned that since Damon came aboard, sales had increased 20 percent. It took hours of pleading from Frank before Pee Wee and Duck finally relented. They made it clear to Frank, though, that the next time they heard a complaint from Damon, it would be the last time they ever heard a complaint from him. Frank had gone out on a limb for Damon, and his reward had been death. After talking to Duck and Pee Wee, Frank laid down the law.

He informed Damon that either he stopped complaining or make his bones somewhere else. Damon had plotted to get rid of Frank and take over his lieutenant's spot from that moment on. His opportunity finally came when Frank let it slip that he planned to take a female friend to the movies one Friday night. Damon then hired a thug named Roach to go to the same theater, wait till the lights went out, and blow off the back of Frank's head. Damon even provided Roach with the silencer-attached pistol to carry out the hit. When Roach met with Damon to collect his money, Damon shot him in the face and tied up the loose end.

When Duck and Pee Wee found out about Frank, they suspected that Damon was somehow involved. Since they couldn't prove it, they let the matter go. Even though they still didn't like him, it hadn't been lost on Darnell and Turiq how much Damon had been earning for the team, so they slid him into Frank's spot. Duck and Pee Wee didn't like it, but their hands were tied. Had Turiq known about Damon's complaints, it's quite possible that Damon would have been executed. Darnell would have also been amazed at how two of his capos could have let that situations get so far out of hand. So to stay on Darnell and Turiq's good sides, Duck and Pee Wee decided just to let sleeping dogs lie.

Sitting directly across from Damon was OG Hann. Except for Darnell, Hann had been in the game the longest. He was actually offered the second in command position before Turiq was, but he turned it down, causing Darnell to question his commitment to the game. Unlike the rest of Darnell's crew, Hann didn't see slinging poison in the hood as a lifelong occupation. He wasn't flashy like Trey, and he rarely spent any money. He had a few legitimate businesses that no one knew about, and he was actually married. However, because of the dangers of being in the dope game, he kept that a secret from everyone. Not even Darnell knew about his wife. At 35 years old, he planned on being in the game another five years and then ride off into the sunset.

"Yo, Duck, pass these around for me, my dude," Darnell said, as he opened the envelope and handed its contents to Duck. Duck walked around the table and placed an eight-by-ten photograph in front of each lieutenant. Damon smirked as he looked down at the picture of Detective Warren's shot up body. He never liked the man and was pissed when Pee Wee brought him into the fold. It wasn't until that moment that he realized that Pee Wee wasn't in attendance.

"I neva did like you, cracka muthafucka," Damon mumbled.

"Yo, what's good with this, D? Why is Jeff lying there with a fuckin' hole in his skull?" Trey asked.

"Because his name ain't Jeff. It's Anthony Warren. As in *Detective* Anthony Warren."

At the mention of the moniker "Detective," all four lieutenants' heads snapped up.

"Damn, man, that muthafucka was 5-0?" Blue asked, obviously surprised.

"Yeah, he was," Darnell said. He pulled out his cell phone and went to an app that controlled an overhead projector. A video of Pee Wee's car sitting in front of his house appeared on the wall. Everyone's head turned to Duck when they saw him getting out of the vehicle.

"The fuck is that shit about, Duck?" Damon asked.

"Nigga, just shut up and watch the damn video," Duck barked. He was still pissed that Damon's snake ass had been promoted. Damon seethed as he slowly turned back toward the video. He didn't like the way Duck was talking to him. When his time came, he would make sure that Duck was the first one to catch it. Everybody in the room jumped when Pee Wee's car exploded.

"Yo, was Pee Wee in that car?" OG Hann asked.

"You damn right he was in that muthafucka. That dumb-ass nigga let a cop infiltrate my fuckin' empire, so he had to go."

Darnell looked into the eyes of each man. He wanted all of them to know that he meant business and wasn't going to tolerate any more fuckups. "From now on, nobody else comes aboard unless *I* bring them in. Is that clear?"

Darnell's second in command, his two capos, and his four lieutenants all nodded their heads in agreement.

"Good. Now, let's get down to business." Darnell nodded at Turiq, and his second in command placed an empty duffle bag on the table. OG Hann and Trey each picked up the duffle bags they'd brought and emptied stacks of money onto the table. Damon stood up and removed the backpack he had on and did the same. Blue simply emptied both of his pockets and threw his portion into the bag. Lard then picked up the bag and carried it to another table, where he and Duck began counting it. While they were counting the money, Darnell let the rest of his crew know how appreciative he was of the job they were doing. All of them were making money by the truckload, and to show them how much he appreciated their efforts, he told them that whatever they made for the next thirty days, they could keep. The lieutenants looked at each other and smiled.

"Damon, I need to holla at you for a second," Darnell told him.

As the rest of the crew continued to chop it up with each other, Darnell gave Damon a very important job to do. Damon nodded and smiled as Darnell was filling him in on the details. By the time he was done, Damon was rubbing his hands together in anticipation of carrying out his assignment.

"I got you, dawg. I'm just the man for the job," he said, smiling wickedly.

Chapter 9

Flora's forehead produced a loud thud as she dozed off and fell face-first onto her desk. It had been a week since Darnell and his minions had paid her a visit. Since then, sleep hadn't come easy to her. Even when she was lucky enough to catch a few z's, the nightmares she'd started experiencing would cut them short. She nearly jumped out of her skin when one of her coworkers touched her on the shoulder

"Girl, you all right?" she asked.

"Yeah, just a little sleepy."

"Yeah, I see. You've been coming in here like that for the last week. Yo' man been keeping you up or something?"

"Something like that," Flora lied.

"Girl, I'll be back. I'm going to get you a cup of coffee. And tell that damn man to leave you alone and let you get some sleep."

"Thanks," Flora said, trying to force herself to smile. Not only was she dealing with the grief of losing her lover, but she was also so paranoid that she was continually looking over her shoulder. And if that wasn't enough, she was being weighed down by a tremendous amount of guilt. Two days ago, she'd attended a memorial service for Pee Wee. She didn't want to but knew that there was no way she could not be there for Rhonda. As Rhonda cried on Flora's shoulder, the weight of screwing Pee Wee behind her back nearly caused her to collapse. Throughout the entire service, Flora was never once able to look Rhonda in the eye. Her guilt almost made her confess, but the thought of losing Rhonda's friendship was too much for her to bear.

"Here, girl, drink this," her coworker said, handing her a cup of coffee.

As Flora sipped from the cup, she thought about the offer her sister had made her. Her sister, who worked as a schoolteacher in Dayton, had offered to get her a job as the school's secretary. Flora had the skills for the job. She just never had the desire to move. In her opinion, Dayton was a small, country type of city. She liked the excitement of being in a bigger city such as Cleveland. But ever since the threat from Darnell, she'd been a nervous wreck.

A frown crossed her face as she thought about Darnell. In the span of a week, she had truly grown to hate him. Nothing would please her more than to see him get what was coming to him. She may have been wrong for sleeping with her friend's man, but Darnell was a thousand times wrong for killing him. Her lover was dead, and her best friend had fallen apart. At that point, Flora didn't give a damn about Darnell's threat. She made the decision right then and there to take up her sister's job offer. She loved Cleveland, but she just couldn't deal with the guilt that her actions were causing her. Before she left, however, she would make sure that Darnell paid dearly for his role in Pee Wee's death.

After leaving work, Flora decided to stop by Rhonda's. As hard as it was going to be, she wanted to tell her face-to-face that she would be moving. There was no way in the world Flora would be able to continue their friendship, knowing that it was based on deceit and disloyalty. On the way over, she went back and forth, thinking about whether she should confess. In the end, she decided not to. She concluded that it was better for Rhonda to grieve her man and miss her friend instead of hating them both for what they had done.

As soon as Flora turned on Rhonda's street, a lump formed in her throat. The charred smell of Pee Wee's car still lingered in the air. The scent of burnt flesh hovered over the area where body parts once were. However, that was nothing compared to the pain in her chest, which was sure to get worse the second she laid eyes on her friend. After turning off her car, Flora sat there for ten minutes before getting out and making her way toward the front door. She raised her hand to ring the doorbell but never got the chance.

"Hey, girl. Come on in. I was hoping that you'd come by," a teary-eyed Rhonda said as she opened the door. Flora's heart broke into a thousand pieces. The guilt riding her back damn near broke her spine.

"How are you?" she asked, genuinely concerned.

"I've been better. I still can't believe that Pee Wee is gone. I mean, I'm not gonna fool myself into thinking that he wasn't fuckin' other bitches. I'm not that damn stupid, but he was still my damn man. Whatever he did in the street, he *kept* it there. He never brought any of that bullshit home."

Flora tried to find words of comfort but fell short. She was shocked to see Rhonda pick up a small mirror with a marginal amount of cocaine on it.

"Don't look at me like that, Flora. I know you've never seen me do this, and there's a reason for that."

After snorting a line through her right nostril, she paused for a few seconds before repeating the process through her left one.

"How long have you been doing that stuff?" Flora asked.

Rhonda shrugged her shoulders.

Once again, Flora felt like a fool. She'd been feeling that way a lot lately. Rhonda was a good friend of hers, and she had no idea that her friend was sniffing blow. Rhonda dropped her head for a second before lifting it and staring directly into Flora's eyes. What Flora saw in them convinced her that she was doing the right thing leaving Cleveland. The hurt that Rhonda was experiencing seemed to be transferring into Flora's soul.

"The reason I stopped by is that I wanted to tell you that I'm going out of town for a couple of weeks. I hate to leave when you're hurting like this, but my mother just had surgery, and she's going to be laid up, so I have to go and take care of her," Flora lied.

"Okay. When are you leaving?"

"Tomorrow. If I don't get there soon, she'll be calling me everything but a child of God."

Rhonda smiled. It was the first time she'd done that since finding out about Pee Wee.

"You know, it was nice of his friend Darnell to send all those flowers to the memorial. I know the two of them were friends."

Bitch, if you only knew, Flora thought. All she could do in response to that statement was nod silently.

"You wanna smoke something?" Rhonda asked.

"Nah, I'm good."

Rhonda gave Flora a sideways glance. She knew that Flora liked to smoke weed, so she was curious about why she was turning down a free high. Shrugging her shoulders, she let the matter go. The two women talked for another thirty minutes before Flora reminded Rhonda that she had to get home and pack. They hugged each other for a long time before Flora finally left.

Flora had barely gotten into the car before bursting out into tears. She couldn't take back what she did, but she was damned sure determined to bring Pee Wee's killer to justice.

She took out her cell phone with trembling hands and dialed the number for the Cleveland Police Department. As the phone rang, a thousand thoughts went through her head. She thought about the threat that had been issued on her life. She thought about Victor and how he'd just been an innocent bystander who was killed to send her a message. More guilt. Deep in her heart, Flora knew that she was doing the right thing. But when an officer spoke on the line, she froze.

Flora opened her mouth and tried to push the words from her throat, but they resisted. Without uttering a single word, she quickly hung up. Her nerves were frayed. She now felt like an ass for turning down Rhonda's invitation to smoke a blunt. She needed something to help her calm down. She called her cousin again to see if he'd re-upped yet. Much to her delight, he had indeed copped a few pounds of weed from his supplier. That was music to her ears.

After swinging by his house to pick up a bag of the head banger, she made her way home. It took her a little over an hour to pack up everything she wanted to take with her. The rest she would just leave behind.

Flora then dropped down on her couch and took out the twenty-dollar sack of weed she'd bought. After expertly preparing the blunt, she lit the tip and inhaled. A calming effect washed over her as the smoke descended into her lungs. Flora held it there for a few extra seconds before blowing it into the air. She smiled as she ignorantly thumbed ashes onto the floor.

"Fuck this place," she spat. Had she and the landlord been cool, Flora wouldn't have done that. But since Mr. Parker was an asshole, she didn't give a shit about his property. After smoking half the blunt, Flora walked to the kitchen and poured herself a shot of vodka. She tossed it back and grimaced as the hot liquor burned her chest on the way down. Normally, Flora wouldn't drink alcohol straight, but she needed nerves of steel for what she was about to do. Taking her cell phone out of her purse, Flora took a deep breath and dialed the number to the police station once again.

Chapter 10

Sweat bubbled up on the top of Detective Little's bald head as Captain Moore's eyes stared lasers at him. It had been five minutes since he'd been called into his boss's office, and Moore still hadn't said a word. Now and then, he would grunt. The phone rang a couple of times, but when it did, Moore would simply pick it up and slam it back down on its base. He ignored the knock on the door, but when it was apparent that whoever was there wasn't going to leave, the captain snapped.

"Come in, and this shit better be important!"

Slowly, the door opened, and one of the beat cops looked in.

"Uh, is this a bad time, Captain?" he asked.

Moore looked at him like he was the stupidest person to walk the face of the earth. "The fuck do you want, Gaines?"

"Uh, I just wanted to give you that report you asked for and—"

"Gaines, I asked you for that report yesterday morning, and you wait until I'm in the middle of something to bother me with this bullshit? What the fuck is wrong with you? Put it on my desk and get the fuck out of my office."

The embarrassed cop did as he was told and got out of there as fast as he could. As he walked past Little, he raised his eyebrows and gave a low whistle as if to say, *Man, what the hell did you do?*

Captain Vincent Moore was old school through and through. He didn't trust many people and that included cops. He'd seen too many of them take bribes, use unnecessary force, and even break the law when it suited their purposes for him to believe that any cop was 100 percent genuine. But even though he didn't trust many of his fellow law enforcement brothers and sisters, he didn't dislike them as he did criminals. He hated crooks. To him, a drug dealer was the worst kind of criminal there was. Even if a murderer killed ten people, in his mind, it didn't compare to a drug dealer slowly killing an entire community by feeding them poison in a bag. That's why he was so upset about what had happened with the botched bust.

Captain Moore had deemed this bust top secret. Only Detective Warren, Little, and he knew about it. Everyone else would find out when it was time to put Darnell McCord and the rest of his crew in handcuffs. But now, that wasn't going to happen. The big fish had wiggled off the hook, and Moore wanted to know what the fuck had happened.

"Let me ask you a question, Little. Are you going to honestly sit up here and tell me that you didn't know anything about Warren going after McCord himself? You mean to tell me that I've got cops that stupid working under my command?"

Harold weighed his options. He didn't want to dishonor the memory of his partner by ratting him out, but he didn't want his captain to think that he was stupid enough to go along with Warren's idiot plan. When he didn't speak fast enough, his boss barked at him.

"Answer me, dammit! Did he do that dumb-ass shit on his own, or were you a part of that silly shit?"

Fuck it, he thought, *I'm not putting myself on the captain's shit list just because my dumb-ass partner wouldn't listen to me.*

"Captain, I swear to God, sir, I had nothing to do with Warren's decision to do that."

"Did you know he was going to do it?"

"No, sir, I didn't," Little lied. The captain stared at him for another ten seconds before slowly nodding his head.

"Okay, Little. I believe you. But if I find out that you're lying to me, I'll have your fuckin' badge. Is that clear?"

"Yes, sir."

"Good." Captain Moore wiped his brow. He too had begun to sweat.

"I swear, you incompetent motherfuckers are going to be the death of me. Lucky for me, I only got six months until I leave all this bullshit behind. Now, do you remember when that poor slob was killed and left on the front porch a few days ago?"

"Yes, sir, I remember it. Why?"

"Because the girl that lives there is the one who's giving us the lead."

"Say no more, Cap. I'm on it."

"That's what I wanted to hear. And hurry up. This could be the break we need to bring that bastard down. The desk sergeant has the address. I told her to give it to you."

Hoping to crack the case, Little flew out the door and headed for his vehicle. He may not have been able to stop his deceased partner from making a deadly mistake, but he would like nothing more than to take down the scumbag that was responsible for his death. Even though Warren was a borderline racist, he was still Little's partner, so he had to try to make his death an honorable one.

***

Little picked up his phone, glanced at the screen, and tossed it back on the seat. He smirked and shook his head, knowing that he would have to hear his wife's mouth when he got home. He was supposed to take her to the movies, but he had to follow up on this lead. Surely, she wouldn't be in such a pissy mood when he told her why he wasn't able to make it. Or, at least, he hoped she wouldn't. If Little were being totally honest with himself, he would admit that his wife had been very understanding of his job as a detective, and it made him feel bad that he couldn't give her the time she deserved. Tracy was a good woman, but if he didn't start spending some quality time with her, he would turn her into a bad one. He kept that in mind as he turned on Flora's street. His cell phone buzzed, letting him know that he had a text message coming through. He didn't even have to look at it to know that it was Tracy wanting to know where he was. For shits and giggles, he decided to look at it anyway.

Harold, where the fuck are you?' I know damn well you ain't gonna cancel on me again!

Harold sighed deeply. If he had had more time, he would have texted her back and let her know what was going on, but he was fast approaching Flora's place. He skidded to a stop in front of her house, grabbed his phone, put it in his pocket, and got out of his car. Right away, something felt off to him. He couldn't put his finger on it, but something just didn't feel right. Carefully, he walked up the steps and up to the door. He raised his hand to ring the doorbell but stopped when he noticed that the door was slightly open. His gut was telling him to take his gun out, so he listened. The door creaked as Little pushed it open.

"Hello?" he said as he continued to walk in. A chill snaked up his spine when he realized how dark it was inside.

"Ms. Matthews? Are you in here?"

Little eased through the foyer and into the living room area. As soon as he turned the corner, he saw Flora's silhouette.

Little held his gun tightly in his right hand while searching for the light switch on the wall with his left. When he finally found it and flipped it on, he wished he hadn't.

"Oh my God," he mumbled softly. Seeing her silhouette in the dark was one thing. But seeing her actual body in the full light was something altogether different. Little shook his head sadly as he stared down at Flora's bloody corpse. Her eyes were wide open, but the life in them had long since been extinguished. Dried streaks of blood stained her face. A large hole rested in the center of her head.

Little pulled out his cell phone to call it in but never got the chance. No sooner had he dialed the first number, a heavy blow to the back of his head knocked him out cold.

Chapter 11

The affluent, upscale suburb that Darnell's residence was located in housed some of the city's most elite personalities. Plastic surgeons, high-powered attorneys, business owners, and corporate CEOs all had elegant, pricy homes in the area. Like many drug dealers, Darnell sold most of his dope in the inner-city neighborhoods and purchased homes far away from there. But moving out of the hood did not make him a sellout. Over the years, Darnell had anonymously donated to various charities that benefited the inner city. Darnell knew where he came from, and he wasn't ashamed of it. The lessons he'd learned as a teenager shaped him into the man he was today. However, there was a major difference in remembering where you came from and wanting to remain there.

When Darnell first purchased the land, he took inventory of how all the other houses in the area looked. Had he wanted to, he could have easily had a home built that would have put the surrounding houses to shame. But Darnell, doing the smart thing, had something constructed that was more along the lines of the other homes. The front yard was immaculate. The lawn was neatly manicured, and every blade of grass was the same shade of dark green. The circular driveway consisted of a smooth concrete pavement that was void of any cracks or unevenness. The best feature about the driveway, however, was that it was heated. This ensured that the driveway wouldn't turn into an ice sheet even when it snowed, or the temperature dropped below freezing. Halfway around the driveway, it veered off to the garage. Inside of the garage was a door that connected to the basement. The basement was where he usually entertained his guests.

Darnell's backyard was just as nice as the front. The grass was evenly cut and was surrounded by a cement patio where a huge barbecue grill sat. On rare occasions when he did have some free time, Darnell would call up Turiq and sometimes OG Hann to see if they wanted to have a few drinks or play a few games of dominoes while something was cooking on the grill. OG Hann was the only one of his lieutenants that he'd ever allowed at his house. Trey talked too much for his own good, and Darnell didn't trust him to keep his mouth closed. Being in the position that he was in, Darnell had quite a few enemies. The last thing he wanted was to wake up in the middle of the night with a gun pointed at him. Or worse yet, one pointed at Sunny.

Blue had too much of an attitude problem for Darnell to deal with in a social setting. The fact that he was the shortest person in the room 95 percent of the time put a chip on his shoulder the size of Ohio. Darnell didn't need or want that type of negative energy around him. Damon? Well, Darnell just didn't trust Damon. On countless occasions, he'd thought about replacing him, but for some reason that not even Darnell could explain, he kept him around. As grimy as Damon was, there was something about him that made Darnell want to see him succeed. But that didn't mean that he trusted him enough to invite him to his home.

Most of the time, it would be Darnell sitting on his patio thinking of power moves he needed to make, or him, Turiq, or OG Hann, bragging about who was better at dominoes. But today, something different was happening. The long-overdue party for Sunny was in full swing. It was catered by one of the finest barbecue places in Cleveland. It wasn't as large as Hot Sauce Williams or B&M, but Murphy's Ribs and Wings could run circles around those places when it came to taste. The only negative aspect was the threat of rain.

Large, dark clouds hovered in the sky, making it a less-than-ideal day to be throwing a barbecue. The meteorologist had promised everyone that it would be nice and sunny, but God had other ideas. Darnell had wanted to cancel the cookout and have it another day, but Sunny wasn't having it. She'd been waiting on this for a long time and wasn't about to let the slight threat of rain ruin it for her. Plus, this was the day that her father had promised to buy her a car, and she wanted everyone in attendance to see it, especially her new friend Jazmine. Since that night at her place, Jazmine and Sunny had become quite the pair. Their fathers were shocked when the two girls started hanging out and going shopping together, but they were also pleased. Darnell and Turiq had the same way of thinking. Neither of them wanted their kids to grow up wanting for anything. White America wasn't going to hold them back and deprive them of anything just because they were Black women. Their fathers were going to see to that.

"Can you believe this shit?" Darnell asked Turiq. "They're over there shootin' the shit like they been best friends all they damn lives."

Turiq shrugged and took a sip from his Cognac. "That's what we wanted to happen, right?"

"Indeed. And now it begins," Darnell declared.

The two of them held up their glasses and clicked them together. Turiq nodded his head in agreement. Although Darnell had broached the subject of taking over his drug empire to Sunny, he had yet to bring it up to Turiq. That could wait. In the coming weeks, he would sit Sunny down and begin to school her on the ins and outs of the drug game. Both fathers were happy that their daughters had settled their beef. They knew that loyalty and trust had to be present for them to prosper in the drug game. They also knew that although many drug dealers didn't place much stock in friendship, Darnell and Turiq both knew that being friends with your friends was an underrated aspect of being in the game. If you're not friends with someone, there was no way in the world you would ever be loyal to them, let alone trust them.

"My dude, I'm not gon' lie, though. I was surprised as hell to see the two of them laughing and joking around and shit. I just knew when I got home, Jazmine would be choking your daughter." Darnell cut his eyes toward his friend.

"Or Sunny would be choking *your* daughter."

"Nah, playa. My daughter's a beast."

"And you think mine's not? Nigga, she learned from the best," Darnell said, throwing playful jabs at Turiq.

"A'ight, my nigga. Let's just say we both got beasts for daughters." The two friends laughed as they clicked glasses again.

"So, what's good with that nigga you caught trying to slide outta ya' crib?"

"I got Damon taking care of it."

Turiq raised an eyebrow. He knew what type of goon Damon was and wondered if his friend was going overboard in his attempt to send the young man a message.

"Damon? You sure you wanna do that, bro? You know how savage that muthafucka is."

"Yeah, I know. Don't worry, though. I told him to just rough up ol' boy a little bit, not put him in the dirt." Darnell tossed back the last remnants of his drink. Not thirty seconds later, Turiq did the same.

"Time for a refill, bro," Turiq said, handing his glass to Darnell. Darnell looked at the glass and then back at Turiq.

"Nigga, what the fuck wrong with yo' legs?"

"The same thing that be wrong with *yo'* legs when you come to *my* house," Turiq said, laughing.

"Yeah, a'ight, nigga. I'ma bring back yo' ass a glass of water, nigga," Darnell said, walking back into the house. He then made his way over to a shelf with several different liquor bottles on it and grabbed a bottle of Rémy Martin. After refilling both glasses, Darnell held his nose down to one of the drinks and took a long sniff. He smiled and nodded his head at the potent aroma. He was just getting ready to turn and go back outside when he felt something cold and hard press up against the back of his head.

"Your next move is your last move. Turn around slowly, and don't make any sudden moves," a sweet, silky voice said from behind him.

With two glasses of Cognac in his hand, Darnell was at a distinct disadvantage, so he had no choice but to do as he was told. He slowly turned around and stared directly into the barrel of a pistol.

"I guess I'm supposed to be scared now," he said, his facial expression unchanged.

"If you had any sense, you'd *definitely* be afraid."

"Sorry to disappoint you, but that little pea-shooter you got there doesn't scare me."

"Oh, really? Well, maybe *this* will," she said as she lowered the gun to his groin. Darnell looked down at the weapon and then back at the intruder. He cocked his head to the side and smirked. Shrugging his shoulders, he shook his head. His smile faded when she pulled back the hammer.

"Okay, now, yo' ass is playing a little too much," he said.

"Oh, so *now,* you're scared?"

"Move that damn gun away from my nut sacks," he demanded. The intruder laughed and set her gun on the table. As soon as she did, he put down the drinks, grabbed her, and pulled her into his arms.

"You know what? You play too damn much. What if that thing woulda went off?" The woman reached into her pocket and pulled out a clip. She smiled at him as she held it up to his face.

"The gun's useless without this. Besides, baby, I don't wanna do anything to hurt this thing," she said as she grabbed his penis. Darnell's dick swelled in her grasp. She was turning him on in a major way, and there was nothing he could do about it. Not that he was complaining. Had it not been for the fact that he was hosting a party for his daughter and several other teenagers, he would have gladly taken her into his bedroom and blown her back out. Joy was her name, and being sexy was one of the things that she did very well.

She had long, black hair, which she usually kept in a ponytail. Her cocoa-brown skin was soft and smooth. She had a perfect set of white teeth that caused her smile to illuminate whenever she parted her lips. Joy had high cheekbones and slanted light brown eyes. At first glance, she would appear to be a dark-skinned Vietnamese woman, but she was African American through and through. At five foot ten, she was nearly eye to eye with Darnell, and from the first moment he laid eyes on her, he felt that she was the sexiest woman that he'd ever seen in his life.

"Joy, you need to stop playing," he said, lust filling his voice.

"Who's playing?" She squeezed it harder.

"Damn," he grunted.

"You like that?"

"You know damn well that I do." She leaned in and licked his lips, then pushed her tongue between them, forcing Darnell to open his mouth. The two kissed passionately for a few seconds before Joy broke the lip-lock. Grabbing his hand, she started pulling him toward the bedroom.

"Wait. My daughter and her friends are out there."

"And what does that have to do with anything?"

"Shit, nothing, I guess."

"Then bring yo' ass on. Hell, I just want a quickie, not some two-hour marathon."

Darnell was just about to take her up on her offer when Turiq walked in.

"Man, what's taking yo' ass so lo . . . I shoulda known," he said when he saw Joy. "Hey, Joy."

"Turiq, has anyone ever told you that you have the worse timing?" Joy laughed as she walked over to him and hugged him.

"Nope. Can't say that they have."

"Well, you do," Darnell said, frowning.

"My bad, dawg." Turiq cocked his head and looked at Joy.

"Wait a minute. How in the hell did you get into this house without us seeing you?"

Joy smirked and placed her hands on her hips. "You really got the nerve to ask me some bullshit like that? Nigga, you know a bitch got skills." Joy smiled as she brushed the imaginary haters from her shoulder.

"Yeah, whatever. Man, you better bring yo' ass back outside. I didn't come over here to watch a bunch of teenagers while y'all go upstairs and screw like rabbits."

Joy looked at Darnell and shrugged. With an "oh well" look on her face, she picked up one of the drinks and walked outside. Darnell stared at the door for a second or two, then turned his eyes on Turiq, who was trying hard to suppress a smile. Darnell, however, saw right through it.

"You think that shit is funny, don't you, ol' cock-blocking-ass nigga."

"What?" Turiq asked innocently. All Darnell could do was shake his head. He grabbed the other drink that he'd poured and headed out behind Joy.

"Hey, man, ain't that my drink?"

"Nah, nigga, she took yo' shit. Better hook yo'self up another one," he said, gesturing toward the bottle. While Turiq was busy pouring himself another drink, Darnell went outside to be with Joy. The frown on his face caused her to burst out laughing.

"Nah, baby, don't put that shit on me. Ya' boy Turiq is the one cockblocking."

"Yeah, I know." Darnell leaned in close to Joy and whispered into her ear. "Did you take care of that little 'situation' for me?"

"You know I got you, baby. That bitch is outta here. Check this shit out, though, baby. Not even five minutes after I put something hot in that bitch, one of the detectives pulled up. I was barely able to duck inside the closet before he came in the door."

"So, what did you do?"

"I waited for him to drop his guard and cracked him in the back of the head."

"Did you kill him?"

Joy shrugged. "Don't know, don't care," she spat.

Darnell laughed. He knew how ruthless Joy could be and was glad as hell that she was on his side.

Joyce Green had been a cop for the last five years. To understand her story, you have to know about her childhood. She grew up with her older brother Marcus in the Glenville area on Cleveland's East Side. While their father was doing twenty-five to life on an armed robbery-turned-murder charge, their mother, Sarah, was busy holding down two jobs to keep food on the table and clothes on their backs.

Sarah was a woman who commanded respect. She didn't tolerate foolishness and ran her house with an iron fist after her live-in boyfriend and kids' father Ronald got locked up. She was hard on Marcus but was three times as strict with Joy. Being raised in the inner city herself, Sarah knew of the dangers and temptations that it presented every day, especially for females. She constantly preached to Joy that the city was a dangerous place to live in and made sure that Marcus always kept his eyes on his little sister. Although Marcus was three years older than Joy, the two siblings were close to each other. It wasn't until he started high school that he began to find his own niche. At 15 years old, his hormones had just begun to jump, and at 17, they were raging out of control. He routinely snuck young girls in and out of the house.

With Marcus starting to spend more and more time with girls his own age, the green-eyed monster in Joy started rearing its ugly head. Knowing that whenever she wanted to go anywhere, her mother wouldn't let her go without Marcus chaperoning her, Joy would often pick times when she knew her brother had plans. She would also play sick at night so that her mother would stay up longer, which would make it nearly impossible for Marcus to sneak out. Marcus knew what she was doing, and it pissed him off to no end. Still, he loved his little sister.

Then came the hot summer night that changed everything. The date was July tenth, and the sun was just beginning to go down. Marcus had promised to take her to the movies. However, one hour before they were supposed to go, a girl that Marcus had a crush on called him out of the blue wanting to hang out. Marcus, not wanting to blow a chance to spend time with a girl he'd been chasing for months, told Joy that they were going to have to reschedule their outing. Joy was livid. She couldn't believe that her brother was canceling on her to hang out with some tramp. When she couldn't talk him into changing his mind, she brought out the big guns.

"Either you take me to the movies tonight like you promised, or I'm going to tell mama that you had a girl in here while she was at work."

"What the hell are you talking about?" Marcus asked, trying to act as if he didn't know what she was referring to.

"You *know* what I'm talking about and stop cussing at me."

"Girl, get the hell out of my room. I'm about to get dressed and roll out." Marcus pushed his little sister out of his room and continued getting ready. Two minutes later, his cell phone buzzed, indicating that he had a text message coming in. When he picked up his phone and looked at it, his jaw dropped. It wasn't a regular text message his sister had sent, but a video text message. It was a video of him kissing one of the girls from his school. Had that been the only thing on the video, he may have been able to sweet-talk his mother into giving him a pass, but there was no way he was going to keep her from blowing her top when she saw that his hand had disappeared under the girl's skirt. Marcus had no idea that Joy was even at home. As far as he knew, she was supposed to be at cheerleading practice at that time. He stormed to his door, slung it open . . . and was greeted by his smirking sister.

"You sneaky little—"

"Uh-uh-uuuh," Joy said, wagging her finger. "Don't say something you're gonna be sorry for. I'm going to get dressed," she said as she sashayed back toward her room. Marcus wanted to be mad, but all he could do was laugh. His little sister had one-upped him, and in a strange kind of way, he admired her for it. He picked up his phone to call and cancel his meeting with his high school crush, but before he could, it vibrated in his hand.

"Speak of the devil," he said to himself. He answered the call, ready to get cussed out for bailing on her at the last minute. But before he had a chance to say anything, she began apologizing for having to cancel on him. Marcus breathed a sigh of relief. Considering the circumstances, it was the best thing that could have happened. He pretended to be upset but didn't want to appear to be too angry. He pumped his fist and smiled when the girl told him that she would make it up to him. Marcus had only had sex twice and was looking forward to experiencing the act again.

He didn't have a car, so he and his sister had to catch the bus to downtown Tower City. After the movies, Marcus called his mother to tell her that he and his sister were on their way back home, but they would stop and get some ice cream first.

"What? No, it's too late. You and your sister bring y'all asses home," she'd told them.

Marcus disconnected the call, looked at his sister, and shrugged his shoulders. "No ice cream tonight, li'l sis. Mama said we had to come home ASAP."

Joy pouted but knew better than to disobey her mother when she gave them an order. The two of them went to the bus stop and waited for the bus. While they were waiting, a police car passed them. The officer sitting on the passenger's side eyed them suspiciously. Marcus snorted.

"Punk-ass police," Marcus spat.

"What you got against the police, bro? Don't you know that they only want to protect and serve? At least, that's what the words on their cars say."

Marcus looked at his sister like she were crazy. Shaking his head, he grabbed her hands and looked into her eyes. He figured that it was time to school his little sister on the real ways of the police.

"Sis, let me hip you to something. I know that you like to watch all those shows where the police are the good guys, and they come to ya' rescue every day, but that shit just ain't reality, at least not when ya' skin is dark like ours."

Joy frowned. In her young life, the only thing a policeman had done so far was wave at her. It was hard for her to believe that a police officer could harm her in any way. Since they lived in a rough neighborhood where crooked cops came through and regularly harassed people, Sarah kept a tight rein on her. She was only allowed to be outside no longer than two hours and absolutely, positively, had to be in the house before the streetlights came on.

"Bro, you been watching too many hood movies," she laughed. "You need to——"

"No, yo' little ass needs to listen to what the fuck I'm telling you. You think you know what's going on out here, but you don't. These cops don't give a fuck about our black asses, and the sooner you learn that, the better off you'll be."

"Why are you yelling at me?" Joy asked with tears in her eyes. Marcus had never in his life talked to her like that before, and it threw her for a loop. He hurt her feelings, and it was exhibited as a tear ran down her cheek.

Marcus felt like shit. In trying to school his baby sister about the ways of dirty cops, he'd inadvertently caused her pain. He grabbed her and pulled her close to him.

"I'm sorry, sis. I didn't mean to yell at you like that. I was just trying to let you know what time it was, so you don't get fooled by so-called officers of the damn law."

Marcus held his sister in his arms and rocked back and forth. They were the only two people at the bus stop, but Marcus didn't care if there were a hundred people there. All he cared about was comforting his sister. When he looked up, he saw the same police car that had passed them a few minutes earlier, stopping on the other side of the street. His eyes remained on them as he watched them get out of the car and walk their way. Joy must've felt him tense because she pulled away from his embrace and looked into his face. Following his eyes, she turned her head and saw the cops approaching.

"Hey, is your name Rodney? Rodney Byrd?"

"Who?"

"Rodney Byrd. Is that your name?"

"Nah, man. My name's Marcus. Marcus Green."

The two cops looked at each other and then back at Marcus. One of them then whispered into the other one's ear.

"Let me see some ID."

"For what? Man, you asked me my name, and I told you. Why y'all messing with me?" Marcus asked angrily. He didn't like the way the cops seemed to be accusing him of something.

"You getting smart with me, boy? Maybe we should do something about that slick mouth of yours."

Marcus saw red. As bad as he wanted to tell them to go to hell, he knew that would only lead to more trouble. He especially didn't want to get into a confrontation with them boys with his sister present. Figuring that the sooner he showed them ID, the sooner they would get the fuck on and leave them alone, he reached into his pocket.

"Hey! What the fuck are you doing? Get your hand out of your pocket!" the younger of the two officers yelled.

"Man, you asked me for my ID, so I'm—"

That's as far as he got before a bullet ripped through his chest and knocked him off the bench. Marcus collapsed onto the ground. He coughed up blood as he lay there, fighting for his life.

Joy's screams threatened to shatter the glass enclosure. She reached for her brother but was held back by the older cop. Lying on the ground was Marcus's school ID. Since they'd already asked Marcus for it, he figured that it was safe to take it out of his pocket. Now, he was lying on the cold pavement fighting for his life. The cops took their time calling for an ambulance. By the time it got there, Marcus was gone.

After the shooting, Sarah suffered a complete emotional breakdown. The only thing she had to cling to was that her son would be vindicated in a court of law. Because Sarah didn't want to put her daughter through the pain of remembering what had happened to her brother, she refused to allow her to testify. Her lawyer reminded her that without Joyce's testimony, there was a good chance that the officers would get off scot-free. Still, Sarah didn't budge. In her eyes, not only was she protecting her daughter from emotional trauma, but she was also protecting her against potential re-

taliation from the police. In the end, the shooting
was deemed justifiable. Even though the police
had instructed Marcus to show them his ID, the
powers that be claimed that the officer's expla-
nation that Marcus may have been reaching for a
gun gave them just cause to fire their weapons. It
was bullshit, and the entire community knew it,
but they were powerless to do anything about it.
Even though Sarah eventually filed a civil suit, no
amount of money could extinguish the pain of her
losing her child.

Despite her best efforts, Sarah was never able
to recover. Because she was always on the edge
of snapping, the state had no choice but to take Joy
away from her. This completely broke her spirit
and robbed her of her will to live. On the eve of her
forty-eighth birthday, Sarah was found dead in
her bathroom. Both of her wrists were slit.

Joy, who at such a young age couldn't understand why everything seemed to be getting taken
from her, went into a deep depression. That lasted
nearly a year. When she turned 18, the state released her from its custody. Upon her release, she
was approached by a lawyer, who told her that her
paternal grandfather had passed away. Joy didn't
blink. She'd never met the man, so she didn't really have any feelings about it one way or the other.
The lawyer also told her that he'd left her a sub-
stantial amount of money in his will. This bit of

good news came at just the right time for her. With nowhere to go and not a dime to her name, she needed a cash infusion in the worst way.

Because both her mother and brother were deceased and her grandfather had no other known relatives, the lawyer told Joy that the proceedings should move along quickly. He informed her that it would take no longer than thirty days for her to receive the inheritance. This still, however, presented a problem. Although the money was coming, she still had none at the time. How in the hell was she supposed to secure a place with no money? she'd asked him. Luckily for her, her grandfather owned the home where he lived. So as it turned out, she could live there without having to pay any rent. Things were looking up for her, but the memories of what happened to her brother and mother still haunted her. Every time she saw a cop, she wanted to throw up. She hated cops with a passion. Not only because of what they did to her brother but also because they had the nerve to pretend like they had given a damn. The entire situation made her wonder how in the hell they could sleep at night.

Joy wasn't so naïve that she believed every single cop was a bad one. But she did feel that the bad ones got away with bullshit because the good ones wouldn't hold them accountable. It was called the "blue wall," and she would bet her life that it was first invented by a racist-ass cop to trick ignorant-ass Black cops into keeping their mouths shut, even when their own people were being mistreated. But what could she do? Then, like a bolt of lightning, a wicked idea struck her. If she couldn't beat them, she would join them and corrupt everything she could from the inside out. Of course, Joy knew that she couldn't take down an entire police department. But what she could do was secretly look after the people that the corrupt cops usually targeted. While other cops were taking the pledge to protect and serve, Joy was secretly plotting to steal evidence and fuck up investigations. She blamed the entire police force for what happened to her brother. And she would feel that way until they put her in the ground.

"It looks like your daughter is having a good time," Joy said, bobbing her head to the music. "I see that DJ you hired is getting it in," she said.

"Yeah, he kinda fly." Before he knew it, Darnell also found himself moving to the beat. He looked over and saw Joy singing along to Jay-Z's song, "Brooklyn Go Hard."

"Damn, that shit bumping," Turiq said, coming out of the house, sipping on his drink.

"Yeah, we were just talking about how the DJ's killing it over there," Joy said. She cocked her head and looked around. There was something strange about the party, but she couldn't put her finger on it. Then it hit her. There were no young men there.

"Hey, Darnell, did you ever take care of that creeping situation?"

Joy cut her eyes at Darnell. "Creepin' situation? What creepin' situation?" she asked.

Darnell laughed. He thought it was funny the way she acted jealous sometimes. "Be cool, ma. It ain't what you think."

"Yeah, Joy, stop acting so jealous all the damn time," Turiq added.

"Whateva." Joy folded her arms and waited to see what they were talking about.

Darnell looked at Turiq and shook his head.

"What?" his friend and head capo asked.

"Nigga, are you drunk already? You asked me that one time already, remember?"

Turiq scratched his head and thought. "Oh shit, I did, didn't I?"

"Yeah, nigga, you did. I told you that I had Damon on it."

"Is someone going to fill me in on what the fuck is going on?" Joy asked impatiently. Darnell really didn't want to disclose that matter to her. However, he knew from experience that if he didn't tell her, she would bug the shit out of him until he did. He went ahead and told her about seeing Jamaal sneaking out of his house. When he finished, Joy frowned.

"Now what, Joy?" he asked.

"Baby, you shoulda let me take care of that little nigga. I woulda scared the shit out of his ass."

"I'm sure you would. But I don't want him only scared. I want his ass to *feel* something behind that disrespectful shit. And Damon is just the man for the job."

"Hold up. Is that why there are no boys here? You're punishing her?"

"You damn right. She's lucky I'm still giving her that damn car I promised her."

The three of them continued to shoot the shit until Darnell glanced over to where Sunny and some other girl were nose to nose.

"Now what?" he said, rubbing his face. He was just getting ready to go over and see what the problem was when the other girl abruptly stormed off.

"This is some bullshit," Sunny said, leaning back with her arms crossed.

"Tell me about it, girl. Yo' dad is waaaay outta bounds for this shit," her friend Kim cosigned. She was a short, thick, dark-skinned chick who Sunny had been friends with for nearly twelve years. While most of the young men gravitated toward Sunny, Kim seemed to drive them away like tear gas. Her attitude was stank, and her mouth was rancid. But to Sunny, she was a good friend and one of the funniest people she'd ever met. Standing next to her was Stacy. Stacy lived a few houses down. Although Sunny and Stacy weren't the best of friends, they were cool enough that Sunny felt comfortable inviting her to the party. Kim didn't particularly care for Stacy and hated it when she was around. The fact that Stacy and Sunny were eye candy and she wasn't caused her to become jealous whenever the three of them were together. Kim did a quick count of the guests and shook her head.

"Twenty bitches and no muthafuckin' niggas. Where the hell they do that at? Ain't enough dicks in here," she complained as if she regularly got laid. The truth of the matter was that she'd only had sex once. Kim wasn't a pretty girl, and she knew it. So to compensate for her lack of beauty, she often threw herself at the opposite sex.

"Kim, keep your damn voice down. Don't you see my dad over there watching us," Sunny said.

"Sunny, I don't know why you're so mad," Jazmine said. "This shit is your own fault. If your ass hadn't gotten caught sneaking that simple muthafucka out of your house, there would be some dicks swinging around here."

Butter and Dani, who came to the party along with Jazmine, snickered.

"Bitch, what the fuck you laughing at?" Sunny asked, looking directly at Dani. Butter was cool with her, but she didn't like Dani. There was just something about how Dani sauntered around like she was queen bitch that rubbed Sunny the wrong way. Sunny couldn't place her finger on it, but Dani just looked sneaky to her.

"I'm laughing at the same thing Butter is laughing at," Dani said, pointing at Butter. "Don't get mad at me because your daddy won't let you have any male company up in this piece."

"Bitch, who the fuck you think you're talking to like that? Jazmine, you better get ya' girl before I beat the brakes off her ass in here."

"Come on, y'all," Jazmine said, "calm the fuck down."

"No, *you* calm the fuck down. This broad is always popping fly at me, and I'm getting tired of that shit," Dani stated. Before anyone could stop her, Sunny had quickly invaded Dani's space. Jazmine quickly moved to separate her two friends. Although she'd known Dani longer, she and Sunny had gotten as thick as thieves in the last week or so.

"Dani, why don't you chill out?"

"Chill out? Why the fuck you telling *me* to chill? Tell that bitch to chill out. She started it."

Sunny pushed Jazmine out of the way as she got nose to nose with Dani. "I'll tell you what, ho. If you call me out of my name one more time, I'm gonna fuck yo' ass up."

"You know what? I don't even have to be at this boring-ass party. I'm going over to my man's house and lie up under him. At least I can get me some dick over there."

With that, Dani stormed off.

Chapter 12

Detective Little sat on the steps holding a handkerchief to the back of his head. He'd only been out for about twenty minutes. To him, it felt like two hours. When he finally came to, he had a splitting headache and a golf ball-sized knot on the back of his head. His vision was slightly blurry, and he feared that he might have a concussion. The last thing he remembered seeing was a potential witness sitting on the couch with a hole in her head. He had just dialed the number to call it in when someone cracked him in the back of the head. Luckily for him, his car was equipped with a LoJack, and they were able to zero in on his location. His vision was just beginning to clear when two black Crown Victorias came skidding to a stop in front of the curb. The first Crown Victoria hadn't even come to a full stop yet before Captain Moore yanked open the door and bolted toward his injured detective. While he was attending to Little, the other detectives made their way inside of the house. Little was surprised to see his captain there. Usually, he didn't come out to crime scenes.

"Little, are you okay?" he asked.

"I think so, sir," Little said. His voice was groggy, and Moore could tell that he was in pain.

"What the hell happened?"

Before Little could fill his captain in on what had gone down, one of the other detectives stuck his head out the front door. With a somber look on his face, he just shook his head.

"Cap, I think you'd better come take a look at this." Moore alternated looks between Little and the detective. The captain pulled his hand down the front of his face and walked into the house. Moore had been in law enforcement for a long time, so he wasn't surprised by what he saw when he entered the house. The thing that did surprise him was that someone had managed to sneak up on one of his best detectives and get the jump on him. Moore looked around the room and tried to spot anything that would give him a clue about what had gone down.

"Smith, get a forensic team in here ASAP. I want this place combed from top to bottom."

Both Moore and Little knew that Darnell was probably to blame for the young lady's brains being scattered all over the floor. Apparently, he had gotten word that the young lady was going to blow the whistle on him and made sure that she would never get the chance. Moore walked back outside disgusted. He hated that Darnell seemed to be untouchable. He wanted to see the arrogant drug dealer get the needle for killing one of his officers. Detective Warren may have been an asshole, but he was an asshole protected by a shield. The fallout from Warren's murder hadn't fully hit the precinct yet, but it was only a matter of time before his father caused a shitstorm to rain down on the police department. It was always bad whenever a cop got killed. But the shit was really about to hit the fan since it was a judge's brother that got murdered, especially when the judge and the mayor of the city were close friends.

"This shit stinks," he yelled.

"Tell me about it."

"No, I mean, this shit *really* stinks. Think about it. I send you over here to get this woman's statement about a murder, and someone gets here before we do and kills her? What does that tell you, Little?"

The detective didn't have to think long before figuring out what his captain was getting at. From what he was told, he and Moore were the only two to know about the witness. They gave each other a knowing look. There was a crack in the blue wall.

"Jesus, I hate to think that someone in my department is dirty, but obviously––" Moore's cell phone buzzed in his pocket before he got a chance to finish his sentence. When he took it out and looked at the number on the screen, the situation had officially gone from bad to worse.

Mayor Thomas Brackens and Judge Ryan Senters had been best friends since junior high school. Their mothers worked as police dispatchers and were good friends. Their fathers owned a carpentry business together and tried hard to get them to enter the business with them, but neither of the boys was interested. Both of them had a fascination with the law. From the time they sat around watching cop shows on television until they were seniors in high school, the two friends dreamed of the day they could stand side by side and arrest criminals. In their eyes, people who committed crimes deserved to be in jail, no matter what the situation was. They just couldn't understand why people who lived in the inner city had to resort to such drastic measures to survive. Their similar way of thinking was the catalyst for their strong bond. And although they took different career paths, they still had the same mentality and remained great friends. That's why it hit Brackens just as hard as it hit Senters when Warren was killed.

The two of them sat stone-faced inside of Captain Moore's office, awaiting his arrival. Every now and then, Brackens would place his hand on the shoulder of Senters and try to comfort him. Senters was struggling to keep his composure. He and his brother hadn't spoken to each other in five years, and the guilt was weighing on his soul like an anvil. As much as he wanted to yell and scream, he had to act only as a concerned citizen and not the grieving brother that he was. Brackens was already looking into the future. He would pull every string he could to ensure that he, and he alone, would be the judge who tried the guilty party when they were finally caught. His beady eyes stared daggers at Captain Moore and Detective Little as the two of them entered Moore's office.

Little chose to remain standing as Moore dropped down to the large leather seat behind his desk. For a few short moments, everyone just stared at one another.

"Well," Mayor Brackens said, breaking the silence, "do you have any leads on this damn case, Captain Moore?" The mayor folded his arms and glared at Moore. While he was doing that, Senters was doing the same to Little. He knew that Little was Warren's partner and wanted to know why in the hell wasn't he there when his brother had gotten murdered.

"Well, actually, we had a lead, sir, but—"

"Well, what the hell happened then, Captain? Why isn't the perpetrator in custody?"

"Because the witness is dead, sir. That's what I was trying to tell you. I sent Little here over to the witness's house to question her, but when he got there, he found her sitting on the couch with a bullet hole in her head."

The mayor's face went slack. Closing his eyes, he just shook his head.

"So, let me get this shit straight, Moore. One of this precinct's officers goes undercover to help take down that piece of shit drug dealer Darnell McCord and gets murdered in the process. And now, you're sitting in here telling me that the only potential witness to the crime had also been murdered? Is that what the fuck you're trying to tell me, Moore?"

"Uh, yes, sir, that's about the size of it, sir."

The mayor opened his mouth to say something, but before he could, Senters jumped up and stormed across the room. It first appeared that he was heading in Moore's direction, but at the last second, he stopped, planted his foot on the floor, and turned to face Little.

"Jesus Christ, Captain! What the fuck kind of idiot do you have working in this fucking department?" The question was directed to Captain Moore, but Senters was staring at Detective Little. He was standing so close to Little that the detective could smell what he had for breakfast. Little looked at Senters like he'd lost his mind. For the first time since he'd followed his captain into his office, he wondered what the hell a judge was doing there.

"First of all, Judge Senters, I'm going to need you to back the fuck up out of my face. And second, I had no idea that Anthony was going to do what he did. What the hell are you doing here anyway?"

"What do you mean, you didn't know? You're his goddamn partner. How could you *not* know?" Senters said, ignoring Little's question. Brackens quickly walked over and grabbed his friend. He didn't want Senters to do something that they both were going to regret.

"Easy, my friend, easy." He then turned his attention to Little. "Detective, this man is here as a friend of mine. He stopped by my office to see me when I was just getting ready to come over here," Brackens lied. "And, like I said, he's a good friend of mine, so I would appreciate it if you would show him the same fuckin' respect that you show me. Are we clear on that, Detective?"

"Yes, sir, Mayor," Little said through clenched teeth.

"Well, the last time I checked, this was still my office, and I don't appreciate your friend barging into it accusing my detective of being an idiot, sir."

"Well, what the hell do you call it, Captain?"

"We're still gathering the facts, sir. I have a forensic team over there right now combing through the victim's place, trying to find any clues or evidence that may be helpful to our investigation."

The mayor took a deep breath and rubbed his forehead. He would never say it publicly, but he needed to do something to ensure the community's faith in him with the election coming up. Drugs had been running rampant throughout the neighborhood. The best chance he had at getting reelected was to take down some of the city's dealers.

"Look, Captain, both of us have been on this job long enough that we know there are no such things as coincidences. Sure, this could have been random, but I seriously doubt it. I'd bet my next five paychecks that McCord had something to do with both of these murders. Piece this fuckin' puzzle together so that we can put this asshole behind bars."

The judge then turned to face Detective Little. "Detective, I apologize if we've offended you in any way. Let's remember that we're all on the same team here."

He held out his hand for Little to shake. Little thought about spitting on it. He was still pissed over the way Senters had talked to him, but he decided to let bygones be bygones. With a slight smile on his face, he reached out and shook Senters's hand. He was about to do the same for Brackens, but before he had the chance, the judge abruptly turned and stomped out of the office. Both Moore and Little waited until the two unwelcome visitors were on the elevator and headed downstairs before voicing their opinions.

"Okay, is it just me, or was that some strange-ass shit?" Little asked. He turned to look at Moore, who had his head cocked to the side with a twisted expression on his face. He was still staring at the elevator thirty seconds after it closed.

"No, it wasn't just you. That was *definitely* some strange-ass shit," he said.

Chapter 13

All Rick could do was laugh and shake his head. His little cousin, Jamaal, was getting schooled on the basketball court, and Rick was enjoying every minute of it. For some reason, his cousin thought that he was the second coming of LeBron James. He starred on his high school team, and although he was a talented player, he still had a lot to learn. When he wasn't chasing girls, the youngster could often be found on the courts alone practicing or embarrassing some of the lesser-talented players on the court. His ego had grown to enormous proportions. Rick, being the asshole that he was, decided to bring him down a peg or two. The young man had no way of knowing it, but the guys he was playing against today were former high school superstars who didn't have the grades to attend premier colleges. They were old enough to be able to play circles around the young man without breaking a sweat but were young enough so that he wouldn't get suspicious. Rick spat out a portion of the beer he was drinking when one of the players crossed over his cousin and dunked on him.

"Damn, nigga, you got took," Rick yelled out. His cousin, clearly embarrassed, gave Rick the finger in response. At first, the players told Rick that they were too busy to be bothered with his bullshit, but it was amazing what some weed heads would do for a bag of smoke. As his cousin continued to get taken to school, Rick continued to agitate the situation.

"Damn, cuzzo, that shit was nasty," he said when another one of the players went behind his back and nailed a jumper in his cousin's face.

"Man, fuck you," the youngster spat.

"Yo, don't get mad at me 'cause them niggas putting something on your ass," Rick said, laughing. After looking around the park to make sure no cops were trying to creep on him, Rick took another swig of his beer.

Richard "Rick" Baker had once himself been an outstanding basketball player. As a matter of fact, he received a partial scholarship to play at Cleveland State University, but his desire for fast money derailed his chances. He was busted twice for selling weed. The first time he was caught, the university chalked it up as a youthful mistake. The second time was the kiss of death. After that, Cleveland State quickly rescinded its scholarship offer. Instead of being seen as a rising star, he was seen as a knucklehead who didn't have the discipline or common sense to stay out of trouble.

When Rick's father grew tired of his antics and finally threw him out, he had no choice but to sell weed full time to survive. Later, while strolling through the mall, he ran into Jazmine.

After about thirty minutes of back-and-forth, the two of them discovered that they had something in common . . . weed.

The two of them had been hooking up for a few weeks before he found out who her father was. Had he known that she was the daughter of a drug-dealing murderer, he would have never even given her the time of day. He didn't need or want that kind of smoke, but it was too late now. They'd already consummated the so-called relationship. Rick was on edge every time she suggested getting together. He just knew that at any moment, the hotel door would fly open, and five goons would come inside and beat him within an inch of his life. So far, that hadn't happened . . . yet.

He was supposed to hook up with her a day or so ago, but he hadn't heard from her. And he was just fine with that. Rick looked up to see his little cousin storming toward him with an attitude.

"Man, I am ready to roll," he said.

Rick checked the time on his cell phone.

"Already, little cuz? What, you tired of them niggas dunkin' and rainin' threes on your ass?"

"Whatever, man." Rick's cousin dropped down on the hard bench and used his shirt to wipe excess sweat from his face. It amused Rick to see him pouting like a spoiled child. Although he felt bad about setting up his cousin, it was a lesson he thought he needed to learn.

"Let's roll, cuz," Rick said, as he stood up and headed toward his vehicle. Rick was still laughing as the two of them got in his whip.

"Man, what the fuck is so fuckin' funny?"

"You, nigga. Every time something don't go yo' way, you start pouting and acting like a child. Nah, you know what? Check that. Nigga, you actin' like a bitch."

Rick's cousin looked at him with a hurt look. He couldn't believe his cousin was talking to him that way. "Whatever, man," he said, leaning back on the headrest and staring out the window. Rick looked at his cousin and suddenly felt bad about the way he'd talked to him. His little cousin looked up to him, so he needed to do something to rectify the situation.

"Look, cuz. I'm sorry I talked to you that way. But you really need to stop wearing ya' heart on ya' sleeve like that. When people see you do that, they take advantage of it." Rick looked at his gas gauge and saw that he was low, so he detoured from his destination and headed to the nearest gas station.

"What are you doing? I thought you were gonna get me a rib dinner, and then we were gonna smoke something."

"Nigga, you wanna be walking? I need some damn gas. We can go after that. But check this shit out, dawg. I can't hang out with yo' ass too late. Hell, I don't know about you, but I got some pussy lined up for later."

His cousin frowned, remembering the last time he came close to getting his dick wet. His cousin noticed the look on his face.

"The fuck wrong with you, cuz?"

The youngster looked at him and wondered if he should say anything to Rick about what happened. He'd already been clowned one time today and didn't want to suffer embarrassment anymore.

"Dude, get the fuck outta yo' feelings," Rick said, reading his cousin's mind. "If something is on ya' mind, you know damn well you can tell me what the fuck is going on."

With a deep sigh, Rick's cousin told him about what had gone down recently. When he was done telling his story, his cousin glared at him like he'd lost his ever-loving mind.

"Nigga, is you fuckin' crazy? Don't you know how much time you can get for some shit like that?"

"Man, didn't nothing happen."

"It don't fuckin' matter. All she needs to do is say something happened. Li'l nigga, you better get yo' head on straight before they send yo' ass up the road. The best thing you can do now is stay as far away from that bitch as you can," Rick advised his kinfolk as he got ready to get out and pump gas.

"You right, fam. Fuck both of those bitches. Sunny and her friend Jazmine can kiss my ass."

Rick froze in his tracks. The name his cousin said rang in his head like Christmas bells.

"Jazmine? Cuz, did you say her name was Jazmine?"

"Yeah, so?"

"Cuz, let me ask you something. What does this bitch look like?"

As the young man described Jazmine's appearance to Rick, the color began to drain out of Rick's face, and a migraine started to creep in.

"Dude, after I pump this gas, we gotta have a fuckin' talk." Rick got out of the car and walked into the gas station to pay for his gas. "I can't believe this shit," he said, shaking his head all the way there.

Chapter 14

Moon's eye's swept back and forth as he sat on the steps of the now dilapidated East High School. For the last six hours, he'd been posted up there doing what he needed to do to survive. At 20 years old, Moon had learned early what it took most individuals a lifetime to learn . . . that the world didn't give a shit about you. Moon had been on his own since he was 17 years old. A disagreement between him and his mother led to her kicking him out. For three years, he survived on the streets of Cleveland by robbing and stealing. So far, he hadn't graduated to murder yet, but with a heart as cold as Moon's, it was just a matter of time. The young man had brutish features. His hands were larger than an average person's. He was only five foot ten, but he was powerfully built. Moon never felt sorry for himself, but he did wonder how long he was for this world. In his mind, nothing was as bad as living on the street and wondering where your next meal was coming from. Death struck no fear in his heart. He reasoned that even if he did die, he would be free of the world and its bullshit, and he didn't see anything wrong with that.

In time, he and his mother made amends. She wanted him to move back into the house, but he refused. She'd thrown him out once. Who's to say that she wouldn't do it again when she got mad? At least, that's the way he saw it. But Moon did love his mother, and he helped her whenever he could. Her job didn't pay much, so she was always behind the eight ball. His father had died when he was 15, and he hadn't completely gotten over it, but he knew that life went on. His big break, so to speak, came when he got caught breaking into the car of a ruthless drug dealer. The few dollars he found in the console was less than nothing to the dealer. But to Moon, the twenty dollars meant that he would eat for the rest of the day. After stuffing the money in his pocket, Moon was just about to get out of the truck and flee the scene when something hard pressed up against the back of his skull.

"Don't move, muthafucka."

For a brief second, Moon thought about trying his luck but then reasoned that if he were going to die, he wanted his killer to look him in the eye before pulling the trigger.

"Nigga, get the fuck outta my whip," an angry voice shouted.

When Moon had gotten all the way out, he was spun around and shoved roughly against the vehicle. The gun that had been pointed at the back of his head was now resting on his cheek.

"You tryin'a rob me, nigga?" Damon asked him.

Moon shook his head.

"No? Then what the fuck do you call yo'self doing?"

"Just trying to make a living, man."

"Well, let me put you up on something. Dying ain't much of a living, my nigga." Damon reached into Moon's pocket and pulled out the crumpled twenty-dollar bill.

"Twenty muthafuckin' dollars," Damon spat. "You 'bout to get yo' ass whupped over twenty punk-ass dollars. Yo, Slab, show this li'l thief what we do to muthafuckas who steal from us."

Slab smiled. He was Damon's henchman and a man who loved violence more than life itself.

Damon could look at Moon and tell that he was just a young kid. It was the only reason he hadn't splattered his brains across the cement. Still, the kid had violated, and he needed to be taught a lesson.

Slab grabbed a fistful of Moon's shirt and yanked him forward. With an evil grin on his face, Slab drew back to slap the youngster, but that was as far as he got. Before he knew what had hit him,

Moon thrust his head forward and headbutted Slab in the nose. The pain forced Slab to release the grip he had on the young man. Slab staggered back but quickly regained his bearings. Rage filled his eyes as he rushed Moon. He took a wild swing, but Moon easily ducked it. Before he could gather himself to throw another punch, Moon hoisted *him* in the air. With a show of strength Damon hadn't seen in a long time, Moon threw Slab across the hood of Damon's truck. Angry and embarrassed, Slab headed back around the truck. He no longer wanted just to kick the young man's ass. Now, he wanted to kill him. He was just about to go at Moon again when Damon stopped him.

"Hold up, Slab," he said, cocking the hammer on his pistol. "Li'l nigga, you know you just signed your own death warrant, right?"

"Do what you gotta do, fam. I ain't never been scared to die, and I damn sure ain't gonna just stand here and take an ass-whoopin' from this pussy-ass nigga," Moon said, cutting his eyes at Slab.

"What you say, li'l nigga?" Slab said, moving closer to Moon.

"Damn, bro, ain't you done had enough?" Paul asked smirking. "You better leave that li'l nigga alone before we have to call the meat wagon for yo' ass."

Paul was another one of Damon's cronies. Throughout the fight, he was trying hard to resist the urge to laugh. He hated seeing his partner in crime getting manhandled like that, but the shit was funny as hell.

"Fuck you, nigga," Slab spat. His nose was bleeding, and his vision was blurry.

Damon looked into the young man's eyes, searching for fear, but his voyage came up empty. He looked at his clothes and concluded that they probably hadn't been washed in quite some time. His shoes were worn and scuffed. He looked back at Slab and found it nearly impossible not to laugh. Damon had seen Slab put some of Cleveland's toughest customers in the hurt locker, and the young kid damn near rendered him unconscious.

"What's ya' name, li'l nigga?"

"Moon," the young man answered.

"Moon? Now, I know damn well that ain't ya' government, li'l nigga."

"Nah, it ain't."

"Well, what the fuck is it?" Damon said impatiently.

"Why the fuck they call you Moon?" Paul asked.

"Long story," Moon said, relaxing a little.

"Well, Moon. I got a question for you. How would you like to make some real bread?"

"What? My dude, I know you ain't about to let this li'l nigga eat off——"

"Slab, shut the fuck up before I have this li'l nigga fuck you up again!"

Slab was tight, but he knew better than to go against his boss.

"So, what's good, Moon? You wanna make this cheese or not?"

"Doing what?"

"Li'l nigga, does it fuckin' matter? You ain't doin' shit now but breaking into cars and puttin' ya' life at risk. I'm offering you a chance to move up on the food chain. You'd be a fool not to take it."

Moon looked at the attire of the man standing before him. His jeans were crisp and clean. An Odell Beckham jersey hung loosely from his frame. The platinum and diamond bracelet on his wrist shined brightly. Even his flunkies were dressed nicely. Moon may have been proud, but he was far from a fool.

"Good, good," Damon said as Moon nodded his head in agreement. He would have to run it by Duck and Pee Wee, who, in turn, would have to talk to Tariq and Darnell. But for all intents and purposes, Moon was now a soldier in Darnell's army. That was a year ago, and Moon had more than proven his worth.

After selling his last pack, Moon pulled out his cell phone. He was just getting ready to call Damon and let him know that he needed another pack when a Lexus truck came peeling up in the parking lot. Moon instinctively reached behind a large rock where he kept his burner stashed. He was more than ready to issue lead to anyone trying to creep on him.

"Be easy, cowboy. It's me," Damon said, rolling down the passenger-side window.

"Damn, man, when you get that?" Moon asked.

"I'll tell you on the way. Let's roll."

"On the way where?"

"Li'l nigga, stop asking so many questions and get in the damn truck."

Damon hit a button and unlocked the doors. When Moon got in, he reached into his pocket to give Damon the day's profit. "Later for that, fam," Damon said, holding out his hand to stop him. "We got something to handle right quick."

"Oh, yeah? What's good?"

"Well, apparently Darnell caught some li'l nigga on camera sneaking out of this house, so he wants us to go straighten dude's ass out."

"Word? Damn, it's been awhile since I swung these hammers," Moon said, shadowboxing.

"Pump your brakes, killa. You just there to flank a nigga. I got this. I ain't got my hands dirty in a minute, so I need the practice," he said sneering. "Oh, and let me put you up on something else too, fam. I'm not supposed to say anything yet, but sometime in the next few months, Darnell's gonna be calling a meeting."

"So what?" Moon said, not giving a fuck. None of the soldiers had ever even seen Darnell, let alone been in a meeting with him as far as he knew.

"If yo' li'l ass would listen, I'll tell you so what. You know what?" Damon said, getting annoyed. "You need to start closing your damn mouth and listen. I couldn't even get this out of my mouth before you start questioning shit."

"My bad, man."

"Now, like I was saying, he's putting together a meeting. It's the first time that I've heard that he's going to bring the first and second soldiers in on it."

Moon raised an eyebrow. This *was* big news. Something was going on, and he was glad to be a part of it.

"Keep that on the low, youngster."

"Fo' sho', big homie. You ain't got to worry about me saying nothing."

"I know that, little nigga. Why the fuck you think I am telling you? I knew from day one that you were a stand-up nigga. That's why I . . . Shit, we got here just in time," he said as he watched the young man get into the passenger side of a Nissan Altima.

"That's gotta be his bitch's car. I don't know no muthafuckin' brotha who drives a fucking Altima," he said, laughing. Damon followed the car for ten minutes.

"Bingo," he said when the car pulled into a gas station. Not wanting to look suspicious, Damon pulled up next to the pump three lanes across and waited for the driver to get out. They watched as he went into the gas station and came back to the pump. As soon as he started pumping gas, Damon turned to Moon.

"Go inside and make sure that no one calls the police. And get that surveillance tape too."

Being the good soldier that he was, Moon tucked his gun into his waistband, got out, and made his way into the gas station store. He looked around and was glad to see that there were only a few people in there. He didn't want to hurt anyone, but he would if he had to. Two of the customers were still shopping, while the other one looked to be heading toward the bathroom. Moon glanced at the cashier and saw that he was too busy on his cell phone to notice anything. He looked back out the door and gave Damon the sign that everything was a go. Damon nodded his head and smiled.

With a slow creep toward the man pumping gas, he took out his gun. The man turned his head just in time to see the butt end of a pistol coming down across the side of his head. The man collapsed to the pavement. He still had his hand on the pump, so he inadvertently pulled the pump out of the gas tank when he fell. Gas squirted all over the side of the car. Damon peered into the car and saw that the young man did not know what was going on. Crouching down, he crept around the side of the vehicle. He prayed that the door was unlocked. The last thing that he wanted to do was smash the window to get in. He grabbed the handle and pulled. He smiled when he heard the door click. With a strong pull, the door came open. The unsuspecting young man looked up with fear in his eyes.

"Come here, li'l bitch-ass nigga," Damon snarled as he tried to snatch Jamaal out of the car. Jamaal's body jerked as the seat belt prevented him from being pulled out. Damon reached down and unclicked the seat belt just before yanking him out of the car. As he looked down at the young man, Damon noticed the fear in his eyes.

"I heard you got caught being someplace you wasn't supposed to be at, li'l nigga."

"Huh? What the fuck you talkin' about, man? I don't even know you," Jamaal said.

"Nah, li'l nigga, you don't know me. But I bet you know my boss, Darnell. And I damn sure know that you know his daughter, Vanessa."

At the mention of Sunny's legal name, Jamaal nearly shit himself. He thought that he'd gotten away with trying to rape Jazmine, but obviously, he was wrong. He had no way of knowing that he was being roughed up because he'd been seen on camera leaving Darnell's home. He was just about to open his mouth and snitch on himself when he saw Rick stagger around the car.

"Yo', man, what the fuck you doing? Get the fuck away from my little cousin, man."

Damon raised his pistol and pointed it at Rick. "And what if I don't, nigga? What the fuck you gon' do about it? A few seconds ago, you felt how this gun feels after being hit with it. The next time, yo' ass is gonna feel what comes out of the end of it. Now, just stand there and shut the fuck up."

Damon slapped Jamaal upside the head with his gun. Jamaal's legs gave out, but because Damon had him by the collar, he couldn't fall. As badly as Rick wanted to rush Damon, he knew that it would be a fool's move to do so. The hardened look in the killer's eyes told him that he would be dead before he even took the first step.

"Now, like I was saying, li'l nigga, Darnell wanted me to let you know that he didn't appreciate you sneaking around in his house when he wasn't home. All you had to do was go over there like a man, introduce yo'self, and let the chips fall. But y'all li'l niggas always wanna try to be slick."

Even as he was giving his speech, Damon wanted to laugh. Darnell hadn't said any of the shit he was kicking to Jamaal, but it made him feel like a big man bestowing some great amount of knowledge on someone of lesser intelligence.

"And, oh, yeah, he told me to tell you something else." Damon's words came in the form of his pistol crashing down on top of his head. "The next time I have to pay you a visit, I'm gonna give you more than a knot on the top of yo' fuckin' head. You feel me?"

All Jamaal could do was nod his head. Truth be told, he was happy as hell that the attempted rape of Jazmine hadn't been mentioned. Damon looked in the direction of the gas station entrance and gave Moon the signal to come out. Moon walked out with his head whipping around and the surveillance tape in his hand. He quickly jumped in the car, throwing the video in the backseat.

"Remember, nigga. The next time I have to come see yo' ass, I ain't gonna slap you around with the burner. I'ma let it make love to yo' ass." With his gun still trained on Rick, Damon made his way toward the driver's side of his truck. He backhanded Rick with his pistol for good measure, causing the man to fall to his knees, clutching his face.

"That's for trying to look tough, bitch-ass nigga." After hopping inside the truck, Damon mashed the gas, and the two goons peeled out of the gas station and sped down the street.

"Now, *that* was some gangsta-ass shit. But on some real shit, what the fuck is this meeting about?" Moon asked.

"The fuck if I know. But if he's asking for all the lieutenants and their right hands to be there, then it must be hella important."

Chapter 15

After the situation with Jamaal was resolved, Damon swung by the house of a broad Turiq fucked with and picked up another package for Moon. Damon was becoming quite impressed with the young man's loyalty as well as his hustle game. His make-money-first mentality was a welcomed attitude and proved that he was all about his business. Damon frowned as he recalled how Duck had spoken to him. He wanted to punch the arrogant capo in the face but knew that it would mean certain death if he did.

"You gon' be the first muthafucka to go, nigga," Damon mumbled as he thought about Duck's disrespectful ways ever since he was a street soldier. Damon felt that it was his destiny to be on top. Being a soldier was a start move. Being a lieutenant was even better. Being a capo? That was cool too. But the only thing Damon ever wanted to be was the boss. In his opinion, Frank held him back from being that, so he had to go. Damon was sure that Duck and Pee Wee had their suspicions about what happened to Frank, but since neither of them had any proof, there was no way that they could go running to Turiq or Darnell, so that was that. Damon was far from stupid. He knew that to over-throw the throne, you needed two things. One was your own pipeline to the supplier. He was work-ing on that. The other thing that Damon was going to need was a crew, and regardless of whether he knew it, Moon was going to be his first recruit. He wanted to have at least four more money-hungry killers on his team before he made his move.

As Damon made a right on Euclid Avenue, he saw a man putting his infant son in a car seat. His mood instantly turned sour. A wave of jealousy washed over his heart. He'd never met his father, but from the little his mother told him, the man was a piece of shit. She didn't like to discuss him much, opting only to say that the day they split up was the best day of her life. She tried to tell Damon that his father never knew that she was pregnant with him, but Damon refused to believe her. He felt in his soul that she was protecting the asshole, and for the life of him, he couldn't figure out why.

It took Damon another ten minutes to get to his place, and when he finally did, he saw a familiar vehicle waiting there for him. It was a green Honda Accord with tinted windows. Damon didn't need to see inside to know who had come to visit him. The head of the individual sitting in the car bobbed up and down to a catchy beat from Dr. Dre. Even if the windows hadn't been tinted, it still would have been virtually impossible to identify the person through the thick cloud of smoke circulating throughout the whip unless you knew who it was. Damon just shook his head as he got out of his truck and made his way over to the Honda. The closer he got, the more his annoyance level grew. The music was so loud, the car vibrated. The bass coming from the speakers threatened to shatter the windows.

"Young bitches," he mumbled as he tapped on the glass. As soon as the window was halfway down, Damon barked at the driver.

"Bitch, what the fuck is wrong with you blasting that shit out here like that? Turn that shit down."

"Sorry, babe, I was just getting into my zone."

"Getting into your zone? What the fuck are you talking about? You know what? Never the fuck mind! Just turn that shit off and come the fuck on." Without waiting for a response, Damon turned and headed for his front door. Dani, the young lady, quickly got out of her car and followed him. She was a sexy, dark-skinned chick who Damon had shot game to at a traffic light one night. From the way that she was eyeing his whip, Damon could tell that she was one of "those" types of broads. He invited her back to his place the same night. A half bottle of Hennessy and a thick blunt later, he was standing behind her pounding away at her sweet little pussy. Because he didn't want to pony up the money for a hotel, he had made the mistake of taking her to where he lay his head. Now, he couldn't get rid of the bitch. He'd thought about telling her to stay away from his crib but knew that she was the type of broad that would cause a scene.

"You wanna hit this, baby?" she asked when they got inside the house.

"Yeah, let me hit that shit." Damon pinched the blunt from her fingers and raised it to his lips. With a deep pull, he drew the smoke into his lungs and held it in. A few seconds later, he expelled it into the air. Damon had no idea where she copped her weed at, but she always bought some premium shit.

"Go pour me a drink," Damon ordered. He figured that since she was there once again, she might as well make herself useful. Damon went to his basement and turned on his seventy-five-inch television screen. For the rest of the day, all he wanted to do was relax, fuck, drink, and relax some more.

"So, how was work today, baby?" she asked, coming down the stairs. Damon heard her before he saw her. But once she came into view, his eyes did a double take. Holding drinks in both hands, the young lady sexily sashayed over to him in her bra and panties. Damon's dick immediately jumped to attention. To be so young, she knew exactly how to turn a man on.

"Damn," he said, gawking at her. "Are you sure yo' ass is 20 years old?" he asked. She smiled and nodded as she handed Damon his drink.

"Well?" she asked.

"Well, what?" Damon asked, damn near drooling on himself.

"How was work today?"

"Oh, it was cool." The young woman had no idea that Damon was a lieutenant for one of Cleveland's most notorious kingpins. Whenever she asked him what he did for a living, he would always give her a vague answer and quickly change the subject.

"Come and sit on my lap," he commanded. His manhood wasn't fully erect yet, but it was damn sure close. The young woman eased down on his lap, wiggling her ass on his dick as she did.

"Somebody's ready for the good stuff," she said. They both took a large sip of the brown liquor they had in their glasses. They eyed each other hungrily. The young woman reached behind her back and undid her bra, allowing it to fall into her lap. She then poured a small amount of liquor on her left nipple. With a sexy look in her eye, she picked up the bra and threw it around Damon's neck and slowly pulled his head toward her plump, dark areola.

Damon's lips parted as he let the nipple enter his mouth. Soft moans escaped her throat as he sucked it gently. Her hands began to probe. She let them glide over his jeans and took hold of the monster inside of them. As he continued to suck her nipples, she undid his belt buckle and unbuttoned his jeans. Expertly, she unzipped them and snaked her hands inside of his underwear until she found what she was looking for.

Hard.

Thick.

Meat.

After stroking it a few times, she got off his lap and motioned for him to stand up. When he did, she pulled his pants down to his ankles. She licked her lips and decided not to waste any time. In less than a second, she devoured his penis. Just when Damon was getting ready to bust off, she stopped.

"Fuck you doin'?" he asked. As an answer to his question, she got up from her knees and pushed him back down on the sofa.

"Give it to me, baby," she said, straddling him. Warm tingles swam through Damon's nuts as her wetness engulfed him. Dani winced as Damon's manhood filled her up.

"Oh God, baby, yes," she moaned. Hearing her sexy voice caused Damon to thrust harder. Wanting to get into every crevice of her sweet walls, Damon picked her up and laid her on the floor. The young woman wrapped her legs around his waist and crossed her ankles. It didn't take long for both of them to release their love juices together.

"Oh my God, baby, I needed this," Dani said. She'd been so stressed out from the argument at Sunny's party that this was just what she needed to help her relax. Jazmine, Butter, and Dani had known each other for years, but it had only been recently, about six months ago, that they'd started hanging out. Dani and Butter were the first of the trio to become friends. They were hanging out with each other at the mall when they ran into Jazmine at the food court. The three of them struck up a conversation and quickly became friends. That's why it bothered Dani so much that neither of them came to her defense when Sunny tried to style on her. She wanted to beat Sunny's ass, but the hurt and betrayal she felt from her so-called friends went deeper. Both of them had tried to call her after she stormed off, but Dani was in her feelings and didn't want to be bothered with either of them.

As she drove away from Sunny's house, the only thing on her mind was getting high, getting drunk, and getting fucked and not particularly in that order. It wasn't the first time that the three of them had had a spat. But it was the first time that her two friends didn't have her back, and it stung. Dani had heard the rumors on the street about who Sunny's father was but didn't know if they were true. She had also heard that Jazmine's father was in the game as well. She'd come close to asking Jazmine about it on a few occasions but always chickened out.

Dani moaned as she felt Damon's dick hardened. It had only been three minutes since he busted his last nut, but he was ready for round two.

"Ooooh, yes, baby, seconds. I love it when you give a bitch seconds."

Searing heat rushed through Damon's loins as he plunged back into Dani's sweetness. Her inner walls felt like warm silk, and the sensation suddenly reminded Damon of why he kept Dani around. Typically, after getting a nut, men could last forever the second time around. But those were the men who hadn't fucked Dani. Her pussy was so good that Damon was only ten strokes in before he was ready to bust again. "Fuck, you got some good-ass pussy," he told her.

"Uh-uh. You like this pussy, baby?"

"Fuck, yeah," Damon said, withdrawing his penis. Getting up from the floor, he went into the bathroom to relieve his bladder. The way she'd just put the pussy on him made him rethink any plans he had to get rid of her in the near future. However, he still planned to keep her in the dark as to how he made his living. That part of his life was none of her business.

After finishing up in the bathroom, Damon came out ready to get nice. The glass of liquor that Dani had brought him was still half full, and he planned on drinking that and a lot more before the night was done. His ego swelled as he looked down at Dani and saw that she was still panting. A smile was plastered on her face. Even though he had decided to keep her around a little while, he was still going back and forth in his mind about whether he wanted her to stay the night. When he looked down at her nude body again, the decision became an easy one.

"Hey, if you want to stay overnight, it's cool. But don't be asking me about moving in and shit. Feel me?"

"Oh, I felt you, baby. I felt you like a muthafucka," she said sexily while playing with herself.

"You trying to be funny, huh? You know what the fuck I'm talking about."

"Okay, baby, okay. I won't bring it up."

Although Dani was disappointed to hear Damon make such a decree, she quickly brushed it off. She knew that there would be other times to bring it up. Dani was really beginning to like Damon. He may have been a square when it came to what he did for a living, but there was nothing wrong, she reasoned, with a man bringing home a steady paycheck. Dani lived in a one-bedroom apartment. Her bullshit job paid just enough to pay her rent and buy groceries. She wasn't with Damon for financial reasons, but she sure as hell wasn't going to turn down any help he wanted to give her. Suddenly, both of their cell phones buzzed at the same time.

"Yo, what up?" Damon asked the caller.

"'Sup, nigga? Darnell wants to know if you took care of that little problem," Turiq said.

"Oh, fo' sho', dawg. I definitely took care of that shit."

"Then how come you ain't call and fuckin' tell us?" Turiq barked.

"Oh man, I——"

"Forget it, nigga. From now on, when we give yo' ass something to do, let us know as soon as it's done."

Before Damon could even respond, Turiq hung up in his face. Damon looked at the phone and snarled. He knew that Turiq didn't care for him, but he was getting tired of getting disrespected by upper management.

"Bitch-ass nigga," he spat. He quickly downed the rest of his drink and was about to tell Dani to get him another one when he saw her animatedly talking on her cell phone.

"Fuck all that. You bitches were supposed to have my back. I thought we was fuckin' friends. What? Y'all just gon' let this Johnny-come-lately bitch take my spot?" Dani listened for a few seconds before speaking again. "Yeah, whateva. I'll talk to you hoes later. I got shit to do."

Dani hung up without saying another word.

"Damn, what the fuck was that shit all about, shorty?"

As soon as the question rolled off his lips, Damon wished like hell he could take them back.

Like most women in America, Dani couldn't answer a question in one sentence. He only half-listened as she rambled on about how her friends dissed her at some party. It wasn't until she mentioned Sunny's name that Damon started paying attention.

"Wait, who? What did you say her name was?" Damon had no idea that Dani even knew Sunny.

"Her name is Vanessa, but they call her Sunny. Why? You know the bitch or something?" Dani asked with an attitude.

"Miss me with that whole jealousy shit, shorty. Ain't nobody on that bullshit."

"I ain't on the bullshit either. I'm just asking you if you know her ass."

Damon ignored her as the wheels started turning in his head. This could be just the lucky break he needed to accelerate his ascension to the number one spot. By that time, he planned to have a team of goons to help him with his takeover. He glanced at Dani, who was still looking at hime sideways, and smiled. A wicked idea formed in his head. What better way to take down an empire than from the inside out? But as with any great achievement, there comes great sacrifice. Still smiling, he slid up next to Dani and threw his arm around her. He suddenly began to realize that she could be the most critical piece on the chessboard. But in order to get her in the game, he had to put her on his team.

Chapter 16

"Is it done?" Darnell asked Turiq. "Yeah, that silly muthafucka got it done."

Darnell noticed the tone in which his question was answered. Turiq had never much cared for Damon, nor had he ever hidden his feelings about it.

"What's good with you and that li'l nigga, 'Riq? Every time that nigga's name is mentioned, you get in ya' feelings. What? That nigga fuck yo' bitch or something?" Darnell asked. Darnell hadn't gotten this far in the game by not being able to read the body language of other people. Whenever Damon's name was brought up, both Tariq and Duck tensed up like they were getting ready for war.

"Nah, man, it ain't nothing like that. I just don't trust that li'l nigga. He seems kinda sneaky to me. You remember when Frank got killed? Everybody was getting ready to go to war and ride for our comrade. But that nigga was as cool as a fuckin' cucumber. He didn't seem rattled at all. That shit doesn't seem suspect to you, fam?"

Darnell had long ago thought about the words Turiq was now saying to him. Of course, he had his own suspicions as to what had gone down, but he didn't have any proof, and he wasn't about to kill a member of his organization without it. His gut feeling told him that either Duck or Pee Wee had suspicions as well, but since neither of them brought anything to the table, Darnell decided to let the matter die.

"Yes, it did. But let's just suppose that Damon did have something to do with Frank's death; we have no way of proving it, so give me one good reason that we should push the matter further."

Turiq sighed. All he had was a hunch, and the fact that he didn't like the young man mattered very little to Darnell. His boss wanted proof, and Turiq didn't have any. After figuring that he'd waited on Turiq long enough, Darnell shrugged his shoulders and said, "Exactly, my friend. You don't have one. Now, all I know is that when Frank died––"

"Was murdered," Turiq corrected him.

"Died, murdered, what-the-fuck-ever," he said, irritated. "When he left this world, Damon stepped in, and the money train didn't stop. As a matter of fact, the profits grew, did they not?"

Turiq hated to admit it, but Damon did seem to be a better earner than Frank.

"Yeah, I guess so," Turiq said.

"Then that's that, my dude. Let this shit go." The way Darnell said it, Turiq knew that it wasn't a request.

"A'ight, man. I just have one more thing to say on the subject."

"What's that?" Darnell asked, rubbing his temples. He was getting tired of this subject and wanted to move on.

"Let's just say for the sake of argument that I'm right and that the li'l nigga did have something to do with Frank getting killed. No, I don't have any proof, but if I'm correct on my assumption, we need to keep an eye on that li'l nigga. If he had the balls to knock off Frank so that he could take his spot, how long do you think it will be before he gets it in his head to try to take one of us out?"

Darnel pondered the question. It wasn't like he didn't know that a bull's-eye was on his back and that some ambitious upstart was always gunning for his crown. He just didn't think any of his own people would be foolish enough to try to do it. He remembered the look in Damon's eyes when he ordered him to handle the Jamaal situation. There was a hint of disappointment in them when Darnell told his lieutenant to just slap him around instead of ordering the young man's death. There was also another look in Darnell's eyes. It was one of recognition, like he'd seen Damon somewhere before, even before he'd started making money for the squad. Still, Darnell knew that his friend had a point. Anyone thirsty enough to kill a member of his team needed to be watched closely.

"Well, I hope that li'l nigga is smart enough to keep dumb-ass ideas like that out of his head."

"Me too. I just think we need an extra set of eyes and ears on that muthafucka to make sure that he doesn't start feeling himself a little too much."

Darnell sighed. He hadn't planned on telling Turiq or anyone else, but it seemed like his friend was going to bug the shit out of him about the situation, so he decided to let the cat out of the bag. A slight grin creased his lips and soon turned into a broad smile.

"I'm already on it, my nigga."

"Huh? Since when?"

"Since the day Frank was murdered."

Chapter 17

Marvin sweated profusely as he pumped in and out of the young woman's juicy nectar. His penis was only five inches long, and there was no way in the world that he would ever be able to satisfy the young vixen. Had it not been for his long tongue and deep pockets, she would have never even given him the time of day.

Angela "Butter" Vincent grew up in a financially challenged household where bills were often behind, new clothes were scarce, and having seconds at the dinner table was considered a luxury. Eighty percent of the time, her father was either drunk or absent. He couldn't find a decent-paying job, so he was forced to work two minimum wage jobs just to make ends meet. His inability to adequately provide for his family frustrated him to the point where his only solace could be found at the bottom of a Jack Daniel's bottle. He loved his wife and his kids, and it hurt his soul not to be able to give them some of the things that other men gave their families.

Butter, her younger brother Terry, and her older sister Melissa all loved their father deeply, so much so that they never asked for anything. They would much rather see their father at home with them than watch him work nineteen-hour days between two jobs so that they could have the latest designer clothes. John was never aware of their sacrifices, but it meant the world to their mother, Christine. She was ecstatic that her kids knew the meaning of true love. That all changed, however, when the two younger sisters became teenagers.

Being in high school presented an entirely different set of problems. It was in that setting that peer pressure first reared its ugly head. Day after day, they witnessed young ladies their age walking around wearing nice clothes and having money in their possession. One of the girls took a liking to Melissa and befriended her. Melissa was shocked to learn that the girl's father didn't live with her and that her mother didn't make much money.

"Joan, how in the fuck can you afford such nice things when you're just as broke as I am?" she asked her friend. Joan smiled and patted her pelvic area.

"Because I know how to use what I have to get what I want."

This disturbed both Melissa and Butter. They'd always been taught that taking money from a man in exchange for sexual favors pretty much made you a prostitute. Joan, however, had been raised differently. Then one day, out of the blue, Joan asked them a question that would change their entire way of thinking.

"Let me ask y'all something. If a man offered y'all twenty dollars to give him some pussy, would you do it?"

"Hell no," the two sisters said in unison.

"Okay, okay," Joan said, holding up her hands. "Now, what if that same man offered you five grand? Would you do it then?"

Both sisters looked at each other. Neither of them said a word at first.

"Joan, there's a big-ass difference between twenty dollars and five grand."

"So, is that a yes or a no?" Joan pressed the issue.

Melissa looked at her younger sister. She didn't want to set a bad example, but she didn't want to appear fake either, so she decided to keep it one hundred.

"I mean, I guess so, probably."

"Probably my ass, bitch, and the only reason you're acting all coy and shit is because Butter is standing here. You know damn well, if a nigga offered you that much bread to give up the coochie, you'd beat him getting in the damn bed."

"Whateva, bitch. What the fuck is your point?" Melissa asked.

"My point is this. In one way or another, we all accept money for pussy. Let me put it to you another way. If you didn't give a man some ass, do you think he would do anything for you? Hell no. And if you were married or even had a boyfriend, and he didn't do shit for you, why in the fuck would you spread your legs for his sorry ass? You wouldn't, would you?"

As much as Melissa hated to admit it, her friend had a point—a very good point.

"But don't you worry about your reputation?" Butter asked.

"Fuck no. It ain't like I'm messing around with a bunch of different dudes. There's only two, and one of them don't even go to this school."

"What school does he go to?" Melissa asked.

"He doesn't. He's out of school."

"Damn, girl, you messing around with a nigga that old?"

"Rule number two," Joan said, laughing. "If you gonna try to get some coins out of a nigga, make sure that he's older than you. Most of these muthafuckas our own age are just as broke as we are. Now, let's roll up to the food court and get something to eat. Don't worry about it. I got it," Joan said, flashing two fifty-dollar bills.

From that moment on, the seeds of manipulation were planted inside of Butter. Five years later, at the tender age of 20, her sexual skill level was at an all-time high. She caught Marvin at just the right time. His wife had just passed away from breast cancer, and he was lonely and vulnerable. What he thought would be a simple release of tension and sexual frustrations one night turned into Butter pussy-whipping the hell out of him. After putting it on him again the following morning, Butter had Marvin eating out of the palm of her hand. He fell hard for her. He practically begged her to move in with him, and she'd been there ever since. But tonight, all she wanted was for Marvin to hurry up and come so that she could hop in the shower and be ready by the time Jazmine got there to pick her up.

Trying to hurry the process along, she started talking dirty and moaning loudly. She knew that Marvin loved it when her mouth went to the gutter in the bedroom. It actually turned him on more than the act of having sex. Her plan worked to perfection. Less than ten seconds later, Marvin was coating her insides with his semen. Breathing heavily, he rolled off her and collapsed onto his back.

"Okay. I gave you what you wanted. I'm about to take a shower and go out with my girls."

"Okay, baby. You need some money?" he asked as Butter knew he would.

"Yeah, I do."

"Well, go get it, baby. You know where it is."

Butter got out of bed and walked over to the closet. After opening the door to it, she kneeled on the floor and entered the combination to the floor safe. There was another larger safe in the basement, but she was only going out with her friends, so she didn't need that much. Had she been going shopping, she would've gone downstairs and taken out some real bread. For some reason, Marvin didn't like to put his money in banks, at least not all of it. The majority of his cash, he kept in his home. Butter had tried to get him to put most of his money in the bank, citing that it was dangerous, but he didn't budge. Unbeknownst to Marvin, however, Butter's pleas were just a front. She loved the fact that so much cash was at her disposal. She knew Marvin well enough to know that he wouldn't change his mind about putting it in a bank, and she was very happy about that.

Butter took out three one-hundred-dollar bills and closed the safe. When she turned around, she saw that Marvin had fallen asleep. That had been expected. He always did that after busting a nut.

Jazmine pulled up to the curb of the small apartment building and cut the engine. For the third time since it was brought up to her, she said a silent prayer and wondered how in the world she ever let Dani talk her into such a time bomb waiting to happen. The way Sunny spoke about her after she left was wicked, and there wasn't a doubt in Jazmine's mind that the two of them were never going to be friends. That put her in a bad spot. She and Jazmine had gotten extremely tight over the last few weeks. Add that to the fact that their fathers were business partners, and the whole thing made for a sticky situation. Jazmine had to admit, though, that she was supremely shocked when Dani called her and asked if she thought she and Sunny could ever be friends. That in itself was strange.

Dani wasn't the type of person to kiss someone's ass if they didn't want to be bothered with her. She would simply tell them to go fuck themselves. Jazmine had already accepted the fact that her two friends would never see eye to eye, so she would just have to find a way to divide her time and friendship between them. When Dani called, she was expecting her to go off because neither of her friends had defended her. Jazmine wanted to say something, but it was Sunny's party, so she decided to remain neutral. When Dani didn't bring it up, Jazmine was stunned.

Jazmine knew that she was taking a big chance with what she'd schemed up. The four girls were going to a club to hang out, but Jazmine was the only one who knew that both Sunny and Dani were going.

When Jazmine looked at her watch, she realized that she had been sitting in front of Butter's
house for nearly fifteen minutes. She was just
about to lay on the horn when Butter came out
dressed to kill. She wore a pair of tight-fitting light
blue Capri pants that fit her like a second skin.
The V-neck white blouse she wore revealed just
enough cleavage to get men interested but covered
her boobs enough for her not to look like a ho. Her
toenails were freshly painted, and her hair was no
longer in a ponytail. It was now lying on her shoulders.

"Damn, hurry up, bitch. We don't have all night.
I've been out here waiting for damn near an hour
for your ass," Jazmine lied.

"Bitch, stop lying. I looked out the window
twenty minutes ago, and your ass was nowhere in
sight," Butter said, catching her friend in a lie.

"Damn, bitch, you trying to catch a man tonight
or something?" Butter asked Jazmine as she got in
the car and closed the door.

"Shit, girl, you never know. I just might."
Jazmine had on a pair of form-fitting jeans that
showed off her ass and legs. Her shirt was cut off
at her belly button so that any and all could see her
flat stomach.

"You mean to tell me that Turiq let your ass
come out of the house like that?" Butter asked.

"Hell no. I changed clothes in a Walmart bathroom," Jazmine said, laughing.

"My dad doesn't normally police what I'm wearing, but he does give me a hard time when he thinks I have on something that I shouldn't. I didn't feel like hearing that shit tonight, though, so I just threw on some bullshit clothes that I knew he wouldn't object to and changed at Walmart."

Butter sniffed the air twice and wrinkled up her nose.

"The fuck wrong with you, bitch?"

"You don't smell that?" Butter asked.

"Smell what, bitch? I don't smell shit," Jazmine said.

"Me either. That's the fucking problem. I don't smell no fucking weed burning in this bitch. Fire that shit up. I know you got some on deck."

"Nah, to be honest with you, I'm out, but I was going to pick up some on the way."

"*That's* what's up. A bitch gotta get right before she goes up in the club."

Butter reached into her back pocket and pulled out a miniature bottle of vodka. After unscrewing the top, she tossed it back, taking the entire small bottle of alcohol to the head. Her face twisted as the liquor burned going down her throat. She took another one out of her back pocket and handed it to Jazmine.

"Screw the cap off for me, bitch. You see I'm driving?"

Butter obliged her friend by taking the top off and handing her the small bottle. The two of them shot the shit for about five minutes when Butter realized they were going in the wrong direction.

"The fuck are you going? I thought we were going to your house to pick up Sunny."

"We are," Jazmine told her. Butter looked around at the scenery, then slowly turned her head to Jazmine. Even though Jazmine didn't return the look, she already knew that the jig was up.

"Jazmine, I know damn well we're not about to go where I think we're about to go."

"Yes, Butter, we're going to pick up Dani."

Butter looked at Jazmine like she rode the short yellow bus.

"Bitch, are you fucking high? Sunny is going to blow her fucking top when she sees Dani. You know as well as I do that those two broads don't get along. Now, your silly ass is going to pick her up and pour gas on that fire? The fuck type of shit are you on?"

"Calm the fuck down, Butter. Dani asked me if she could go with us because she wanted to apologize to Sunny. Believe it or not, Dani actually wants to be friends with Sunny."

"Oh, is that right? Well, that ain't the fuckin' question. The question is, does *Sunny* want to be friends with Dani?"

Jazmine remained tight-lipped. That was a question she couldn't answer, so she decided to change the subject.

"Anyway, that old man still treating you right, girl?"

"You know it. And as long as he keeps breaking off that bread, I'll stay there with his ass. The minute he starts getting stingy, I'm outta that bitch."

"Girl, it's like that?"

"Straight like that. This sunshine between my legs don't come for free."

Jazmine laughed so hard at Butter's comment that she damn near ran a red light.

"Stop, bitch, damn. You trying to get us in an accident before we even get to the damn club?"

"No, girl, I was just laughing at yo' crazy ass."

"Crazy, my ass. I'm serious. If a muthafucka wants to lay up between my legs, he's going to have to bring something to the table besides dick."

"I heard that shit," Jazmine said, giving her friend a high five. As they approached Dani's apartment building, a worried expression formed on Butter's face.

"What's wrong with you?" Jazmine asked.

Butter took a deep breath. "Jazmine, I'm trying to have a good time tonight, and if Sunny is in one of her moods, there's going to be fireworks, and that'll fuck up the whole evening for all of us."

"Well, let's just pray that that doesn't happen," Jazmine said sincerely. She pulled into the parking lot of Dani's building and killed the engine. Then she took out her cell phone to dial Dani's number, but before she could, it buzzed in her hand.

"Yeah, we're outside," she said when she looked at the screen and saw that it was Dani calling her.

"Yeah, I know, bitch. That's why I called to tell you that I was on my way."

"She's on her way down," Jazmine said after the call ended.

"Yeah, whateva," Butter responded. Jazmine cut her eyes at her

"Look, Butter, it's already going to be a hard sell to get Sunny to go along with this shit. Please don't make it any harder, okay? If I didn't know any better, I'd say you had something against Dani too."

"Jazmine, now, you know that's bullshit. Me, you, and Dani have hung out on a bunch of different occasions. I just don't wanna be bothered with bullshit tonight. I want to have a nice time."

"Well, who says you can't? Just because these two hoes have to find a way to get along doesn't mean you can't have a good time. Plus, we're going to have a buzz and high on, so we're gonna be good anyway. And remember, Dani wants to get along with Sunny, so she's going to try everything in her power to make that happen."

"And how do you know that?"

"Well, that's what the bitch said she was going to do," Jazmine said, shrugging her shoulders.

"Let's hope so," Butter said as Dani walked out of the building.

"What's good, ladies?" she asked as she opened the door and climbed in the backseat.

"Shit, hopefully, this night," Butter said. As soon as Dani was comfortably in the car, Jazmine turned around and looked at her.

"Dani, are you sure about this? I mean, you and Sunny did have words the other day at her party."

"Yeah, I know. That's why I want to talk to her. I want to apologize for storming off like that. I really want me and Sunny to be friends. As a matter of fact, I want all of us to be friends. We could have so much fun hanging out together. I'll do my part. Hopefully, Sunny does hers."

Butter raised an eyebrow. "I don't know. Sunny can be a hard bitch sometimes. I was shocked as hell when Jazmine told me that she and Sunny had become friends."

"Bitch, you act like that was a stretch. I told y'all awhile ago that our fathers were trying to push us to be friends," Jazmine reminded Butter.

"Yeah, but from the way you used to talk about her, I didn't think y'all would ever be friends."

"Well, things happen that causes shit to change," Jazmine said, remembering the night Sunny stopped Jamal from raping her. What happened that night brought the two girls together and created a bond that was pretty much unbreakable. Both Dani and Butter saw how close the two of them were getting, but as long as Jazmine wasn't neglecting their friendship, neither had a problem with it.

"So, what happened to bring you two hoes together like this?" Butter asked.

"That's our secret," Jazmine said. Butter was taken aback. For the first time since Sunny and Jazmine had become close friends, she felt a twinge of jealousy.

"Oh, excuse the fuck outta me," she said with an attitude. Butter turned her head toward the window and stared out of it. Jazmine knew that Butter was in her feelings and thought briefly about letting her stay there. But the two of them had been cool too long to let her friendship with someone else come between theirs.

"Come on, Butter, I didn't mean it like that. I'm just saying it's not all of my secret to tell. If you really wanna know, just ask Sunny."

"I'm not asking Sunny. I'm asking you."

"Butter, chill out with that shit now. You're gonna sit up here and tell me that you've told me about every single thing in your life?"

Butter thought on it long and hard and had to admit that there were a few things in her life that she was going to take to the grave. In her opinion, though, this was different. Things she was holding were personal. This wasn't. But even though she didn't like it, she wasn't going to make a big deal out of it.

"Yeah, a'ight, bitch. Let's just forget about it," Butter said, still not liking it. Jazmine pulled into Sunny's driveway and parked. She pulled out her cell phone, called Sunny, and told her that they would meet her at her car.

"Damn, that muthafucka nice!" Butter yelled when she laid eyes on Sunny's silver drop-top Mercedes-Benz. Sunny came out of the house looking every bit the diva she was. The miniskirt she had on wrapped around her thighs and hugged them tightly. The white cami she wore accentuated her breasts perfectly. A twenty-four-inch diamond necklace hung around her neck, shining brightly in the night. An iced-out diamond and platinum bracelet dangled from her wrist. Her friend Kim followed behind her. She wasn't poorly dressed but compared to Sunny, she looked rather average.

"What's up, bitches?" she said, smiling. The smile disappeared from her face, however, when she spotted Dani standing next to her whip. With an evil scowl on her face, Sunny slowly walked over to the three ladies and glared at Dani.

"The fuck is this bitch doing here?"

"She has something she wants to say to you," Jazmine informed her. Sunny walked up to Dani and got in her space.

"You got something to say to me, ho?" Dani swallowed hard. She hated taking shit off Sunny, but she kept reminding herself that she was doing this for the greater good.

"I just wanted to say that I was sorry for the way I acted at your party, and I would like it if we could be friends." Sunny's mouth opened wide as she looked from Jazmine to Butter.

"Is this bitch serious? Am I just supposed to forget about what happened at my party?"

"Sunny, to be fair about it, you did get mad at her for something she didn't even say," Jazmine told her. Sunny looked at Jazmine like she wanted to slap the shit out of her. "Stop looking at me like that. The truth is the light."

"Come on, Sunny. Just let me roll with y'all tonight. If I get on your nerves, I won't bother you again. I just want to be friends."

Sunny once again looked from Butter to Jazmine.

"Fine, bitch. You can roll with us. Get yo' ass in the back and don't get my leather seats dirty with that tacky-ass outfit."

Sunny brushed past her as she walked around to the driver's side. Dani looked at Jazmine, who just shrugged. Jazmine quickly jumped into the front seat, leaving the rest of them to settle into the back. Five minutes of silence went by before anyone said anything. The tension in the car was ultra-thick. It was clear that Sunny didn't want Dani tagging along, and Dani was trying her best not to rub Sunny the wrong way.

"Fuck, I forgot to stop and get some weed," Jazmine said. Sunny gave her the side eye.

"This fuckin' night just gets better and better," she said. "First, you got me going out with this bitch in the back, who I do *not* like, let's be clear on that. Now, we have to go up in the fuckin' club without a buzz."

"I have a couple of blunts on me," Dani said, ignoring Sunny's insults.

"Bitch, don't nobody want yo' dirt-ass weed," Sunny spat.

"You know what?" Butter said. "You can be on that bullshit if you want to, but I'm about to blaze up. Pass me that stick, Dani."

Dani reached into her purse and pulled out a couple of thick blunts. She gave one to Butter and passed the second one to Jazmine. Within seconds, smoke filled the entire car. Sunny felt herself getting a contact high from the fumes.

"Bitch, so you wanna hit this or what?" Jazmine asked her.

"A'ight, I'll try the shit," Sunny said, taking the blunt from Jazmine. Jazmine watched as her friend took a long pull, held, and exhaled.

"Well? How is it?" Jazmine asked.

"It's a'ight," Sunny said, although it was clear that the weed hit was hitting her harder than she was letting on.

"A'ight? Bitch, stop frontin'. You know damn well that's some potent-ass piff."

Sunny took another puff. This time, she held it in longer than the first time before expelling it into the air. A goofy smile appeared on her face as she looked in the rearview mirror and nodded.

"Okay, okay, bitch, I'm gonna give you ya' props. This is some good shit."

"Thank you, but could you please stop calling me bitch? My name is Dani. Please call me that."

"Yeah, a'ight." Sunny gave Dani a half smile.

"Or at the very least make the shit sound like a term of endearment," Dani said, frowning.

"Get the fuck outta ya' feelings, Dani. We call each other bitches all the time," Butter reminded her.

"Yeah, stop being so fuckin' soft," Kim chimed in. She'd been so quiet that they had forgotten that she was there.

"Nah, there's a difference between the way she says it to y'all, and the way she says it to me." The rest of the young ladies looked at each other in bewilderment as Sunny slowed down and pulled over. After putting the car in park, she slowly turned around and glared at Dani.

"Look, bitch," she said harshly, "my bad if me calling you a bitch hurts ya' little feelings. But until I warm up to you, I'll say the shit in whatever tone I want to say it in. I didn't even know that your ass was rolling with us tonight, and the only reason I allowed yo' ass to get in my ride was because my girl wanted you to go with us tonight. Now, like Butter said, we call each other bitches all the time, so suck that shit up. Everybody in this crew is built, so we don't have time for weak bitches. So, either toughen the fuck up, or get yo' ass out and walk back home. Feel me?"

After making her speech, Sunny looked into each one of their eyes.

"Do any of you hoes have a problem with what I just said? Good," she said when no one spoke up. She then reached into the backseat and snatched the blunt out of Kim's hand. She took a long drag, blew it out, and handed it to Dani.

"Now, let's go have some fun . . . bitches." At that moment, the gauntlet had been thrown down. Even though none of them said it, no one had to. From that moment on, Sunny had established herself as the head bitch of the clique.

"So, what's up with this club tonight?" Kim asked. She couldn't care less about the drama between Sunny and Dani. Of course, if push came to shove, she would stand with Sunny. However, in her opinion, she didn't see what it would hurt for them to start hanging out together. She had no idea why Sunny didn't like Dani.

"Because I just don't like the bitch," Sunny would say whenever Kim would ask her about it.

"Girl, I heard this club was the bomb," Jazmine said excitedly. "What's the name of it again, Sunny?"

"Club Château."

"Club Château? That sounds classy as hell," Kim said.

"Yeah, it also sounds like it has an age restriction," Butter said, frowning.

"It does have an age restriction," Sunny informed them. The three girls in the backseat looked at each other in confusion. They were all pretty sure that the restriction was at least twenty-one years of age, which none of them were.

"Okay, what's the fucking catch? How are we going to get in if there's an age restriction?" Dani asked. Sunny looked in the mirror and smirked.

"Apparently, you hoes don't know who y'all hanging with. All things are possible when you're kicking it with the boss bitch," she said smugly.

Sunny wasn't telling them that it was her father's construction company that had built Club Château from the ground up. The owner of the place, a sleazy pedophile, named Barton Reeves, had made inappropriate comments to Sunny one day when she rode with her dad to Akron to check on the progress. She had been only 17 years old at the time, but much like now, Sunny wasn't a slow leak. She pretended to agree to have sex with him, all the while recording on her phone all the lewd and nasty things that he said he was going to do to her. Later that evening, Sunny sent Barton a voicemail message of the recording and let him know that she would let her dad hear the message if he even spoke to her again. It was the last time the two of them had ever had a conversation until she decided that his club would be an excellent place to hang out at. At first, Barton steadfastly refused to allow her and her friends to enter, citing that he didn't want to lose his license for allowing minors into his club. He knew that she was over 18, but the age restriction to get inside the club was 25.

"Do I need to have a talk with my father and let him hear all the things that you said you were going to do to me?" she told him, reminding him of the ace up her sleeve. The threat of Darnell finding out how he'd propositioned his daughter caused Barton to change his mind immediately. Sunny and whomever she chose would have access to the club and put in the VIP section, as well as have drinks brought to them free of charge for as long as they were there.

Twenty-five minutes after Sunny got on the freeway, she was pulling into the club's parking lot. The excitement in the young women's faces was evident as they quickly hopped out of the car. All heads turned as the young vixens made their way to the front entrance.

"Damn, look at this fuckin' line. We're gonna be out here forever," Dani whined.

"No, the fuck we're not," Sunny assured her. "Just follow me." Frowns and hot stares followed Sunny and her crew as they walked past the fifty or so people waiting to enter.

"The fuck is that bitch doing?" Sunny heard someone ask.

"Who the fuck is that?" someone else wondered.

"These hoes sound like they need to be checked," Jazmine barked. She was just about to turn around and go off on the girl who had made the last comment, but Sunny stopped her.

"Jazmine, why would you even waste your breath on these basic bitches? Fuck these hoes."

By the time Sunny and her crew had arrived at the front of the line, nearly everyone in it was staring at them.

"Yo, hold up a minute, li'l girls. The fuck y'all think y'all goin'?" the bouncer said.

Sunny looked the brutish woman up and down. Although she was young, Sunny had been to a few clubs before, but this was the first time she had ever seen a female bouncer.

"Well, after you move the rope the fuck outta my way, me and my girls are gonna roll up in this bitch and let our hair down."

The bouncer looked at Sunny first before letting her eyes travel to the rest of the young ladies.

"First of all, Rihanna," the bouncer said, poking fun at Sunny's hairstyle, "I don't think these folks will take too kindly to me letting y'all jump the line, especially since some of them have been here nearly an hour waiting to get in."

"That's right, little girl. Ain't it past your bedtime anyway?" a light-skinned woman with a high weave asked. Sunny and the rest of the crew turned and glared at her.

"What? You li'l hoes got an eye problem or something? Y'all don't want this smoke," a lady standing next to the light-skinned woman said. She was thicker than the other lady, but they looked so much alike that Sunny figured that they were probably sisters. With a frown on her face, Jazmine looked at Sunny, who gave her a sign to be cool.

"And second of all, we got an age restriction here, and I know damn well ain't neither one of y'all 25," the bouncer said, smugly.

Sunny took notice of the bouncer's attire. Her Reebok tennis shoes were slightly torn. Her blue jeans were so faded that they damn near looked like they were stone washed, but from the looks of them, that was not their original condition. She looked back up at the bouncer and smirked. Without an ounce of fear in her heart, she moved closer to the woman. She had to get on her toes to do it, but Sunny managed to get close enough to the bouncer's ear to whisper into it.

"Look, sweetie, I can tell by those raggedy-ass clothes you're wearing that you really need this job. So, unless you want to be unemployed tomorrow, why don't you do us both a fucking favor and let me and my girls through here before I have to call your boss and get your ass fired?"

The bouncer looked at Sunny as if she had lost her mind. She couldn't believe that this hot-in-the-ass li'l girl had the nerve to threaten her. If there weren't so many witnesses around, she would have grabbed Sunny by her ankles, used her as a human bat, and beat the shit out of the rest of her crew with her.

"Li'l girl, if you don't get the fuck outta my face, I swear on everything I love that I'm going to fuck you up out here."

Sunny smirked before taking out her cell phone. She dialed a number and waited for Barton to answer it.

"Yes, this is Sunny. I'm having a li'l problem with your bouncer out here. Me and my friends are trying to get up in this damn club, and this bitch is acting shitty. I'm going to need you to either come out yourself or send someone out here to let her know what time it is."

Sunny hung up the phone before he had a chance to say anything. She looked at Jazmine, winked, and then smiled at the rest of her crew. After about five minutes, a short, balding man in loud clothes came out. He reached up and pulled the bouncer's shoulders down so that his mouth was level with her ear. The bouncer's face twisted into a mask of anger as she listened to what he had to say. After he got done talking, the bouncer looked at Sunny and took a deep breath.

"Sorry, Miss Lady. There seems to have been a misunderstanding. Please accept my apology and come on in," the bouncer said as she removed the rope. Onlookers and others there to party were outraged. They couldn't believe what was going on and why Sunny and her young-ass crew were being let me in before them. But Sunny didn't give a fuck. As long as she got what she wanted, everyone out there waiting in line could go to hell. The bouncer was pissed. Sunny could almost see the steam rising from her head. The woman was huge. She stood at least six foot one and weighed about 220 pounds. Sunny looked at her left hand and was amazed to see a ring on her finger.

Damn, who the fuck this bitch married to? King Kong? Sunny wondered to herself. Instead of dogging the bitch out like she probably should have done, Sunny decided to handle the situation with class.

"No apologies needed, Miss Lady. You were just doing your job. It's all good," Sunny said as she smiled and walked past the bouncer with her crew following behind. Kim mean mugged the bouncer. She wanted to call her a bitch but knew if she did, she would probably get her ass kicked, so she remained mute. As soon as they got inside the club, loud music bombarded their ears. The base thumped so hard that it caused all of the girls' bodies to rattle. Club Château was much bigger than it seemed from the outside. The dance floor was packed with at least one hundred people, and all of them were surrounded by tables and chairs where people were drinking, laughing, and having a good time. Sunny looked around until she found what she wanted.

"Let's go, bitches. Ain't no fucking reason for us to be down here with the rest of these basic-ass broads."

Sunny walked along the wall until she came to the sign that said *VIP, upstairs*. A winding staircase led up to that area. Sunny smiled to herself. She looked back at her friends, and for the first time all night, she was glad that they were together, even Dani.

"Okay, bitches, let's go wild the fuck out," she said as she started to walk up the stairs. After she had taken only two steps, a large, bald man ran down the stairs and blocked her path.

"Hold up, li'l mama. Y'all can't go up there unless y'all have a VIP badge that looks like this one," he said, showing them a circular patch with the letters VIP on it. Sunny rolled her eyes.

"Shit, don't tell me that we gon' have to go through this shit again." Before Sunny could begin to lose her temper, the same short, bald man that had set the bouncer outside straight quickly came over. Just like he did the butch bitch outside, he whispered into the bouncer's ear. The bouncer shrugged, stepped aside, and allowed Sunny and her friends to venture upstairs. When they got to the second floor, Jazmine looked back and saw Kim still downstairs trying to converse with the bouncer.

"Dani, go down there and get that thirsty bitch," Sunny told her. Dani trotted back downstairs and grabbed Kim by the arm.

"Damn, girl, we just got in here, and you already all up in a nigga's grill? Bring your thirsty ass on," she said, damn near dragging Kim up the stairs. When they reached the top, Sunny just looked at Kim and shook her head.

"What? Shit, don't tell me all you hoes are trying to do tonight is get drunk and high. I'm also trying to get some dick tonight."

"Bitch, we just got in here. Bring your ass on," Sunny said. As Sunny led her crew around the VIP area, men were eyeing them like fresh meat. For the first time since they got there, the girls looked a li'l uncomfortable . . . all except Sunny, that is. She wasn't worried at all. In addition to their crew being treated like royalty, they were also afforded maximum protection. Even though Darnell was a brilliant businessman, Barton also knew him as a stone-cold killer, so there was no way he was going to let anything happen to Darnell's daughter at his club. Sunny was still surveying the scene when a tall gentleman sporting slacks, a silk shirt, and a tie approached her.

"Excuse me. Is your name Sunny?"

Sunny looked at her friends and then back at him. "Who the fuck wants to know?" she asked with an attitude.

"I apologize, pretty lady. I've been instructed by Barton to show you ladies to a table and bring you a bottle of our best champagne."

"Oh," Sunny said, clearly embarrassed. "I'm sorry."

"It's quite all right. Follow me, please."

The man led them to a secluded corner where they could barely be seen but could pretty much see everything that went on. The area that Sunny and her crew were led to had a restaurant-type feel to it. A large table was surrounded by booth-like seats that were comfortable enough to hold ten people. The leather seats were so soft that when Sunny and the rest of the girls sat down, they felt like they were going to sink into them.

"Damn, this shit is nice," Dani said. A few minutes later, a waitress walked over with a bottle of Dom Pérignon. Sunny looked at the bottle and shook her head.

"Nah, you can take that shit back. Bring us two bottles of Cîroc and one bottle of Hennessy."

"And five glasses," Jazmine added. The waitress nodded her head and went to do as Sunny had instructed. When she came back, not only did she have the three bottles of liquor and glasses, but she also had a large tray of complementary barbecue wings.

"Damn, that's what's up. I'm hungry as fuck," Kim said, reaching for a wing before the waitress even had a chance to set the platter now.

"Damn, you about a greedy-ass bitch," Butter said.

"Nah, I'm just a hungry-ass bitch," Kim corrected her.

"Well, at least sanitize your damn hands, nasty-ass broad," Jazmine said as she handed Kim a small bottle of sanitizer from her purse. Kim grabbed the sanitizer and squirted a quarter-sized amount in her hand. She quickly rubbed the sanitizer into her skin. No sooner had she finished than she was grabbing another wing.

"It's a good fucking thing that all of this shit is on the owner tonight," Sunny said, "because your greedy ass would have the bill coming to somewhere around a thousand dollars," she said, laughing.

"Yeah, well, whatever. I'm hungry. You bitches can sit up here and look all prissy if y'all want to, but I'm about to get my grub on," Kim said, not giving a fuck what the rest of them thought. About twenty seconds later, Butter was also reaching for a wing.

"You know what? Kim is right. Shit, I haven't eaten all day. Fuck that 'look cute' shit. I'm about to dig into these muthafuckas too," she said.

Before long, all of the ladies had devoured the wings and told the waitress to bring more. The waitress rolled her eyes but dared not say anything. She had been given explicit instructions to cater to Sunny and her crew. Jazmine picked up the bottle of Cîroc and poured a half glass full for each of them. Then she picked up the juice that was sitting next to it and mixed it with the Cîroc.

"What kind of juice is that?" Dani asked.

"Does it matter? Shit, it's free," Jazmine said.

"Free or not, I want to at least like the shit if I'm going to drink it," Dani said.

"That's the trouble with you hoes. Always complaining about something," Sunny said, laughing.

"I'm not complaining," Dani said. "I'm just saying, if I'm going to drink it, I don't want to be drinking something that I don't like."

"Damn, it's orange-peach mango, you choosy ho," Jazmine told her.

"Yo, Sunny. You think they'll say something if we fire up a blunt in here?" Dani asked. Jazmine, Kim, and Butter all looked at her like she were crazy.

"Bitch, what the fuck wrong with you?" Butter asked. "You trying to get us sent to jail?"

"What? I was just asking," Dani said, feeling foolish. Dropping her head, she picked up her drink and sipped it. When she looked back up, Sunny was looking at her, smiling. There was something unspoken between them that made them think that they were thinking the same thing.

"You know what? Y'all some scary-ass hoes," Sunny said. "Dani, fire that shit up."

The other three girls looked at Sunny like *she'd* lost her mind.

"What the fuck, Sunny?" Jazmine asked.

"Don't worry about it. Like I told y'all before, y'all hanging with the boss bitch, so just sit back and enjoy the ride."

Dani smiled as she pulled another blunt out of her pocket. She lit it and took a deep pull. A couple of seconds later, she blew the smoke into the air.

"Oh shit, here we go," Jazmine said when she saw the waitress rushing over. To her surprise, when the waitress got there, she set three ashtrays down in front of them and left. Jazmine looked at Sunny with wide eyes. She was surprised as hell.

"Damn, I guess your ass *is* a boss bitch," she said to her friend.

The rush of power was intoxicating to Sunny. She loved having her crew listen to every word she said and obey her orders. She loved having

Barton's workers at her beck and call. She nodded her head slowly as she began to give serious
thought to what her father had said about her taking over his empire. If this was what it felt like to
be a boss, then Sunny was all in. As soon as she
got back to Cleveland, she would let her father
know that she wanted to start learning about
his business and what she had to do to be a boss
like him. Since Sunny was driving, she knew that
she couldn't go as hard on the liquor and weed
as her friends could. That was okay, though. She
didn't come out to get tore-down drunk or sky-
high. She just wanted to have a nice time with
her friends, although it did amuse her to watch
them get fucked up. After about thirty minutes,
the liquor combined with the weed had them all
feeling nice. They were dancing at the table, cracking jokes, and bullshitting with each other when
Jazmine spotted a guy staring at their table.

"Hey, y'all, I think that nigga over there checking
us out."

All five of their heads turned and looked at the
dashing young gentleman staring in their direction. He was tall, about six foot four with milk
chocolate skin and a slim but muscular build.

"Damn, that nigga fine as fuck," Kim said, damn
near drooling.

"Kim, could you get any fuckin' thirstier?"
Jazmine asked her.

"Whateva. Y'all know that nigga fine. I don't even know why y'all trying to front."

"Which one of us y'all think he's scoping out?" Butter asked.

"Probably me. Shit, after all, I *am* the finest bitch over here," Kim said. The other four girls looked at each other before bursting into a fit of laughter.

"Bitch, please. You probably the homeliest looking bitch over here," Dani said, teasing her.

"Look, everybody over here is a fuckin' dime piece. Whoever that nigga chooses to holla at, the rest of us will just fall back. We not about to be up in here competing for some random nigga's attention like some thirsty-ass thots. Agreed?" Sunny asked, looking at all of them.

Everyone nodded their heads, although Kim did so reluctantly. She didn't see anything wrong with a little competition. Truth be told, she was insecure about her looks and felt that if she just sat back and let a man come to her, she would never get laid. Since everyone else agreed to Sunny's rule, Kim felt that she had to as well. Even though she and Sunny had been friends for quite a while, even she didn't know the depths of Kim's insecurities. Kim had always come off as a confident young woman, but she never felt like she was attractive deep down inside. After staring at them for a few more seconds, the young man stood up and walked over to their table.

"Here he comes, girl," Kim said, tugging on Butter's arm like an excited kid on Christmas morning.

"Bitch, get off me," Butter said, yanking her arm free. "Thirsty-ass bitch," Butter mumbled to herself. She was the least nervous of the five. Unlike Sunny, Jazmine, and Kim, she had dick waiting on her when she got home, so she had no reason to chase it. They all started to smile as the guy moved closer. By the time he got to their table, all five of the young ladies were staring directly at him. The looks on their faces pretty much told him that they were waiting to see which one of them that he'd come over to meet. A very slight frown appeared on his face as he looked at them all a little closer. No one picked up on it but Sunny.

"Something wrong?" she asked.

"Uh, nah, I was just coming over to say hello and introduce myself to you ladies. How are y'all doing tonight?"

"We're good," Sunny said, once again speaking for them all.

His voice was deep, like Barry White's, and it caused Jazmine to get wet. She hadn't been fucked in a couple of weeks and was desperately horny. The young man stared at the one that he was interested in. From afar, she looked much older than she did now that he was directly in front of her. He weighed his options. It didn't take someone with the best eyesight to see that none of the girls sitting at the table were twenty-five or over. He took another long look at the young lady that he'd come over to see and concluded that she was worth it.

"Well, I was wondering if you wanted to dance," he said, smiling at Jazmine.

"Her?" Kim said, dry hating. Sunny shot her friend a nasty look. They had already discussed this, and she wasn't about to let Kim do as she pleased.

"I'm just asking," Kim said, holding up her hands.

"Sure," Jazmine said, sliding past Sunny.

"Get it, girl," Sunny said as the man led her friend to the dance floor. As soon as they were gone, Sunny and the rest of the girls looked at Kim disgustingly.

"The fuck is wrong with you, bitch? You ain't getting' no dick at home?" Butter asked.

"Oh, I get plenty of dick," Kim lied.

"Well, you damn sure ain't acting like it," Dani said. Kim glared at her evilly.

"Bitch, you don't even need to be talking. You just lucky that my girl let yo' ass come with us in the first place."

"Ain't that a bitch?" Dani said, insulted.

"Ain't it, though?" Kim shot back.

"Both of y'all shut the fuck up," Sunny bellowed. "The fuck is wrong with y'all? Kim, what did we just agree on? This is our first time hanging together, and you cockblocking already?"

Kim opened her mouth to speak, but there wasn't much that she could say to contradict the truth as it was being told. The fact of the matter was that she was indeed cockblocking.

"Sorry," was all she could say while crossing her arms over her chest.

"Damn, girl, I didn't mean no harm. I was just messing with you," Dani said as she inhaled the blunt sharply and tried to hand it to Kim. Kim hesitated before taking it from her and taking a puff.

"You know what? I think I like you hoes," Sunny said, pouring another round of drinks. Although she was just speaking in general, she was staring at Dani as she spoke. "Maybe I have been a little too hard on some of y'all," she said, still looking at Dani.

"Ya' think?" Dani said, laughing.

"You still need to toughen up, bitch. But I guess you a'ight," Sunny said, taking another small sip of her drink. She smiled at Dani, but everything wasn't all good as she led her crew to believe. She still didn't trust Dani. She didn't know what it was, but the broad just seemed phony to her. Sunny figured that she'd hedge her bet. If Dani turned out to be really down with her, then so be it. But if she turned out to be the conniving bitch that she thought she was, then all she was doing right now was giving her enough rope to hang herself.

"Oh shit, what the fuck is going on down there?" Butter asked.

They all got up and looked over the railing. A commotion had broken out on the dance floor. Sunny was hoping that Jazmine was down there, showing off her dance moves, but the feeling in her stomach told her that wasn't the case. She grabbed her purse off the table and headed down the stairs. Although the other girls had no idea what was going on, they followed their leader, showing that they had her back.

Vance held Jazmine's hand tightly as he led her down the spiraled stairs and onto the dance floor. In his opinion, four out of the five young ladies at the table were fuckable. Even the hating one would do for a screw if he had the right amount of liquor in his system. It wasn't that she was ugly; she just wasn't as fine as the rest of them.

"What's your name, pretty lady?" he asked when they got on the dance floor.

"Jazmine. What's yours?"

"Vance."

As the two of them moved to the music, Vance watched her closely. Her curvy figure was turning him on. His eyes roamed over her body so much that he nearly forgot what her face looked like. After seeing her swivel her hips several times,

Vance made his mind up that he would try his best to convince her to go to a hotel with him and blow her back out. He knew she was young but reasoned that she had to be at least 18 years old, which was good enough for him.

"So, what are you doing after you leave here?"

"Well, to be honest with you, I was hoping that I could bounce up and down on your dick."

Her blunt statement caught Vance off guard. Jazmine didn't have time to play games. She wanted to get laid, and she wanted to get laid tonight. She didn't ask him if he was married or had a girlfriend because she didn't give a damn. All she wanted to do was get herself a good nut and get the fuck on.

"Damn, little lady, you sure are direct."

"You damn skippy. Look, I know I'm not that old, but I don't have time for games. I'm not trying to get married or hitched tonight. All I want to do is have some fun. Are you down with that?"

A wry smile flashed across Vance's face. He was already married, so he didn't need any added drama to his life. His wife had gained about twenty-five extra pounds after their kid was born, and he was no longer attracted to her. So, he figured he would come out tonight and get himself a shot of good pussy before he had to go home and hear her mouth.

"Damn right, I'm down with that. The question I have for you is, can you handle all this meat?"

Jazmine looked down at the bulge in his pants and had to admit that he was packing. But she wasn't intimidated in the least. She looked forward to the challenge.

"Oh, I can handle that and much more," she said seductively. The up-tempo music stopped, and a slow song started playing. Jazmine turned to walk away, but Vance grabbed her hand.

"Where are you going?"

"The song is over. We can hook up later, but right now, I'm going back up to the VIP area to chill with my girls."

"Come on. Don't be like that. Let me get this last dance."

"We just danced, nigga."

"Yeah, but that was on some fast shit. I want to slow dance with you. I want to see how it feels to hold your gorgeous body," he said, gassing her up. Jazmine already knew she was fine, but it didn't hurt to hear it from a man.

"Well, I guess so."

As the song began to play, Vance slipped his arm around Jazmine's small waist and pulled her close to him. It got heated as they probed and caressed each other's bodies. Trying to be slick, Vance let his hand fall to Jazmine's ass. He gave it a gentle squeeze.

"Nigga, what the fuck are you doing?"

"What?" he asked, trying to play innocent.

"Did I say you could touch my ass?"

"My bad, li'l mama," Vance said as he pulled his hand back up to the small of her back. Looking up at him with a lustful smile, Jazmine said, "Did I tell you to take your hand away?"

She felt Vance's manhood pressing against her pelvic area.

"Oh, I see you like to play games, huh? Well, I got some grown-up games for us to play a little later," Vance said deviously.

"Is that right?"

"Hell yeah. Baby, I'm gonna knock the bottom outta that pu——"

"Go ahead, baby. Finish ya' statement," Jazmine said when she noticed that Vance had stopped talking. She also noticed that he had stopped dancing. She leaned back and looked at him. Only then did she notice the change of his facial expression. His eyes seemed to be looking past her and at something or someone else. She immediately released him and turned around just in time to see a thick, bronze-skinned woman with short hair and wire-rimmed glasses storming their way.

"I knew it! I muthafuckin' knew it," she screamed. "I'm at home dealing with our sick child, and your ass is in this funky-ass club dancing with some tramp."

Vance looked toward the entrance to see if he could spot the bouncer. He'd paid her fifty dollars to tell his wife that he wasn't there. But what he didn't count on was her paying the bouncer one hundred dollars to let her know if he showed up there.

"Yo, hold up. Who the fuck are you calling a tramp?" Jazmine shouted.

"Bitch, I will get to you in a minute," the woman said without even looking at Jazmine. She was focusing all her energies on her wayward husband.

"Baby, it ain't what it looks like. I was just dancing." The woman looked at her husband like she wanted to slit his throat.

"Nigga, do you think I'm fuckin' stupid? I done caught yo' ass cheating twice, and you gon' tell me that you were just dancing? How fuckin' dumb do you think I am?"

"Pretty damn dumb, if you still wit' his ass," Jazmine mumbled. She hadn't intended to say it quite that loud, but her voice carried, so the woman heard her. The woman slowly turned her head toward Jazmine. She had to do a double take when she noticed how young Jazmine was. After looking her up and down, the woman gave Vance an incredulous look. She put her hands on her hips and shook her head. Turning her attention back to Vance, she got nose to nose with him.

"Nigga, have you lost yo' damn mind? Not only are you out here fuckin' around on me, but you also have the nerve to be fuckin' around on me with a fuckin' teenager."

"I ain't no damn teenager," Jazmine lied.

"Bitch, please! You might have my dumb-ass husband fooled, but I know a young bitch when I see one."

Jazmine took a step toward the woman. "I ain't gon' be too many more bitches," she warned.

The woman looked at her and started laughing. "Little girl, I will take off my belt and whup yo' ass like the child you are."

By now, there was a crowd gathering around. People took out their cell phones in anticipation of recording video footage they could put on WorldStarHipHop later tonight.

"I wish you would try that——"

The rest of Jazmine's sentence went unsaid because before she knew what was happening, the woman slapped her in the mouth. Jazmine never had a chance to right herself as the woman pulled a switchblade from her pocket, grabbed her hair, and pressed the knife to her throat. She didn't intend to kill Jazmine. She just wanted to scare her. She opened her mouth to threaten Jazmine, but her words were drowned out by the clicking sound of Sunny cocking her .380.

"Bitch, if you don't get that knife away from my girl's neck, I'm gonna blow yo' muthafuckin' brains out."

The woman looked at Sunny for signs of fear or nervousness, and when she didn't see any, she wisely removed the knife.

"You ain't got shit to do with this," the woman yelled. Sunny responded by slamming the butt of the gun into the woman's mouth, dislodging two of her front teeth. The woman crumpled to the floor. Vance flinched. He wanted to help his wife but didn't want to get shot.

"I do what the fuck I want to do," Sunny spat. "Let's go, y'all, before I have to put something in this bitch."

On their way out, Jazmine kicked the woman in the face. A sense of power coursed through Sunny's body as she led her crew out of the club.

Chapter 18

Even though she hadn't drunk that much the previous night, Sunny woke up with a slight headache. However, it couldn't suppress the powerful feeling that surged through her being. She had handled herself like a true boss bitch. She'd laid down ground rules for her crew, checked them when they got out of line, and came to their defense when they needed her the most. That was the definition of a boss bitch.

Rubbing her temples, Sunny got out of bed and made her way to the bathroom. That was one of the great things about being the daughter of a drug lord. You didn't live in a shack, so you had your own bathroom and didn't have to share it with anybody. When Sunny came out of the bathroom, her nose was assaulted by the smell of bacon, pancakes, and eggs. She hadn't noticed it when she went in, but her growling stomach made sure that she did now.

After getting herself together, Sunny was about to go downstairs to see about her growling stomach when her cell phone buzzed. Hungry and irritated, she walked over to her nightstand and aggressively snatched it up.

"Yeah?" she said without looking at the caller ID.

"Uh . . . Sunny?" a voice said over the line.

"Yeah, this is Sunny. Who the fuck is this?"

"This is Dani."

Sunny held the phone back from her mouth and looked at it strangely. Although she figured that she knew the answer to the question she was about to ask, she decided to ask it anyway.

"Bitch, how the fuck did you get my number?"

"Oh . . . ah . . . Jazmine gave it to me."

"Oh, she did, huh?" Sunny asked, figuring as much.

"Yeah, I mean, I asked for it."

Sunny held the phone for a few seconds, waiting for Dani to reveal why she called. *The fuck wrong with this dizzy bitch?* Sunny wondered when Dani hesitated to speak.

"Dani, what the hell do you want? Why did you call me?"

"Oh, my bad. I just wanted to thank you for letting me kick it with y'all last night. I had a fuckin' blast."

"Yeah, don't worry about it. Look, I have to go," Sunny said, dismissing her.

Before Dani could even say goodbye, Sunny hung up on her. The growling coming from her stomach was getting louder. Sunny didn't know why she was so hungry. She'd eaten more than her share of wings the night before, but for some reason, she woke up famished.

She quickly made her way downstairs and into the kitchen. She was all set to thank her father for making breakfast . . . until she saw him sitting at the table stuffing a forkful of eggs into his mouth. When Sunny looked over toward the stove and saw Joy stirring a pot of grits, she frowned. It wasn't that Sunny didn't like Joy. She just didn't trust her. For the life of her, Sunny couldn't understand how her drug-dealing father was messing around with a cop. In her mind, no cop could be trusted.

"I see you finally up, huh?" Darnell said, chomping down on a piece of bacon. Sunny smiled weakly as she took a seat at the table.

"You hungry, Vanessa?" Joy asked her.

"Very."

Joy piled a generous amount of food onto a plate and set it in front of Sunny. Sunny tore into the food like it was her last meal on earth. In less than ten minutes, she was walking back over to the stove to get seconds. Darnell patiently waited for his daughter to sit back down before broaching the subject of her taking over for him one day. He was just about to bring it up when she beat him to the punch.

"I was thinking about what you asked me the other day about taking over for you, and to be honest, the more I've thought about it, the more I liked the idea."

Darnell nodded his head approvingly. "Good, I was hoping that you would make the smart decision."

"I was wondering, though, Dad, how is Turiq going to take this?"

Turiq had been Darnell's second in command for a long time, so it stood to reason that he would be next in line to inherit the throne. Sunny was a little worried about how he would feel when he learned that she would be running things.

"Let me worry about Turiq," Darnell said, smirking. Little did Sunny know that her father and Turiq had already discussed the matter. They both shared a plan for their grand exit from the game and weren't going to reveal it until the time was right.

"Now, whatever you got planned for today, cancel that shit. I'm going to get you started right away learning the drug business, among other things."

"What other things?"

"Well, for starters, I want you to know how to shoot a gun."

"Huh? But I already know how to shoot a gun."

"No, you just *think* you do. There's a huge difference between learning how to shoot a gun correctly and just pull a trigger. Just because you shot a dying man from five feet away doesn't make you a good shot. In about an hour, Joy is going to take you to the gun range. When you get back, I'm going to give you the rundown on cocaine. It may take some time, but when I'm done showing you the ropes, you're going to be the female version of me."

During Darnell's talk, Sunny kept thinking about how powerful she felt at the club. It felt great to her to be in charge. For some reason, it felt so natural for her to take control. Darnell noticed the excited look on his daughter's face, and it made him smile. The plan he'd devised would not only keep money flowing into his pocket but would also ensure that the next generation of his family lineage would be set up for life. Thinking about his future grandkids never having to worry about money pleased him to no end. However, his mood soured as thoughts of Debra entered his mind. He quickly pushed them to the back of his thoughts.

The bitch was lying then, and that shit hasn't changed, he thought. The question had haunted Darnell for the last twenty years. *What if she were telling the truth?* Once again, Darnell pushed the thought from his mind. Since there hadn't been any evidence to the contrary, he was always going to assume that Debra was lying. Darnell moved on to his next order of business.

"Now, I want to talk some more about that little nigga being in my house."

Sunny opened her mouth to speak, but a raised finger from her father silenced her.

"Sunny, I know that you're 20 years old, and it would be naïve of me to think that you're not having sex. But . . ."

Darnell looked deep into his daughter's eyes and pointed his finger at her. He wanted her to know that he was deadly serious.

"You will *not* have sex in this house. Is that understood?"

"Yes, sir," Sunny said.

Her father wasn't fucking around, and she knew it. Sunny knew that she should have let the subject drop right there, but curiosity got the best of her. "So, what did you do to Jamaal?" Darnell stared at his daughter for a few seconds.

"I didn't do anything to him. I had Damon have a word with him. You got a problem with that?"

"No, sir, not at all," Sunny said, shaking her head. Truth be told, after what Jamaal had tried to pull on Jazmine, Sunny didn't give a shit what happened to him. She was just nosy.

"Good. Now, go upstairs and get ready."

Darnell waited for Sunny to go upstairs before turning his attention to Joy. "What do you think? Is she ready?" he asked.

"No, but give her a little time. Judging from what I just heard, she has the perfect mentality to take over someday. All she needs is direction."

"Is that right?" Darnell asked, cutting his eyes at Joy. "Turiq said the same thing. Y'all been sharing notes or something? Something you wanna tell me?"

"Stop playing, boy," Joy said, mushing him in the head. "You know damn well this pussy only gets wet for you."

She got up, walked behind Darnell, and wrapped her arms around his chest. "Can yo' ass say the same, nigga?" she whispered into his ear.

"Damn straight," Darnell said, lying through his teeth. While he wasn't screwing everything that moved, Darnell had occasionally dipped his wick into another female's wax.

"Better not be messing around on me, nigga." Joy crept over to where the steps began and looked up toward the top. Switching her ass hard, she sashayed back over to where Darnell was sitting.

"Hey, why don't you take it out and let me suck it right quick?"

Darnell looked at his lover like she'd lost her mind. "Are you crazy? My daughter will be down here any second."

Joy shrugged her shoulders. "I thought you liked living dangerously."

"Not that damn dangerously," he said. Even though the prospect of getting a blow job did turn him on, that was just going to have to wait until later.

"Spoilsport," Joy said as she sat down in the seat next to him.

Not even three minutes later, Sunny came down the stairs. Darnell looked at Joy as if to say, "See, we would have gotten caught."

Sunny looked from her father to Joy and shook her head. "You know what? I don't even want to know," she said, holding up her right palm. Although the house was relatively large, it wasn't uncommon for Sunny to hear Joy and her father screwing. The thought alone nearly caused her to vomit.

"I'm ready, Joy," she said.

"See you later, babe," Joy said and gave Darnell a goodbye kiss.

"Bye, Daddy," Sunny said, hugging her father.

Darnell watched both ladies leave and smiled. He still couldn't believe how much Joy resembled Debra. Thinking back on it, that was probably what attracted him to her in the first place. Debra had been a woman that Darnell was sneaking around with when he was dating Sunny's mother, Trish, and although they knew each other casually, they had no idea that Darnell was screwing them both. Darnell remembered vividly the day he broke it off with Debra. She and Trish were both putting pressure on him to commit to them. Darnell, being the young player he was, wasn't trying to hear that kind of talk from them. For some reason, however, Trish occupied a place in his heart that Debra didn't. Still, he wasn't ready to settle down until Sunny's mother broke the news to him that he was going to be a father. Not wanting to be a coward about it, Darnell drove over to Debra's house to tell her face-to-face that it was over.

When he called to tell her that he was on his way, she didn't answer her phone, but instead of waiting until he was sure that she was home, he went over there anyway. When he got there, he saw a car in the driveway that he'd never seen before. Everything in his gut told him to get back in his car and leave, but curiosity got the best of him, and he proceeded to enter her place without knocking. He eased up to the edge of the bedroom door and stopped. The door was slightly open, so it allowed him to peek in without being seen. Debra was sitting on the edge of her bed with her head down. Sitting next to her was a dude that Darnell had seen around the neighborhood but didn't know personally. He was a short cat, about five foot six, with a tan complexion and a scar running down the middle of his chin. His face was triangular-shaped, and he sported a short Afro. Darnell's blood boiled as he reached over and grabbed Debra's hand and rubbed it. The smile on his face told the story of someone who'd just gotten some good news.

Although he had been messing around with Trish, Darnell felt that Debra was his and his alone, and that this guy was intruding on his turf. Darnell had to hold himself back from rushing inside of the bedroom and going upside both of their heads.

"So, are you sure?" the dude asked Debra. Slowly, she nodded her head. A broader smile appeared on the man's face. Darnell didn't know what was going on yet, but he had an idea.

"How far along are you?" the man asked.

"Six weeks," Debra answered.

Now, Darnell didn't have to guess. He knew now that Debra was pregnant. It had never occurred to him, though, that she had been messing around on him the same way he was screwing around on her. He'd always thought that he had that pussy on lock. Seeing the man sitting next to her smiling obliterated that thought. Debra slowly raised her head and looked the man in the eyes.

"Sammy, I love you, but there is something I have to tell you."

When Darnell heard Debra tell the man that she loved him, he lost it. It would have done him a world of good to listen to the rest of the conversation and find out what Debra had to say, but he just couldn't help himself. Kicking the door open, he barged into the room with his gun dangling by his side.

"Nigga, who the fuck is you?" Sammy asked.

"Oh my God, Darnell," Deborah shouted before Darnell could answer the man.

"Now, I see why you wouldn't answer your phone. You're too busy in here playing house with this muthafucka."

Sammy stood up. He was about to take a step toward Darnell until he looked down and noticed the gun in Darnell's hand.

"Muthafucka, I wish you would. Sit yo' bitch ass down before I lay yo' ass down."

Wisely, Sammy did as he was told. He glared at Darnell hatefully, but he wasn't stupid enough to act on his feelings. Darnell then cast a disgusted look at Debra.

"Baby, I was going to tell you."

"Tell me what, bitch? That you've been fucking this nigga behind my back?"

"Wait a minute, Darnell. Don't act like I'm the only one being unfaithful in this relationship. I know for a fact that you—"

"Bitch, I don't want to hear that shit," Darnell said, cutting her off. Even though she was right, the only thing he could see now was her wrong-doing. And he was never going to admit that he had been fucking Trish. Darnell just shook his head as he realized Karma was coming back on him. He'd gotten Trish pregnant while screwing around with both of them. Now, he had to sit here and listen to how Debra had gotten pregnant by another man.

"So, I guess you about to have this silly muthafucka's baby, huh? Well, you know what? Fuck you, him, and fuck that little bastard-ass seed growing in your stomach," he spat spitefully.

Hearing Darnell talk reckless about his potential unborn child gave Sammy a few pounds of courage. Quickly, he jumped up off the bed and stepped into Darnell's air space.

"Nigga, what the fuck did you just say about my baby?"

A half second after he had spoken the question, Darnell cracked Sammy on the top of the head with the butt of his pistol. Sammy grabbed his head and stumbled back. With Debra screaming, blood spurted onto the bed as Sammy slowly dropped down to the floor.

"You and this bitch-made nigga have a nice life," Darnell said as he turned and headed for the door. Even though he'd come to break up with her, seeing her with another man pissed him off.

"Darnell, wait," Debra pleaded while grabbing his arm. "I have something to tell——"

"Bitch, get the fuck off me," he said, backhanding her to the floor. "I'm going to get the fuck out of here before I kill you and that piece of shit-ass nigga you've been fucking."

With that, Darnell walked out of her bedroom and out of her life. He hadn't seen her since.

"You call that li'l bitch?" Damon asked Dani. He was just coming out of the bathroom when Dani and Sunny ended their call.

"Yeah, I called her," Dani said frowning. She was sitting on the edge of the bed with her arms folded, thinking. Damon's plan sounded like a great one when he'd first introduced it to her. She was still in the pissed off stage after leaving Sunny's party and wanted revenge. Damon convinced Dani that he would be the next king, but to climb that mountain, he was going to need her help. He told her that if she helped him take down Darnell, she would be right by his side when he was king of the hill. But ever since hanging out with Sunny and the other young ladies, Dani was having second thoughts.

"The fuck you frowning for?"

"No reason," she lied.

"Bitch, stop lying. What the fuck is wrong with you? I know damn well you ain't about to change yo' fuckin' mind."

"I'm just saying, Damon, Sunny was pretty cool to me last night and——"

"Cool to you? You mean the same bitch who dissed you at her party? You better wake the fuck up. That bitch doesn't give a fuck about you. What? You think y'all girls, now?" Damon said, laughing. He noticed how short Dani's call to Sunny was, so he used it to plant more seeds of destruction in her head.

"Damn, yo' ass wasn't on the phone long. I guess yo' new friend had better things to do than to be bothered with yo' peasant ass. Shiiiit, I don't know about you, but my friends don't treat me like that," Damon said.

He sat back and watched Dani's face twist. Her confused expression proved that he could bend her mind to think what he wanted her to think. He eased up to Dani, grabbed her chin, and tilted her head up.

"You're a queen, baby. All you need is a king with a throne. Give me a year or two, and I'm gonna be running this whole damn city, and I'm gonna need someone beautiful and intelligent like you to be by my side when I rule. You know what, though? Maybe you ain't cut out for this shit. I need somebody that's gonna be down for me, not get all in their feelings for people who don't give a fuck about them."

Damon let his hand fall just before turning around and walking away. Just like that, he had built her up *and* torn her down. Now, all he had to do was wait for her to break.

"Make sure that the door is closed on ya' way out," he told her.

"On my way out?"

"Yeah, on ya' way out. I just told you that I need someone who I can depend on. I need a bitch who's down for me. Yo' loyalty seems to be with someone else."

Damon reached into his pocket and pulled out a large knot of money. He counted out $4,000 before stuffing the bills back into his pocket. When he looked up, Dani was damn near drooling while staring at his pocket.

"You still here?" he asked.

"You want me to leave for real?" Dani asked, tears in her eyes. She didn't know until that moment how deep her feelings for Damon ran. She'd been sleeping with him for quite some time now and had developed feelings for him. She thought about all the things he said, and the last thing she wanted was for someone else to be standing in her spot when Damon came up.

"Dani, I ain't got time for—"

"No, baby, please, I'm sorry. I didn't mean to act like I didn't want to be by your side. What can I do to prove it to you?"

Damon walked up to her and stared down at her. The desperation in her eyes caused his dick to get hard. Dominating her turned him on.

"Nah, you ain't the one for this." Damon was about to walk away when Dani grabbed his crotch.

"No, baby, please. Let me prove it to you," she said as she slowly got down on her knees and unzipped his pants.

Chapter 19

"May I help you?" the woman behind the glass asked Larry. Larry opened his mouth to answer, and a lump formed in his throat. Up until he got in his car and drove to the police station, he had no reservations about going to the police academy. In fact, he was looking forward to it. Day after day, Larry went to work at McCord's Construction and did his job. It ate him up on the inside to know that his boss had fucked his wife, and there was nothing that he could do about it. Larry never revealed to his wife that he knew how she'd gotten his job back for him. He chose to save that nugget for another day. There was no way in the world that he would let his wife get away with sleeping with his boss to save his job. She was going to pay, and she was going to pay dearly. He was going to make sure of it. He had never revealed it to anyone, but Larry had already plotted to kill his wife once he became a cop. He was just never able to get over Theresa sleeping with Darnell.

Ever since he'd learned about Darnell and his wife, Larry had a hard time performing in bed. On many occasions when they were just about to get intimate, visions of Darnell driving in and out of his wife played in his mind like a video. His confidence took a severe nosedive, wondering if he could measure up to Darnell's bedroom exploits.

"Hey, mister, you high or something? I said, may I help you?" the woman asked again, louder this time.

"Uh, yeah, I'm sorry. I was wondering what I had to do to sign up for the police academy."

The woman looked him up and down. "Wait right here, please," she told Larry after giving him the once-over. When she returned, she was not alone. Following behind her was a large officer with broad shoulders and a potbelly.

Larry took one look at the man and wanted to laugh. He'd heard that to be a cop, you had to be in excellent physical condition, and from the looks of this guy, the only thing he looked to be good at was drinking beer. What he lacked in build, however, the man more than made up for in sheer size. The man looked big when Larry first saw him. But the closer he got to Larry, his massive frame was even more intimidating. By the time he was standing in front of Larry, he looked downright gargantuan. Larry guessed that he was at least six foot seven.

"Afternoon," the man said, sticking out his meaty palm for a handshake. "Gertrude told me that you're interested in signing up to join the police force."

"Yes, sir, I am."

The man studied Larry's face for a few seconds. The way he was gawking at Larry made him nervous.

"What's your name, fella?" he asked when he finally spoke.

"Burns. Lawrence Burns."

"Well, Lawrence Burns, are you sure you want to be a cop, because judging from the look on your face, you don't seem to be sure that you want to be. And this isn't something that you can be hesitant about."

Flashes of Darnell pounding into his wife gave Larry the confidence he needed to push on. He couldn't wait to roll up on Darnell and give him a bullshit ticket or, better yet, bust him selling dope.

"Trust me, sir, I'm more than confident."

"All right, then," the man said as he smiled and nodded slowly. Larry looked exactly like the kind of redneck racist that would fit right in with the force. He walked over to the window and asked the woman to pass him the application to apply for the academy.

Larry was so anxious to fill it out that he damn near snatched it out of the man's hands. As he filled it out, he couldn't help but think how satisfying it would be to get even with Darnell and his cheating-ass wife finally.

Chapter 20

After leaving the gun range with Joy, Sunny returned home and sat through an hour and a half of her father teaching her about cocaine.

"There's much more to learn than this, but I don't want to overwhelm you," he said to her. She was shocked when she walked into the home, and he handed her a notepad and pen. He told her to take notes and, after she committed the lessons to memory, burn them. He made it clear that she would have to retain the information in her head and not have it just lying around on a piece of paper. Darnell knew that his daughter was sharp, so he knew that it wouldn't take her long to memorize what he taught her. Although Sunny would be a boss and would deal mostly in weight, Darnell felt that it was important for her to know about cooking and cutting cocaine. He charged that task to OG Hann. In a couple of days, he would take her to one of the "kitchens," and one of their trusted soldiers would show her the art of turning cocaine into crack. After that, Darnell was going to have Duck show her how to lightly step on cocaine but still have it strong enough so that the snorters would still be getting grade A product. But these lessons would take place in the next few days. Right now, however, Sunny needed to unwind, so she called her girl.

"Hello?" Jazmine answered, sounding like she was in pain.

"Damn, girl, what the hell is wrong with you?" Sunny asked.

"Shit, girl, I don't know. I've been in the damn bathroom since noon."

"Damn, bitch, you got a hangover or something?" Sunny asked.

"Nah, my stomach is fucked up. I've been on the toilet for an hour."

"Damn, what did you eat this morning?"

"Just some sausage and scrambled eggs. I mean, I thought it was a hangover too, at first, but I didn't have a headache, and I wasn't throwing up."

"That's surprising, considering you hoes tried to drink every bottle in the club last night," Sunny said, laughing.

"I know, right?" Jazmine said, laughing as well. Jazmine opened her mouth to tell Sunny what else she had been doing earlier in the morning but decided not to. She didn't want Sunny judging her.

"Spit that shit out," Sunny told her.

"How do you know I was about to say something?"

"Because I heard your ass take a quick breath and hold it in. Now, spill the tea, bitch."

"Yeah, a'ight. I also had a drink this morning."

"What? Already?"

"Yeah. My dad bought some kind of new chocolate liquor, and I wanted to try it. It's called Mudslide or some shit like that. I don't know what the fuck was in the shit, but after an hour of drinking it, my guts started bubbling the fuck up."

What Jazmine didn't know was that Turiq had caught on to her little rouse. For a couple of weeks now, he'd known all about his daughter's dipping into his vodka, so he decided to teach her a lesson. Knowing that his daughter loved chocolate, Turiq purchased a bottle of Mudslide. Then he bought a box of chocolate-flavored Ex-Lax. With a devious grin, he'd melted it down and poured it into the Mudslide, knowing his daughter couldn't resist stealing some of it. While she was in the bathroom sitting on the toilet, Turiq was in his bedroom laughing his ass off.

"Damn, I was gonna see if you wanted to hang out today," Sunny said.

"Oh, I definitely need to get the fuck outta here. It's been almost twenty minutes since I had a bowel movement, so I should be good."

"Ewww," Sunny said, hanging up. After taking a shower and getting dressed, she got ready to leave.

"Where are you about to go?" Darnell asked.

"Me and Jazmine about to hang out."

"Yeah, a'ight. Stay your asses out of trouble. And stop pulling your fucking gun out on people unless you plan to use it."

Sunny's mouth fell open.

"What? You didn't think I was going to hear about what happened at Club Château last night?" he asked. "Just know something, daughter of mine. I always have eyes on you, even when you think I don't. I am always going to protect you and be there for you. I love you. Always remember that, baby," Darnell said as he walked over to Sunny and kissed her on the forehead.

Sunny was still shocked as she walked out the door. She thought back to the previous night and tried to remember if she'd seen someone paying her a little too much attention, but she couldn't think of anyone. Her father's comments also made her wonder when else he'd been keeping an eye on her. She was going to have to be careful and mindful of her surroundings from now on. The more she thought about it, the more pissed off she became. Although she was still living in his house, she was a 20-year-old woman and felt that she deserved some level of privacy. She knew that her father was only doing it because he loved her and was trying to protect her, but still . . . This shit was over the top.

"Now, I *really* need a fuckin' drink," Sunny said to no one in particular. She glanced back at the house and frowned before jumping into her car and starting the engine. It took her nearly the entire ride to Jazmine's house to calm down. As she pulled up, Turiq was coming out of the front door.

"Good afternoon, young lady," Turiq said, walking up to Sunny and hugging her.

"Hey, Uncle Turiq. How's my girl doing?"

"What do you mean?" Turiq asked, feigning ignorance. It was hard enough for him to keep his laughter in check without Sunny bringing it up.

"Well, when I talked to her earlier, she wasn't feeling too good."

Turiq just smiled. He could see the concern in Sunny's face, so he decided to let her in on the secret . . . sort of.

"Oh, she'll be okay. Maybe you should tell your friend that it's not nice to steal her father's alcohol," he said while walking to his garage. Sunny's face twisted as she thought of what he had just said. It didn't take her long to figure out what he'd done, and once she did, she couldn't stop herself from laughing. She walked into the house and called out to Jazmine.

"Hey! Boo-boo girl! Where you at?"

When Jazmine came down the stairs holding her stomach, Sunny lost it. She dropped down to the couch and fell on her side, laughing. Frowning, Jazmine placed her hands on her hips and twisted her lips.

"The fuck is so funny? You laughing at a bitch, and I could be fuckin' dying?"

"Bitch, you ain't dying. But the next time you think about stealing ya' pops' liquor, maybe you should reconsider that shit."

"The fuck are you talking about, bitch?"

Sunny went on to tell her friend about the conversation between her and Turiq.

"Obviously, he slipped some Ex-Lax into that shit."

A stunned expression appeared on Jazmine's face. "Ex-Lax? Dirty muthafucka," she yelled. "I can't believe he did this bullshit to me." Hearing her friend go off caused Sunny to laugh even harder.

"I don't see what the fuck is so funny about this shit. My asshole of a father tries to poison me, and yo' ass sitting up here laughing."

"Bitch, ain't nobody trying to poison yo' thieving ass. You're the one who was trying to be all slick and shit. If you wanna be mad at somebody, then get mad at yo'self," Sunny said, as she continued to laugh.

"Whateva," Jazmine said, although she too was beginning to snicker. "I still don't think that shit is funny."

"You're right, girl. That shit is fuckin' hilarious."

"Fuck you, bitch," Jazmine said, slinging a couch pillow at her friend.

"As a matter of fact, why are you stealing it anyway? Why don't you just go to that Arab store? You know them thirsty muthafuckas will sell to anybody."

"What Arab store are you talking about?" Jazmine asked.

"Shit, pick one, bitch! Those muthafuckas are everywhere."

"I know, right? And they say Black people are ruining the damn country," Jazmine said, giving Sunny a high five.

"Well, to answer your question, it costs money to buy liquor, and why should I spend mine when I can drink my dad's for free?"

"Because that way, your ass won't have to worry about somebody slipping you a shit pill," Sunny said, laughing.

"Damn, you're not gonna let this shit go, are you?"

With a grin on her face, Sunny shook her head. Jazmine dropped down on the couch a few feet away from Sunny. She didn't know what her friend had up for the day, but she knew whatever it was, it was going to be fun. Jazmine and Sunny had become close over the last few weeks. So close, in fact, that they were starting to view each other as sisters. Jazmine could tell that Sunny had something on her mind. She didn't want to pry, but she didn't want to sit up here wondering either, so she reasoned that the two of them were close enough that she could come right out and ask her about it.

"Why are you looking like that?" Jazmine asked.

"Looking like what?" Sunny responded.

"Like you got some shit on your mind."

"Well, actually, I do. And it may or may not involve you."

"Me? What the fuck do I have to do with it?"

"It depends on what your answer is."

"Answer to what? Bitch, stop speaking in riddles and tell me what the fuck is on your mind."

Sunny had been thinking about this ever since her father brought up the subject of her taking over one day, which is why she asked him about Turiq. It stood to reason that if her father was going to step down, it was only logical that Turiq, his second in command, took his place. Since her father wasn't concerned about it, she wouldn't be either, but there was definitely something going on with those two that she didn't know about. Sunny excitedly explained to her friend her father's vision for her in the future. She watched Jazmine closely, trying to get a read on what she thought about it.

When she was done, Sunny remained quiet and waited for Jazmine to reply.

"Sooo, let me get this straight. Your dad told you that he wanted you to take over for him when he gets ready to retire from the game, right?"

"Yep, that's what he said. I was surprised too, but the more I think about it, the more I like the idea. Shit, I'm already a boss bitch in *my* book," she said, laughing.

Jazmine opened her mouth to speak but closed it quickly. She was trying to find the right words without offending Sunny. There wasn't a doubt in her mind that Sunny had the intelligence and street smarts to run the show. That wasn't what was eating at her. Unable to find the right words to express what she had to say, Jazmine decided to just come right out with it.

"Sunny, I have no doubt that you would make a hell of a boss bitch, but what about my dad? I mean, he *is* second in command," Jazmine said with a little more attitude than she meant to.

"Okay, first of all, you can lose the tone with me. And second, I asked my dad about that. All he would tell me about it was that he and your dad had it all worked out," Sunny lied. She didn't want to tell Jazmine what her dad really said because it would have sounded too negative.

Jazmine rolled her eyes. "Congratulations," she said, folding her arms.

"Jazmine, come on, now. If they say they got it worked out, then they got the shit worked out. Our fathers have been friends for a long-ass time, so whatever is going on, I'm sure that they are both on board with it."

Jazmine thought about what Sunny was saying. She thought about how close their fathers were and what they had been through together. She tossed her head back and forth as if contemplating what she was going to say.

"Okay, girl, you right," she said, cracking a half smile. "Congratulations, for real," she said, hugging Sunny. After the embrace, Jazmine stepped back and shook her head.

"Look at my bestie, about to become the boss bitch of the city." Now it was Sunny's time to cock her head. With a chuckle and a smirk, she shook her head.

"You still don't get it, do you, bitch?"

"Get what? What the fuck are you talking about?"

"I'm talking about you being my right-hand girl. My number two. My second in command."

"For real?" Jazmine asked, surprised.

"Okay, bitch, now *I'm* offended."

"Offended for what?"

"Okay, you talking kinda stupid right now. Who the fuck else did you think I was gonna make my second in command? Kim?"

"Well, she was your friend long before I was," Jazmine said, shrugging.

"That's true, and she will always be my girl, so she will always be a part of our crew. But she's not second-in-command material. Now, if you don't want the position, I can always give it to Butter."

"Hell nah! That broad ain't takin' my spot. *I'm* the number two bitch in this town," she said, snapping her fingers.

"Well, all right, then, bitch. Go get dressed so that we can go out and celebrate."

Jazmine looked down at her clothes and frowned.

"Get dressed? I *am* dressed."

"Nah, bitch. You better go put on some other clothes. You just got promoted. You gotta look the part."

"Damn, you act like we about to take over tomorrow or something."

"No, but we have to get our mentality right."

Jazmine looked at Sunny, and for the first time, she noticed how nicely Sunny was dressed.

"Be right back," she said as she went upstairs to change. When she came back down, Sunny had lit the blunt that was in the ashtray and was puffing on it.

"Damn, bitch, help yo'self."

"Whateva, bitch. You should be thanking me for getting rid of this dirt-ass weed."

"Dirt weed? You crazy as fuck. You know that shit is the bomb."

"It's a'ight. It ain't like that good shit Dani had last night, though. Speaking of which, who in the fuck told you to give that ho my cell phone number?"

"Come on, Sunny. Stop being so hard on her. She only wanted to call you 'cause she wanted to thank you for letting her hang out with us last night."

"Still, the next time you feel like giving my number to someone . . . don't," Sunny said sternly.

"Damn, Sunny, my bad," Jazmine apologized. She didn't think that Sunny would get so pissed off at her for giving a member of their crew her phone number, but she was wrong. Seeing the look on her friend's face caused Sunny to soften a little.

"Look, I'm not trying to get in your shit about it. I'm just saying that a little heads-up would've been nice."

"It's all good. Let's roll," Jazmine said, throwing her arm around Sunny's shoulders. "Where are we going?"

"To the mall. We can hit up the food court. Then we can get our shop on."

Chapter 21

Debra sat in her living room, tired as hell. She'd just worked a twelve-hour shift, and all she wanted to do was pour herself a glass of wine and relax. She was nearly in full-blown chill mode when her buzzing cell phone interrupted her. After looking at the caller ID, she waved her hand at it and took another sip of her wine.

"Not tonight," she mumbled, seeing the name of her on-again, off-again fuck buddy Yancy. For the past month, Yancy had been trying to get closer to Debra, but she'd resisted his advances. She wasn't in the market for a man. All she wanted to do was dress, rest, and occasionally to relieve her stress. From the gate, Debra had warned Yancy that she had comeback pussy, but because he was younger than she, he assumed that she wouldn't be able to keep up with him. Before their first sexual encounter, Debra had regularly shot Yancy down, rebuffing his advances at every turn. But Yancy was relentless in his pursuit. Even though she was quite a few years older than he was, Yancy felt that

Debra was one of the sexiest women he'd ever seen. For weeks, he begged and pleaded for her to give him a chance.

To say it was hard for Debra to resist, though, would be a gross understatement. She'd been celibate for a little over a year now and hadn't had sex regularly for five years, ever since her live-in lover Sammy suffered a massive heart attack and died in front of the television watching an episode of *Martin*. Suffering the loss of her loved one devastated Debra, but the secret she never revealed to him covered her in a shameful blanket of guilt. From the moment Darnell walked out of her bedroom all those years ago, she'd let Sammy think that the baby growing in her stomach at the time was his. She'd even gone so far as to name the child after Sammy. But as time went on, the guilt started to weigh on Debra, so one day, she decided that she would tell him the truth and let the chips fall.

She'd fixed his favorite food, rolled him a thick blunt, and planned to make sweet love to him just before she told him. Unfortunately, she never got the chance.

Figuring that he should be done eating, Debra walked into the living room in a silk, red sheer robe. Sliding up behind him, she wrapped her arms around his neck and hugged him.

"Let's go in the bedroom, baby," she'd told him. When Sammy didn't answer, she figured that he'd fallen asleep, so she got on her hands and knees and crawled around until she was directly in front of him. With a smile on her face, she reached for his zipper. However, her smile soon faded when she glanced up and saw a grotesque expression on his face. It was then that she noticed that he was clutching his chest. As fast as she could, Debra jumped up and raced to her cell phone. Although the ambulance quickly got there, Sammy was dead before they even took him out of the house. Not a day had gone by that Debra didn't think about Sammy and the lie that she'd let him believe all those years.

For the second time in less than thirty minutes, Debra's serenity was broken by her cell phone. This time when she looked at the name on the screen, she smiled. It was a name she never got tired of seeing.

"Hey, baby, how you doing today?" she asked.

"I'm okay, Ma. Open the door. I got something for you."

Debra sighed and shook her head.

Her son treated her well, and she appreciated it. She got up and went over to the door. Unlocking it with a smile, she pulled it open, wondering what surprise he had in store for her this time. Last week, he surprised her with a big-screen television. The week before that, he gave her $2,000 and told her to go shopping. Debra didn't have to ask her son how he was able to give her money like that. She wasn't a fool and knew that the only way her son could afford to do the things he could do was by selling drugs. Since he was now a grown man, there wasn't much that she could say to him. His temper had never allowed him to keep a job, so all she could do was pray that he didn't become a victim of the streets or the crooked-ass Cleveland Police Department.

When Debra opened the door, she nearly fainted. Parked in front of her house was a large truck. On the side of it was the name Reynold's furniture company. She looked at her son, who just stood there smiling.

"What's this?" she asked.

"What does it look like? It's your new furniture."

Tears welled up in Debra's eyes. All she could do was walk up to her son and throw her arms around him. She hugged her son for what seemed like half an hour. When she finally did let go of him, she grabbed his hand and tried to pull him into the house.

"Hold up a second, Ma."

Debra's son ran out to the truck and gave the workers instructions. His mother watched as he peeled off a few bills and handed them to a man standing behind the truck. Tears ran down her eyes. She could no longer stand it. The things her son was doing for her only added to the guilty feeling that simmered in her soul. While the workers were exchanging the old furniture for the new, Debra grabbed her son's hand and led him down the stairs into the basement. The small basement only had a table and two chairs in it, but Debra's son had already promised her that he would furnish it in the future.

"Have a seat, son. I have something to tell you."

Debra's son looked at his mother and saw a sadness in her eyes that he'd never seen before. It worried him. His mind immediately led him to the wrong conclusion.

"What's wrong, Ma? Did that punk-ass nigga Yancy do something to you?"

"No, and watch your mouth, Sammy!"

"Sorry."

Sammy knew that his mother meant business when she called him by his government name.

"What's up?" he asked.

Debra stared at her son for a long while before getting up and walking over to him. She kissed him on the cheek and told him that she would be right back before rushing up the stairs. Sammy sat there, confused. Something was going on, and his gut, combined with her sudden attitude, was telling him that it wasn't something good. The wait for her to come back seemed like an eternity. Just when he was about to go upstairs to see what was taking her so long, Debra reemerged with a photograph in her hands. She sat down in front of her son and smiled weakly. Her hands trembled as she handed the picture to him. It was an old picture, and Sammy's face twisted as he stared at it. He looked back up at his mother and shrugged his shoulders as he looked at the photo again.

"This picture supposed to mean something to me? Who the hell is this nigga?"

Debra took a deep breath. The moment of truth had finally arrived. It was time for her to shit or get off the pot. She said a silent prayer that her son wouldn't hate her for not telling him the truth from the beginning.

"That's your father."

Slowly, Sammy lifted his head and stared at his mother. His eyes narrowed into slits as he shook his head.

"My father is dead. I don't know who the fuck this nigga is."

"No, your father isn't dead. He's very much alive."

"Wait a minute," Sammy said, rubbing his head. "You mean to tell me that the man who I thought was my father wasn't? And now you wanna tell me that this nigga here is?" Sammy said, raising his voice.

"Lower your voice and watch your damn tone. I'm *still* your mother."

"Everything good down there?" one of the workers asked, hearing the commotion. Sammy's eyes turned cold as his head snapped around and looked at the stairs.

"Nigga, mind yo' muthafuckin' business and do what the fuck I'm paying y'all to do," he yelled. His eyes watered slightly as he turned his attention back to his mother.

"Ma, why didn't you tell me that the man who raised me wasn't my father?"

"I wanted to, baby. I swear to God, I did. It just never seemed to be the right time."

Sammy shook his head. He couldn't believe that the only person alive in the world he loved other than himself had deceived him so badly.

"Foul, Ma. This shit is just foul!"

Debra opened her mouth, but she honestly didn't know what to say. Her son had a right to be upset, and she knew it. After a brief silence, a sudden thought occurred to Sammy.

"Ma, don't tell me that you let that man die, thinking that he was my biological father."

All Debra could do was hang her head in shame. "I meant to tell him, baby, I really did, but the day I was going to tell him was the day he died. That guilt has haunted me every day of my life since then. That's why I'm choosing to tell you the truth now. This guilt is unbearable," Debra said, her tears now falling freely.

Sammy wanted to hate his mother. He wanted to despise her for obviously depriving him of a relationship with his birth father. But looking at her break down, he couldn't do it. Sammy was pissed, but seeing his mother's tearful face only made him feel sorry for her.

"Wait a fuckin' minute," he said, realizing something else. "You mean to tell me that some nigga out there in the city knew that he had a son and never even tried to get in contact wit' a nigga?"

"He didn't know he had a son, baby. When I was pregnant with you—"

Debra stopped abruptly. It suddenly occurred to her that if she told her son the whole story, she would look like a slut.

"Look, I'm sorry that I didn't tell you all of this years ago. But just know that this is not your father's fault. We were broken up at the time," she lied.

"So, in a way, he was also lied to, huh?" Sammy asked, making his mother feel even worse. The workers called downstairs to inform Sammy that they were done. After paying them the rest of the money, Sammy kissed his mother on the cheek, gave her a little pocket change, and headed out the door. He needed time to process what his mother had just told him. Stuffing the photograph into his back pocket, Sammy hopped in his vehicle and sped away.

Chapter 22

Dani grabbed her car keys and headed for the door. Her lower regions were sore, but in her mind, it was worth it. The $1,000 that Damon gave her more than made up for the beat-up pussy he'd inflicted on her. She thought that he was done fucking her for the rest of the day, but he left for an hour and returned in a foul mood. It didn't take long for him to take it out on her coochie. Dani's pussy was on fire. Damon had really done a job on her. Usually, she enjoyed a good fucking, but what Damon put on her should have netted her much more than what he'd given her.

"Hey! Ain't you forgettin' something?" Damon asked just before she walked out the door. He was standing in the hallway leading to his living room in his birthday suit. "Get yo' ass over here and let daddy know what you thought about that good-ass fuckin' I gave you earlier."

Dani gingerly made her way over to Damon. Kneeling in front of him, she kissed the head of his dick. She could tell that he was getting aroused, so as sore as her sex box was, she quickly made her way to the door and left. When she got to her car, she carefully got in and exhaled. As she started her car, she heard her stomach rumble. She hadn't eaten anything since gobbling down the wings at the club the previous night. She was just getting ready to pull off when Damon came running out of the house.

"Hey, hold up a second," he yelled.

"The fuck this nigga want now?" she asked herself. Thinking that he was going to be on some bullshit, she instantly caught an attitude. Much to her surprise, though, he gave her another $500.

"Here ya go, baby. I know I put a hurtin' on that pussy this morning, and you took it like the down-ass bitch that you are, so I figured I should hit you off with a little more bread."

Dani's attitude disappeared as quickly as it had come. A smile grew on her face. "Thanks, babe," she said.

"You're welcome. Now, I'm not gonna be here for the next couple of days. I got some business to handle out of town," he lied. "Just remember the mission."

Dani nodded and pulled off. She wasn't a fool, so she knew that Damon would probably have some other bitch in his place the next couple of days. As long as she was his main bitch and he kept other bitches out of her face, she could deal with it, especially now that she knew that she played a part in his master plan to become the next king. Dani couldn't help but fantasize about how it would be when she was standing side by side with the biggest drug dealer in the city. She would be able to shop at the most expensive clothing stores and eat at the best restaurants. The best perk of all, though, would be that she wouldn't have to bow down to bitches like Sunny. She despised those types of hoes. But after going out with her and the rest of their crew, Dani was starting to warm up to Sunny and thought about changing her mind. But Damon quickly mind fucked her and convinced her that she could be so much more than a mere part of a crew if she stuck with him.

"Why be a part of a crew when you can be the leader of the crew?" he'd told her.

In her mind, it made perfect sense. Unfortunately for her, however, Dani was far too trusting of a man without morals. Her stomach growled a second time as she made her way back to her place. She thought about how good the food from Asian Chow was when she'd had it a few nights ago and decided that's what she wanted. It went through her mind to call Jazmine and see if she wanted to meet up but decided not to.

She's probably sniffin' up Sunny's ass, she thought. Dani made a right at the light and pulled into the parking lot. Since it was a Saturday, the lot was filled. It took her two trips around the parking lot to find a space. Her stomach growled for a third time, causing her to race into the building and make a beeline toward Asian Chow. After ordering, she waited for what seemed like forever for her food to get prepared. When it was, Dani wasted no time sitting at a table and tearing into it. She ate like she was starving. Other patrons looked at her like she was a savage, but Dani didn't give a damn. For all she cared, they could go fuck themselves.

After finishing her meal, Dani decided that she needed a few new items for her wardrobe. An hour later, she was walking out, carrying two large bags from Saks Fifth. She was smiling from ear to ear . . . until she heard a familiar voice.

"Since when they let basic bitches in Saks?"

Dani's head turned to the left, but she didn't see anybody. When she turned it back to the right, she saw someone who made her blood boil. Standing there smirking was a woman who went by the name of Janine. Posted up next to her was her flunky, Rita. Janine was once Damon's main bitch, but since Dani slid into her spot, she was now relegated as a last resort for Damon when he wanted to fuck and couldn't get in touch with Dani. Janine hated being reduced to the role of side bitch and blamed Dani for her demotion. Dani smiled. It was the first time she'd seen Janine in nearly six months, but the bitterness between the two of them was still there. She looked at the bags in Janine's hand and laughed.

"The fuck is so funny, bitch?" Janine asked with an attitude.

"Yeah, what the fuck are you laughing at?" Rita cosigned.

"What's funny is that yo' ass got the nerve to call me a basic bitch, but you carrying around bags from Target," Dani said, laughing harder.

Janine looked at her bags and frowned. She was trying to belittle Dani with her statement but ended up getting trolled herself.

"I see you got jokes, bitch. Maybe me and my girl should come over there and beat the funny outta yo' ass," Janine said, balling up her fists.

Dani looked at the two of them and started to reach into her back pocket for her box cutter. She silently cursed herself when she realized that she'd left it in her car, and there was no way in hell that she was going to be able to get to it before the two women got to her. Even though she knew that she had no wins in the situation, Dani wasn't about to go down without a fight.

"Whateva you hoes wanna do, I'm game," she said, setting her bags down on the ground. Janine and Rita looked at each other and smiled deviously. The last time Janine had seen Dani, Jazmine was with her, so it was an even confrontation. But now that the odds were in her favor, she was more than willing to get it popping.

"Let's teach this bitch a lesson," she told Rita, as the two of them advanced on Dani.

Dani stood in a fighter's stance and got ready for battle. Chances were that she was about to get her ass handed to her, but she wasn't going out like a scared little punk. Just as the three women were about to engage in fisticuffs, another voice spoke.

"We got a fuckin' problem over here?" Sunny said as she and Jazmine came over, holding shopping bags. The second they saw Sunny, Janine and Rita stopped in their tracks. Both of them knew Sunny and who she was connected to, and neither wanted a problem with her.

"Nah, ain't no problem. We were just about to teach this bigmouthed bitch what time it was. You know this ho?"

Without saying a word, Sunny walked up to Janine and backhanded her. Rita opened her mouth to say something, but a hard look from Sunny silenced her.

"Yes, I know this queen. She's a part of my inner circle, and if you've got a problem with her, you've got a problem with me. Do I make myself clear?"

The two women were so afraid to talk, they simply nodded their heads.

"Good. Jazmine, grab those bags."

"The fuck you sluts got in here?" Jazmine asked, picking up the bags from the ground. She took them over to Sunny, and she and Sunny looked at each other and shook their heads in laughter.

"Here! Take this cheap-ass shit and get the fuck on," Sunny spat.

Silently, Janine and Rita looked at each other and walked away.

"Don't worry about it, Rita. That bitch will get hers one day," Janine said. But she was no fool. She made sure to say it low enough that Sunny couldn't hear it.

"Thanks, Sunny," Dani said, feeling slightly guilty that Sunny had stepped in and saved her, and she was plotting her father's downfall.

"Don't worry about it. Ain't nobody checking for my fuckin' crew," she said proudly. "Jazmine, call the other two. I'm calling a meeting tonight," Sunny said, feeling more and more powerful by the second.

Red's was a plush, upscale eatery on the outskirts of Cleveland. It was a seafood restaurant best known for its lobster and swordfish. The establishment oozed class. The valet attendants were sharply dressed and approached every customer with extreme politeness. Smiling greeters held the door open for every single patron that entered or left. By all standards, the place was immaculate. The entire inside had wall-to-wall tinted windows. The carpet was thick and soft. It didn't matter if you wore dress shoes, Air Force Ones, or

Tims; your feet still felt like they were walking on clouds. Red's was the epitome of class, which is why Sunny needed to talk with Kim's ghetto ass before they entered the place.

"Look, Kim, this ain't Popeye's, so don't take your ass in here acting all hoodish and shit."

"Huh? Sunny, why are you singling me out?" Kim asked with a hurt look in her eyes.

"Because I know how you get sometimes."

Butter chuckled, prompting an angry response from Kim.

"The fuck are you laughing at?"

"See, that's what the fuck I'm talking about," Sunny said, feeling that Kim had proven her point for her. "Chill out with that shit."

"Yeah, a'ight," Kim said with an attitude.

Sunny knew that her friend was pissed, but she didn't give a damn. She wasn't about to have Kim embarrassing her as if she didn't have any home training. The five young ladies stepped into the entrance with a purpose. Sunny had intentionally picked this place because she wanted her crew to get used to the finer things in life. Jazmine was, but she couldn't speak for Butter or Dani. The only time Kim went to nice places was when she was tagging along with Sunny.

Sunny asked for a booth seat in the back, facing the door. She wasn't afraid, but she wanted to be completely aware of her surroundings and make sure that no one could easily eavesdrop on their conversation. Sunny told her crew to order whatever they wanted because it was on her. Kim, of course, loved this. Her ghetto ass ordered the most expensive steak on the menu.

"What type of soft drink would you young ladies like to order?" the waiter asked.

"Soft drink?" Kim asked about to get ignorant. Sunny shot her a look that instantly closed her mouth.

"Sir, we won't be having soft drinks. What we will have is a bottle of your best champagne."

The waiter looked at each one of them and chuckled. Jazmine flinched. She wanted to bark at him so badly that it ached her soul. Sunny placed a reassuring hand on her friend's shoulder, letting her know that she had everything under control.

"Champagne? You do know that I'm going to have to see some ID from all of you, right?"

"Of course," Sunny said as she reached into her purse and pulled out her wallet. She continued to stare at the handsome waiter as she took out five one-hundred-dollar bills. After placing them on the table, she slowly pushed them across the table until they were sitting right in front of him. The waiter looked down at the money and took a deep breath.

"You know, I can really get in trouble if I sell you young ladies wine."

Sunny smiled. "Look, sweetie, you can either take this money *and* the generous tip that my friend here was going to give you," she said, gesturing to Jazmine, "or we can leave, and you can be just as broke then as you are now."

The waiter thought about it for all of five seconds before reaching for the money. Just before his hand touched the crisp bills, Kim grabbed it.

"Oh, and we'll be needing your phone number," she said, smiling at him. Butter shook her head. She couldn't believe how thirsty Kim was.

"Kim, let that man's hand go!" Sunny ordered. Reluctantly and sadly, she released the waiter's hand.

"Nah, it's cool," he said. "You can have my number," he told Kim.

A broad smile popped onto Kim's face. In her mind, she was already picturing bending over for him and letting him have his way with her. Dani rolled her eyes. The waiter was an attractive dude, so she couldn't help but wonder what the hell he saw in Kim. He quickly scribbled his number on his order pad and slid it to her.

"Well, when you two are done flirting, we would like to have our champagne, please," Jazmine said.

"Coming right up," he said, strolling away. From the second he turned to walk away until he disappeared into the back, Kim's eyes were glued to his ass.

"You are one thirsty-ass bitch," Butter said.

"Don't hate, bitch," Kim responded.

"A'ight, enough of that bullshit y'all talking. Let's get down to business."

Sunny looked around carefully before lowering her voice and getting to the nuts and bolts of why she'd called them all there.

"Wait. What?" Jazmine said when Sunny revealed more of her plan. She'd only told Jazmine a small portion of what she had in store for the city.

"You heard me. I don't only want to control the dope game. I want to start a loan business and an escort service."

"In other words, you want to be a loan shark *and* a pimp," Butter said.

"Tomato, tomahto," Sunny said, smiling.

"Hold up. How are we even gonna get started in this shit? Ain't no telling how much money it's gonna cost us even to get plugged into the dope game, let alone become loan sharks," Butter said. Sunny looked at Jazmine and Kim. As far as she knew, they were the only ones sitting there who knew about her father.

"Jazmine, tell them who our fathers are," she told her second in command.

As Jazmine revealed to them how she and Sunny were already connected to the game, Dani sat there listening like she didn't already know what time it was. Roughly thirty minutes later, Sunny gave each of them the option to get down with her plan. Although Kim felt slighted by Sunny because she thought that she should've been second in command based on her longtime friendship with Sunny, she wasn't pissed enough to let the opportunity to make a ton of money and have elite social status pass her by. Sunny also revealed to them what had happened at her father's house.

"How did it feel?" Butter asked Sunny.

"How did what feel?"

"Killing someone," Butter said, a little louder than she needed to.

"Bitch, lower your damn voice," Jazmine said.

"My bad," Butter said, her eyes and attention still focused on Sunny.

It fascinated her to know someone who'd committed murder. Sunny rolled her eyes and stared up at the ceiling while contemplating her answer. Despite what she'd told Jazmine when she'd saved her from Jamaal, she really didn't feel anything about killing the officer. It was the first time since it happened that she'd thought about it. It scared her that she wasn't feeling any remorse about taking another human being's life. But it was a trait that would serve her well going forward.

Chapter 23

Carol Walker had worked as a police dispatcher for the last ten years. She was a single mother but gave up her parental rights at the age of 24 because she wanted to run the streets and have fun instead of raising a child and being a good mother. The father, a high school janitor at the time, was thrilled to get custody of his son and get him away from such an irresponsible mother. Although she and her son's father couldn't stand each other now, the two of them had some good times earlier on in their relationship. They partied like rock stars and played even harder, having sex two to three times a day. It was foolish of them to think that she wouldn't eventually get pregnant, considering that neither one of them used any form of birth control at the time.

Once Carol finally did get pregnant, the issues between her and Malik started. He was happy as hell to be a father and wanted to tell the world. Carol, on the other hand, wanted no part of motherhood. She was too busy having fun to even think about raising a child. Being pregnant meant no more smoking weed, and more importantly to her, no more occasionally indulging in cocaine. Malik saw it much differently. As soon as he found out that Carol was pregnant, he did away with his cocaine vice, although he still smoked weed now and then. When Malik found out that Carol was planning on getting an abortion, he was crushed. For weeks, he begged Carol to let his child live. It wasn't until he agreed to take custody of the child that Carol relented. Because she didn't trust his word, she made him put it in writing. Carol had seen a few men who were proud fathers before the child was born only to get in the wind once the baby appeared. She wasn't falling for that trap.

The one thing Carol hadn't counted on, however, was Malik losing his job. Since he was unemployed, and she wasn't, Carol had to pay Malik child support. She made enough money to have a decent living, but once child support began to cut into her pockets, her finances were crippled. So, when Joy volunteered to pay her to keep Joy informed of what calls were coming in and whatever else she could keep her eyes on in the department, she jumped at the chance. Carol didn't see any harm in it. She was making a few extra bucks on the side, and as long as no one got hurt, it was all good. But after hearing about what happened to the witness, Carol knew that she had gotten in over her head this time. She knew that it was just a matter of time before everything led back to her telling Joy about the witness, and then she would be in deep shit. Not only would her job be on the line, but also her freedom would, which was why she called Joy and asked her to come over. She needed to be assured that her flapping tongue wasn't going to come back to bite her in the ass.

Carol had just finished her third cigarette and was about to fire up her fourth when a knock on her front door nearly caused her to jump out of her skin. She was a nervous wreck. She just knew that at any moment, Detective Little was going to kick in her door and haul her ass off to jail. Carol cautiously walked over to the door. She looked through the peephole, but all she saw was darkness. Her heart began racing.

"Who is it?" she asked nervously.

"Bitch, it's me. Open the damn door," Joy said.

Carol breathed a sigh of relief as she let her coworker in. Joy strolled in with all the confidence in the world. She didn't seem to be bothered or worried about anything. Carol couldn't understand that. She couldn't tell her what she wanted over the phone, but her frantic voice should have alerted Joy that something was wrong. Joy walked over to Carol's couch and sat down.

"Now, what the fuck did you call me over here for?" she asked angrily.

She had planned on spending the night at Darnell's, but now she had to be bothered with this bitch. Joy had a feeling she knew what Carol wanted but didn't want to say anything in case she was wrong. Carol opened her mouth to speak but looked around first as if someone could be listening.

"The fuck are you looking around for? Look, I'm busy. Say what the fuck you have to say."

"Joy, I think someone knows I gave you the witness's address."

"And just how do you know that?" Joy asked.

"It's just a feeling I have," Carol said, shrugging.

"A feeling? Bitch, you're in law enforcement. When the fuck do we go by feelings? If you don't have any proof, stop wasting my fuckin' time."

"Look, first of all, stop fucking talking to me like that. Second of all, I am not going to jail over some bullshit that you're involved in."

Joy took a deep breath. She figured that Carol would be on edge, so she came prepared to reel her back in. She reached into her pocket and pulled out a small bag with a white substance in it.

"Here," she said, tossing the bag to Carol. "Maybe this will calm your shaky ass down a little bit."

Carol looked at the bag, and her mouth started to water. It was just what she needed to take the edge off. She quickly sat down and sprinkled some of the powder on a mirror that was sitting there.

After separating the powder into three separate lines, she pulled a dollar bill out of her front pocket. Putting the dollar bill to her nose, she quickly snorted it into one nostril, then the other. She sat back and closed her eyes, allowing the cocaine to affect her system and brain. After a few minutes, Joy started smiling. She had successfully brought Carol back into the fold.

"You okay now?" she asked.

"Yeah, I'm good," Carol said in an even tone.

"Still, Joy, although I appreciate you giving me this shit for free, I hope we have everything in order because I meant what I said a few minutes ago. I am not going to jail over some bullshit that I know nothing about."

"I understand, Carol. Trust me; I have everything under control."

Although she hadn't brought it up to Joy, Carol was beginning to wonder what was really going on. She knew that she shouldn't have asked, but curiosity got the better of her. "Joy, what—"

"Carol, don't even ask me that question. The less you know, the better. You know that."

"Yeah, you're right," Carol said, staring at her.

It only took Joy a few seconds to detect the snitch in her. She made small talk for the next few minutes before getting up to leave. When she got to her car, she pulled out her cell phone and called Darnell.

"Yeah, we may have a problem. I'll be there in ten minutes to explain." Eight minutes later, Joy was walking through Darnell's front door.

"Babe? Where are you?" she called out.

"Down here," Darnell shouted from the basement.

When Joy walked down the stairs, she instantly got moist. It had been about a week since she'd felt his sweet stick in one of her holes, and she was getting horny for it. But first things first. She needed to inform him of the little "situation" involving Carol. Darnell listened as she told him about the conversation. Even though his hands were clean of the matter, he didn't want Joy to get popped on some bullshit. He had to take care of it, and he would.

"I'll take care of it," he told her.

"That's good to hear. Now, how about taking care of *me*?" she asked, crawling on his lap.

Slowly, she began grinding her soft ass on his dick, causing it to harden. Feeling his manhood grow, Joy moaned softly. She climbed off his lap and pulled her pants down. After discarding them, she got down on her hands and knees and tugged at his gym shorts. Her mouth watered when his dick revealed itself. Joy wrapped her hands around it and stroked it slowly before lowering her mouth onto it. Instead of going fast, she took her time and savored the taste and feel of her lover's sweet stick in her throat. With his long dick damn near on her tonsils, Joy slid her tongue back and forth across his balls. Darnell could barely stand it. He was seconds from busting his load when Joy abruptly stopped sucking him.

"Oh shit," Darnell said, panting. He didn't know what had gotten into Joy, but she was putting it on his ass. With a seductive look in her eye, she climbed back on top of his lap and inserted his rock-hard pole into her wetness.

"Ooooh, yeeesss," Joy purred. She was so turned on that it only took a few humps for her to come. But Darnell was far from done. Grabbing her hips, he picked her up and slammed her down on his cock repeatedly. Figuring that Darnell's daughter wasn't home, Joy figured she could let her hair down sexually. The harder Darnell fucked her, the louder and dirtier she talked.

"Oh yes, baby, fuck me. Fuck the shit outta this pussy," she screamed. Her nails dug deep into his chest as she exploded for a second time. This time, however, she wasn't alone. With an animalistic grunt, Darnell released his love deep inside of her.

"Whew, oh my God, baby, that was fantastic," she said, placing kisses on his face and chest. Darnell wrapped his arms around her and hugged her tightly. The two of them had been embracing for less than a minute when Darnell heard Sunny's car pull up.

"Oh shit, my daughter's here," he said.

Joy hurriedly got up and put her undergarments and pants back on. Darnell pulled his shorts up just in time as Sunny entered the house through the garage and walked into the basement. Darnell and Joy sat there like they had been watching television, which Sunny could tell wasn't what went down.

"Hey, y'all. What's going on?"

"Not much. Just chillin'. Where you been all day?"

"Well, after we got back from the gun range, I had a meeting with Jazmine."

"A meeting about what?" Darnell asked.

Sunny thought about lying. She didn't know if her father wanted her to say anything about his proposition to Jazmine. She ultimately decided that since Jazmine would be her second in command, she might as well tell her father and get it over with. Because no matter what he said, that wasn't going to change.

"Well, I was talking to her about being my right hand when I take over."

"Is that right?" Darnell asked, rubbing his chin. "I guess you two have finally become friends, huh? Me and Turiq knew that if y'all spent enough time with each other, the ice between y'all would eventually start to thaw."

Sunny shrugged her shoulders. She didn't dare tell her father about what happened to bring them together. If she had, Jamaal would quickly be erased from the planet.

"Yeah, we came to an understanding," she said.

"Good, baby girl, good." Darnell then got up and walked over to his daughter. Placing both hands on her shoulders, he looked her square in the eyes.

"So, how are you doing?"

"Uh . . . I'm doing fine, Daddy," Sunny answered. She was slightly confused as to why he'd asked her that. He smiled at her.

"You sure? I mean, you did take a life just a few short weeks ago."

"Oh, yeah, I'm okay, Daddy. You were right. If we had let him live, that dirty cop would have put you behind bars as fast as he could. It was either him or us. I understand that now."

Darnell looked back at Joy, and the two of them shared a wicked smile. Sunny looked from her father to his lover and frowned. Obviously, something was cooking in their minds, but she didn't know what.

"Okay, what's going on?" she asked.

"So, let me ask you something, Vanessa," he said, ignoring her question, "are you really that comfortable with killing another human being, or are you just saying what you think I want to hear?"

Sunny opened her mouth to speak, but Darnell silenced her by holding up his hand.

"Now, before you answer that question, I want you to think long and hard about the answer."

Sunny cut her eyes toward Joy, who was now intently staring at her. She looked back at her father and saw the seriousness in his expression. Sunny thought about what her father had just asked her. She thought about how Detective Warren's life drained from his body before her very eyes. She searched her emotions for pity or remorse, and much to her surprise, she found none. Taking a deep breath, she looked at her father and told him that she was extremely comfortable with what she'd done to the dirty cop.

"I'm glad to hear that," he said, grinning wickedly. "Because I have another job for you."

Chapter 24

The meeting Sunny had with the other four ladies of her crew was conducted at Gordon Park off Seventy-Second and St. Clair. As soon as she told them what had to be done and what she expected their involvement in it to be, they all stared at her in disbelief.

"You want us to do *what?*" Kim asked.

"You heard me. My father gave me a job to do, and I need my crew to help me carry it out." Sunny didn't need any of them to carry out the hit. However, she did want them to be a part of it to solidify their status within the crew. If they were going to be a part of the organization, all of their hands would have to get dirty. She looked around at her crew's faces and tried to check for any signs of fear or uncertainty.

"What? Did you bitches actually think that y'all were going to rise to the top without getting your hands dirty?" Sunny asked.

"Well, I can't speak for the rest of these broads, but I'm ready to put that work in," Butter boasted.

Sunny gave Butter a strange look. There was something about the young lady that Sunny perceived as sinister. There seemed to be a level of crazy that Butter possessed that the other girls didn't have, not even Jazmine. Sunny had first seen it in her eyes when Butter had asked her how it felt to kill a man. Now, the bloodthirsty look in her eyes had Sunny convinced that she would definitely be ride or die for her team.

"We all know that your crazy ass can't wait to get to blasting, so ain't nobody talking about you," Jazmine said.

"Kim? Dani? You two hoes down for this one eighty-seven?"

Kim and Dani looked at each other. One of them was waiting for the other one to speak first. But instead, it was Butter who broke the silence.

"I think these bitches scared," she spat.

"Bitch, ain't nobody scared," Kim lied.

She couldn't speak for Dani, but she was scared shitless. This is the part of the game that she hadn't thought about. The only thing on her mind was getting rich and getting laid by some fine-ass men. It never once occurred to her that she would have to do any of the dirty work.

Dani, on the other hand, was doing some fast thinking. In her mind, this was her chance to get in good with Sunny. If she could somehow get Sunny to trust her completely, then she would be that much closer to infiltrating the crew and helping Damon destroy Sunny *and* her father.

"Well, I'm damn sure not scared," she said. "Just let me know where to be and what to do." Sunny nodded her head in satisfaction. She then turned her attention to Kim.

"Well?"

"Well, what?" Kim asked as if she didn't know what her friend was talking about.

"Bitch, you know what," Jazmine spat. She was losing patience with Kim and didn't try to hide it.

"Who the fuck are you calling a bitch?"

Jazmine's jaw twitched. Her hands balled into fists. She took a step toward Kim but stopped when Sunny grabbed her arm. Sunny took a deep breath and addressed her longtime friend.

"You know what, Kim? I need to holla at you for a minute." Grabbing her by the hand, Sunny led Kim away from the rest of the girls. When they were out of earshot, Sunny looked Kim in the eye and laid it on the line.

"Look, Kim, I know that I'm asking a lot of all of you. But I need to know where you stand. Either you're down with the fuckin' team, or you're not. If you don't want to be involved with this, I understand. But if you're not, then you can't be a part of this crew. We will always be friends, but I can't have you a part of this operation if you can't get your hands dirty like the rest of us."

Kim took a deep breath. She weighed her options and decided that the money and prestige that came with being down with Sunny's crew far outweighed the risks of being included with it.

"Okay, Sunny, I'm in," she finally declared.

"My bitch! I knew you was a down-ass broad." Sunny threw her arms around Kim's neck and led her back over to the crew.

"A'ight, bitches, my girl is down to do the damn thing. Anybody got a problem with that?"

Although none of them said anything, the other three girls had their doubts about Kim. Her hood pedigree wasn't what was in question. It was her heart that they had concerns about. Before any of them could voice their opinion, Sunny's cell phone rang.

"Hello?"

"Yeah, it's me. I'll be there in thirty seconds," the voice coming from the other end said. Sunny nodded and ended the call.

"Who the fuck was that?" Jazmine asked.

"You'll see in a few seconds," was all Sunny would say.

Approximately thirty seconds later, Joy pulled up. Confused, all the girls looked at Sunny as Joy got out of her car and approached them. Jazmine and Butter recognized her from the party, but Dani and Kim didn't remember her at all. As soon as she got close to them, Joy studied each one of them.

Her eyes lingered a little longer on Dani than it did the rest of them. A sly smirk appeared on her face just before she started to speak.

"So, this is your crew, huh?" she said, nodding her head. "Well, let's get down to business. Did you tell them what was going down?"

"Yeah, I told them. I didn't tell them how we were going to go about executing the plan, though, because neither you nor my father has told me," Sunny said, folding her arms.

"Stop being a smart-ass, Sunny. We didn't tell you because we didn't want to have to repeat it. The more you run your mouth about shit like this, the more susceptible you are to getting locked the fuck up because you never—and I mean *never*—know who's listening."

"You seem to know a lot about shit like that," Dani said. "You about that life or something?"

Joy cocked her head and looked at Dani. There was something about her that didn't sit well with Joy. She'd seen how Dani had stormed away from the party and thought it odd that she was now hanging out with Sunny. Not only did she have firsthand knowledge because she was a woman, but she'd also learned from her experiences on the job that women tended to hold grudges. The fact that Dani was even in Sunny's presence smelled foul to her.

"Don't worry about what the fuck life I'm about, little girl. Just play your position and stop asking so many stupid-ass questions," Joy said, frowning. "Now, I've been studying this broad for a while, so I know her habits. I know where she works, what time she gets off, and most importantly, I know where she's going to be tomorrow evening."

A wicked smile creased her lips as she looked at each one of them in the eye. As a trained police officer, Joy could see inside the heart of individuals. It didn't take her long to form an opinion about the other four girls. Jazmine was solid. There was no need to worry about her. She hadn't noticed it before, but the more she stared at Butter, the more convinced she was that the young lady had a screw loose. The look in her eyes screamed that she was bloodthirsty. There was no need to question her gangsta because it was evident that fear didn't reside in her heart. It took her less than three seconds to figure out that Dani was a sneaky bitch. She didn't trust her as far as she could throw her and was going to tell Sunny the next chance she got. Kim, in her opinion, seemed scary. She tried to put up a brave front, but Joy saw the cowardice in her heart. She decided to bring her concerns to Sunny's attention.

"Sunny, I need to talk to you for a minute," she said, walking away before Sunny could object. Sunny rolled her eyes and followed behind Joy.

"What's good?" she asked when they were out of earshot.

"Sunny, are you 100 percent sure that you can trust these bitches?"

"Joy, why are you asking me some shit like that?" Sunny asked, avoiding the question. After giving Sunny the rundown on her opinion of each member of her crew, Joy asked Sunny again if she could trust them. She was still skeptical when Sunny told her that she could vouch for them, but she let it slide. The only other thing she told her was to keep an eye on Dani. Sunny agreed to take her advice, then the two of them walked back over to the rest of the girls.

"Okay, bitches. Here's the plan, and I'm only gonna say this one time, so listen the fuck up."

Although she never wanted to be a mother, Carol did come to love and care for her son, Deuce. Every Thursday night, she had a standing reservation to have dinner with him at a local eatery that had a game room. Malik didn't have a problem with Carol seeing her son, but he did impose a stipulation. He had to be present whenever she spent time with him. Carol didn't like it, but she wasn't in any position to argue with Malik about it. Carol watched as her son played one of the video games. She and Malik were sitting across from each other, trying to remain civil in the other's presence. Malik had been raising Deuce on his own ever since he was born, and he resented Carol for it.

"He's really getting big," Carol said.

"Yeah, he is," Malik said dryly.

Carol looked at him and smirked. "What the hell is your problem?"

"I don't have a damn problem. I just wish this hour would go faster."

"Oh my God, Malik, you act like I don't have a right to see my own son."

Malik looked at her like she had two heads.

"Carol, I didn't say you didn't have a right to see your son. Stop jumping to fuckin' conclusions."

"Whatever," Carol said with an attitude.

She didn't feel like arguing with her ex, so she occupied her time by scrolling Facebook posts. She had just gotten deep into her nosiness when she felt Malik's hand run up her thigh. Immediately, her eyes went from her cell phone screen to the lustful gaze of her ex.

Typical, she thought. *Just a minute ago, the nigga was talking reckless. Now, he's trying to crack for some ass.*

"What the hell do you think you're doing?"

"I just thought that you might want a little company tonight."

"Oh, really?" Carol panted lightly.

It had been a while since she'd last been laid, so maybe it wouldn't be the worst thing to let Malik crawl between her legs again. Still, she wouldn't make it easy for him.

"Nigga, you got some damn nerve. Ain't you got a bitch?"

"Yeah, and? What she doesn't know won't hurt her ass. Now, are you gonna give me some of that or not?" Malik asked as he pushed her skirt up and slid his hand between her legs.

Carol's breath caught in her throat as Malik moved her panties to the side with one finger and slipped another one inside of her moist vagina. Carol moaned slightly, reminiscing about all the times Malik had brought her to orgasm after raging orgasm.

"If I let you smash, what are you gonna do for me?" she asked, trying to squeeze something other than a piece of stiff dick out of their arrangement. Malik quickly pulled his fingers out of her.

He looked at her and smirked. "Look, don't try to fuckin' hustle me. I ain't giving you shit but this dick."

The smug look he gave Carol made her want to take out her service pistol and pistol-whip him. But his thuggish attitude turned her on like it always did.

"You know what? Fine, then, cheap-ass nigga. But don't make this shit a habit."

Malik smirked, knowing now that he could get the pussy whenever he wanted. After Deuce had used up all the quarters they had given him, he returned to the table.

"Did you have fun, little man?" Malik asked him.

The child nodded his head excitedly. He was smiling from ear to ear. He always liked it when he, his mother, and his father were together. At 10 years old, he had trouble understanding why they couldn't be together all the time.

The only time he'd asked his father about it, Malik didn't have an answer for his son. It caught him off guard that Deuce had even thought about something like that.

"Baby, how would you like to go back to Mommy's house and play some more video games?" Carol asked.

"Yayyy," the young child said, overjoyed.

Carol kissed her son on the forehead and hugged him. She looked around to see if anyone was looking before grabbing Malik's crotch. She leaned in and whispered into his ear. "Don't think that I'm gonna give you some ass every time you let me see my son," she said, as she grabbed her son's hand and headed for the door.

"Deuce can ride with me. You can follow us," she said.

As Malik watched Carol's ass sway from side to side, his already-hard dick grew even harder.

He couldn't wait to slide his pole into her warm, wet walls. As Malik followed Carol to her residence, thoughts of the wild and freaky sex they used to have invaded his mind. Carol was, by far, the best piece of ass that he'd ever had. The only reason that he hadn't tried to screw her more was that he didn't want the potential complication that could come with bedding his ex. But now that his girl wasn't putting out regularly, he figured that Carol's good pussy was worth the risk. By the time they reached Carol's place, his dick was so hard he thought that the head would pop. Malik was so horny that Carol had to fight him off once they got inside of her place.

"Damn, hold up a second, you cock-hound muthafucka," she mumbled through tight lips. Carol led her son into the living room and turned on the television. She had already planned to ask Malik if Deuce could go home with her for a couple of hours, so she had the X-Box all set up for him. She had no idea what kinds of games he liked, so she bought five of them and hoped that he would like one. Deuce looked through the first two games and smiled. However, when he came to the third game, he really broke into his happy dance.

"Thanks, Mommy," he said with a massive grin on his face.

"You're welcome, baby."

Carol didn't even get a chance to see which game had him so excited. Before she could, Malik was dragging her into the bedroom. The two of them were just about to reach their sexual peak when the bedroom door burst open. The couple froze as Sunny, Jazmine, Dani, and Kim walked through the door. Butter, much to her dismay, had been tasked with staying with the child. More than anyone else, she wanted to bust her gun. After quickly pushing Malik off her, Carol instinctively reached under the mattress to where she kept her spare gun. But, much to her surprise, it wasn't there.

"Lose something, bitch?" Jazmine asked, pointing Carol's own gun at her.

"What the fuck is going——?"

That was as far as Malik got before Sunny pulled the trigger on her silenced .45 and put a hole in his head. Dani looked on in shock as Malik's body tumbled to the floor.

"What the hell did you do that for?" she asked.

"Because I fuckin' felt like it. You got a problem with it?" Wisely, Dani kept her mouth closed.

"Look, I don't know what the hell this is about, but I'm a fuckin' cop and——"

"Bitch, shut the fuck up," Jazmine yelled. "We know that you're a damn cop."

A confused look morphed on Carol's face. She knew that Cleveland had some hard-core criminals in the city, but it was beyond stupid to come into a cop's place of residence and commit a murder right in front of her. Something was very wrong with this picture. She wouldn't have to wait long to find out what was going on, however. Carol's eyes nearly popped out of her head when she saw Joy walk into the room. Simultaneously, thoughts of her son ran through her mind.

"Deuce!" she screamed and bolted for the door. Her journey was cut short as Sunny smashed her in the head. Carol crashed to the floor, holding her head. Joy calmly walked over to her and kneeled beside her.

"You don't have to worry about your son, Carol. He's fine."

"What the hell, Joy? What's going on here?"

"Come on, Carol. You know *exactly* what's going on here. We both do. The last time I talked to you, you were scared shitless that Captain Moore was going to call you into his office and feed you to internal affairs. How do I know that you won't run to the captain and tell him about our little 'arrangement'?"

Carol's eyes got wide. She was in grave danger, and she knew it.

"Hold on a minute, Joy. I told you that I wasn't going to say anything."

"That's what you said. But you seem to forget that I have the same training and skills that you do. Your words may have said one thing, but your eyes said something different."

"Come on, Joy. We've known each other too long for you to even think about doing me like this."

"Carol, all that shit sounds good. But I'm not going to jail because you don't have the balls to keep your mouth shut."

Carol scanned the room and damn near urinated on herself. The stern faces staring back at her indicated that they would show no mercy. Having no other choice, Carol lunged at Joy and attempted to wrestle her gun away from her. It was a feeble, last-ditch effort to save her life, but her pursuit was in vain. Joy simply snatched the gun away from her reach and slammed the butt of it into her skull.

"You dumb bitch," Joy said, shaking her head. Carol knew Joy well enough to know that she wasn't bluffing. Her life was nearing an end, and she knew it.

"Oh God, Joy, please . . . please. I don't want to die," Carol sobbed. "Please don't kill me."

Joy looked down at her and smirked. "You're my friend, Carol," she said sarcastically. "I'm not going to kill you."

Carol breathed a sigh of relief. For one brief instant, she actually thought that her life was going to be spared. That thought instantly disappeared, however, as Joy walked over to Kim and handed her the gun.

"She is."

Kim looked around, shocked before pointing at herself.

"Who? Me?" she asked, her mouth hanging open.

"Not me, bitch. You."

Kim wasn't the only person there who was shocked. Sunny, Jazmine, and Dani all looked at each other in amazement. Not even Sunny knew it, but Joy had planned this. From the very beginning, she didn't like or trust Kim, and she was especially concerned about the cowardly trait she saw in her. It was time that she found out what Kim was all about. This was a test, and for Kim's sake, she had better pass it. Joy grabbed Kim by the face and spun her head around so that the two of them were face-to-face.

"Stop stalling. You wanted to be about this life— prove it. Shoot this bitch."

When Joy released her face, Kim turned to look at Sunny, who just shrugged. There was nothing she could do to help, but even if there were, she wouldn't have. She wanted to see if her friend had it in her to do some gangsta shit. With all eyes on her, Kim raised the gun. Her hand trembled as she aimed. Her finger twitched as she waited for Joy to tell her that she didn't have to perform such a heinous act. But all Joy did was fold her arms and wait. Finally, after ten agonizing seconds, Kim dropped the gun to her side.

"I'm sorry, Sunny. I can't do this shit."

"Bitch, give me my muthafuckin' gun. Sunny, I told you this bitch was soft!"

Sunny looked at her friend through disappointed eyes. She knew that they were asking a lot of Kim, but to be in the game, you couldn't be afraid to do what needed to be done.

"Damn, Kim. I thought you was down. Dani, shoot this bitch."

It took Dani less than three seconds to take the gun from Joy and blow Carol's brains out. She didn't have anything personal against Carol. But if she were going to get in good with Sunny and her crew so that she could ultimately take them down, then she would have to go with the flow.

"Now, *that's* what the fuck I'm talking about," Joy yelled. "Somebody who ain't scared to push somebody's shit back," she said, staring directly at Kim.

Although she still didn't trust Dani, she did admire her willingness to do dirt when called upon. Kim dropped her head in shame. She couldn't believe that she had the opportunity to endear herself to her new crew and choked. If she could do it all over again, she would pull the trigger and work it out with God later.

Next time, I'm blowing a muthafucka's brains out, she thought to herself. She watched as Dani passed the gun back to Joy, who pointed the gun at Carol and pulled the trigger. Then they all watched as Sunny fired two shots into Carol's corpse. Sunny then turned her hot glare on Kim as she made her way to where she was standing.

"Here! Blood on our hands, blood on yours. Put one in this bitch."

Kim aimed and pulled the trigger, but to Joy, it didn't matter. When the chips were down, Kim couldn't deliver. It didn't take a whole lot of courage to put a bullet in someone already dead. Joy knew that, and unfortunately for Kim, so did Sunny. Jazmine then fired two shots from her gun into Carol's dead body. The ladies then walked out of the room and made their way toward the living room.

When they got there, Butter was standing over a sleeping Deuce. The young boy had fallen asleep playing video games. Had it not been for the headphones covering his ears, the noise would have surely awakened him. Butter, much to her dismay, was given the task of staying with the child while the other women handled business with Carol. She wanted to be in the room with the action, but there was no reason for her to be there in Sunny's and Joy's eyes. Jazmine was Sunny's right hand, so she was going to be there. Dani and Kim needed to be tested, so they had to be there. But none of them had any reservations about Butter's get down. There was just something in her that screamed that she was about that life.

"Everything good out here?" Sunny asked Butter.

"You damn skippy. Just watching this li'l nigga sleep. Sunny, I can't believe you put my ass on babysitting detail," Butter said, frowning.

"Get over it. Let's get ghost," Sunny said.

"What about this little fucker here?" Dani asked, motioning toward Deuce.

"Oh, that's easy," Butter said, as she pointed her gun at the young boy's face and prepared to fire.

"No!" Dani yelled. A split second before Butter pulled the trigger, Dani pushed the gun away from Deuce's face. The loud bang jolted the young boy out of his sleep. Unlike the other guns, Butter's didn't have a silencer on it. The child sprang up and grabbed his ears. His eyes were open wide, and his breathing was heavy and labored. His head spun quickly as he tried to take in his surroundings. Although he caught glimpses of everyone in the room, one face stood out. It was one that he would never forget.

"Bitch, what the fuck is wrong with you?" Jazmine yelled.

"Ain't shit wrong with me. This little muthafucka is a witness," Butter said.

"Bitch, you really are crazy," Sunny said. On the outside, she was just as shocked as everyone else, but deep inside, she was already thinking about making Butter her assassin.

"Look, your psycho ass ain't about to shoot this child. I'll handle this," Joy said, pulling a burner cell phone from her pocket. After dialing 911 and informing them that she heard a gunshot coming from next door and giving them the address, Joy grabbed the young child by the hand, took him into another room, and told him to stay there.

"Where's my mommy?" he asked with tears cascading down his face.

"She went to get you some ice cream," Joy lied. "Just stay in here until she gets back, and you'll have all the ice cream you can eat."

"What kind is she getting?" he asked, suddenly smiling.

"What kind do you like?"

"Chocolate is my favorite."

"That's what kind she's getting you."

"Yayyy!"

"But you have to stay in here until she gets back, okay?"

"Okay. Can I watch television while I wait for her?"

"Sure, you can."

With a gloved hand, Joy picked up a remote and clicked it on. After leaving the room, she called Sunny into the bedroom, where they had just murdered the child's parents. As she and Sunny made their way away from the group, she looked over her shoulder and glared at Kim. As soon as they got into the bedroom, she whirled on Sunny.

"You know that bitch can't be trusted, right?"

"Come on, Joy. Kim ain't used to this shit. Maybe we should cut her some slack."

"Cut her some slack? Have you lost your damn mind?" Joy asked, trying to keep her voice down. "That bitch is gonna get you and your whole crew locked the fuck up one day."

"Joy, I know her better than you do. And like I said, we should cut her some slack."

"Well, that's not up to you."

"Excuse me?"

"I didn't stutter. I *said* that's *not* up to you."

Sunny placed her hands on her hips and glared at Joy. She didn't have anything against her, but she wasn't about to let his father's fuck buddy tell her what to do.

"And just what makes you think that it's up to you?"

As soon as the words left her mouth, her cell phone rang. Joy smiled at Sunny.

"You're gonna wanna answer that," Joy said.

"Hello?" Sunny answered, looking at Joy suspiciously. When the caller on the other end relayed instructions to Sunny, her face dropped.

"But—"

"But my ass," the caller screamed into her ear. "Just do it."

After hanging up, Sunny stared daggers at Joy. No one was aware of it, but Darnell had been listening to the entire episode. Joy had called him and put her phone on speaker mode just before exiting her car.

"You can stare at me all you want, but we both know that I'm right."

"This is some bullshit, Joy."

"No, this is some *necessary* shit, Sunny. I know you're pissed at me for bringing this to your father's attention, but trust me, we know what we're talking about."

With that, Joy went back into the other room, rounded up the rest of the girls, and ushered them toward the door. When Kim made her way to fall in step with them, Joy stopped her.

"Not you, Kim. Sunny wants to talk to you."

With her head down, Kim walked over to her friend. She knew that she had fucked up by not following orders, but Kim just couldn't bring herself to pull the trigger. She may have been hood, but she wasn't a murderer.

"Hurry up. We haven't got much time before the cops get here." Joy shook her head in disgust as she looked at Kim one last time before walking out the door.

"I'm sorry, Sunny. I know that you're disappointed in a bitch, but I ain't no killer. Give me something else to do in the crew. I mean, let me count the money or some shit like that."

Sunny looked at her longtime friend like she had lost her mind. *Count the money? Is this bitch serious?*

"Count the money?"

"Yeah, I mean, a bitch can do some shit like that. Or I can do some slick credit card shit."

The more Kim talked, the more Sunny realized that she indeed wasn't cut out for the game. No matter how cool she and Kim were, she just wasn't about that life. Joy's words echoed in her head.

That bitch is gonna get you and your whole crew locked up one day.

Rubbing her temples, Sunny turned and walked away from Kim. When she turned back around, she had her gun in her hand. Tears were streaming down her face. Her eyes had already begun to turn red. It was only then that Kim realized the severity of the situation she was in.

"Su-Su-Sunny . . . What the hell are you doing?"

"Kim, you're a liability. I can't have someone in my organization that I can't depend on."

Kim's eyes got big as Sunny pointed the gun at her and cocked the hammer. Seeing that her friend was deadly serious, Kim fell to her knees and began weeping.

"Oh God, Sunny, please don't do this. You don't have to worry about me. Even if you tell me I can't be a part of the crew, I would never ever snitch on y'all."

"I know you won't," Sunny said, just before pulling the trigger.

Chapter 25

Damon sat at his kitchen table, sipping on a glass of Hennessy and chopping up a clump of weed. He was in deep thought as he tried to put the finishing touches on a plan that would put him on the king's throne and put his boss, Darnell McCord, in the grave. He was stressed and needed some relief. He checked the time and frowned. He'd texted Dani seven minutes ago and told her in no uncertain terms that he was horny and wanted to fuck. Although he knew that it took her much longer than that to get there, he still expected her to ask how high whenever he said jump. For the most part, she did, and even Damon himself had to laugh at his unrealistic expectations that she get there faster than humanly possible. It would take her at least twenty minutes to get there, and even that was pushing it. Damon could afford to think like he did. Not only had he dick-whipped Dani to the point where she would do damn near anything for him, but he also had so thoroughly mind fucked her that he could convince her that ice cream wouldn't melt in hell.

"The fuck this bitch at?" he said out loud as he dumped the chopped-up marijuana into cigar paper. After lighting the blunt and taking a puff, Damon closed his eyes and blew the smoke through his nostrils. If Dani's information was correct, he needed to come up with a plan ASAP. He was the next big thing in the city, and he would be damned if he let some young thot nudge him out of his rightful position. Damon had made Darnell a lot of money during his tenure as a capo. Some of his soldiers wondered why he wasn't worried about Turiq becoming the next king, but he would never give them an answer when they asked him about it. He would only smile sinisterly. Only he knew that whenever he cashed in Darnell's ticket, Turiq's was going to be punched as well. He had it all planned out, but now he discovered that Turiq wasn't the heir apparent at all, and it galled the fuck out of him to learn that Sunny was going to be the next boss. He was just about to text Dani again when there was a knock at his door.

"About damn time you got here," he yelled. "Bitch, what took you so muthafuckin' long?" he questioned as he yanked open the door.

"Well, they do give you a lot of time when you do the shit that I did."

When the door was fully open, Damon was surprised to see who had come to visit him. He was an older cat with a block-shaped head and a strong jawline. His thick frame was stacked with muscles, the kind you have when you don't have anything else to do except lift weights and read. His salt-and-pepper hair was matted to his head to the point where the spaces in between the braids were barely visible.

"Oh shit, if it ain't my uncle Eric. What's good, fam?"

The two men embraced and gave each other a tight man hug. Although Eric's body odor was a little on the rancid side, Damon wasn't going to let that stop him from showing his kinfolk some love. The last time Damon saw his uncle, he was being handcuffed on the news. Whether it was bravery or stupidity, and some folks felt that it was both, Eric had come up with the bright idea to single-handedly rob a Brinks truck in broad daylight. The plan was flawed from the beginning, and in the end, Eric ended up getting seven years for attempted armed robbery. Although his lawyer had done a hell of a job to get his recommended sentence reduced, Eric was still angry. In his mind, it was society that had put him in the position of committing crimes. Now, seven years later, he walked out of Grafton Correctional Institution, a free man. However, the problem with that was that he didn't have a pot to piss in or a window to throw it out of. He was flat broke. That revelation was the situation that brought him to Damon's doorstep.

"All right, Nephew. That's enough of this damn hugging," Eric said, pulling away from Damon. "The next thing I wrap my arms around is gonna be soft and tender."

Eric's voice was deep and authoritative and made Damon feel like he was a child again.

"I hear that, fam. Bring your ass in here and have a drink."

"Now *that's* what the fuck I'm talking about." Eric followed Damon into the kitchen. His mouth watered as he watched his nephew pour him a glass of liquor. It had been awhile since the taste of alcohol burned his throat, and he longed for the sensation. He tossed the drink back and frowned.

"Damn, that shit strong. Let me get another one."

Eric didn't drink the second one as fast, preferring to sip this time instead of guzzle. Damon picked up the blunt that was still burning in the ashtray and took a pull. He extended it to Eric, but his uncle quickly declined.

"Nah, man. I can't fuck with that right now, Nephew. At least not until I see my probation officer one or two times. Hmmm," he said, rubbing his chin, "my probation officer is a bitch. Maybe I can slip her a piece of this dick, and she'll look the other way about a drug test."

The hearty laugh from him that followed sounded like a lion's roar.

"So, what's good, Nephew? I hear that you're the man next to the man out here in these streets," Eric said, getting down to business. He'd shot the shit long enough. Now he wanted to talk about getting his paper.

"Huh? Where the fuck you hear that at, Unc?"

"Nephew, you'd be surprised the shit that comes through the prison pipeline. We probably hear more about what's going on in the streets than the niggas who are actually in the streets. What I want to know is, is the shit true?"

Damon smiled. He loved the fact that he was being thought of as a big deal by people in prison. "Yeah, I make a few coins, Unc."

"Good, good. That's just what the fuck I needed to hear 'cause I need to find a way to make some bread. Got a spot for ya' ol' uncle on ya' team?"

The wheels in Damon's head immediately started spinning. Along with Moon and his other soldiers, Damon had already quietly begun assembling an array of rebels looking for their moment in the sun. Adding his cash-thirsty uncle to his squad would only enhance its strength.

"You know, Unc, I think I may have a spot for you after all."

"Good shit, Nephew. Just tell me whose head you want me to crack." To emphasize the point, Eric slammed his fist into his hand twice. "Make no mistake, Nephew. Ya' uncle is down to put in that dirty work if you know what I mean."

Damon knew precisely what his uncle was getting at. His uncle had always been prone to violence.

"I hear you, Unc. As a matter of fact——"

Before Damon could get to the meat and potatoes of the discussion, someone knocked at his door.

"I hope that's a bitch 'cause I need some pussy badder than a muthafucka," Eric said seriously.

Damon laughed hard as he went to answer the door. On his way there, his cell phone buzzed in his pocket.

"The fuck this bitch calling for, and she's at the front door?" he asked himself, thinking that it was Dani.

"Hello?"

"Hey, baby. Look, somebody got me blocked in, and I can't get there. Can you come and get me?"

When Damon heard this, he stopped in his tracks. He wasn't expecting anyone else, so when he heard Dani on the other end of the phone, it made him leery as to who was on the other side of the door.

"The fuck you mean you blocked in?" Damon barked. It suddenly dawned on him that she wouldn't be giving up the pussy tonight unless he went and picked her up.

"Someone has my driveway blocked," she told him. "There's nothing I can do. That's why I asked if you could come and—"

"Bitch, I don't care if you have to drive across the fucking lawn. Just bring your ass over—"

Damon stopped in midsentence when he looked through the peephole and saw who was standing at the door. He smiled and nodded his head as his dick began to harden.

"You know what? Don't worry about it, babe. We can hook up tomorrow," he said.

"Tomorrow? But I thought you wanted some ass tonight. Please, babe, don't do this to me. I need that dick."

"It'll be here tomorrow. Plus, I just remembered that I have some shit to do."

"But—"

That was as far as she got before the line went dead. Dani smelled a rat. As much as Damon liked to fuck, there was no way he would let anything interfere with him getting some pussy. But more importantly to her, she wanted some dick. She *needed* some dick. *His* dick. And being blocked in wasn't going to stop her from getting it. She had hoped that he would come to pick her up, but now that he'd refused, she had to go to plan B.

Chapter 26

After applying her lip gloss and checking herself in the sun visor mirror, Rita leaned back against the headrest and bopped her head to the music. It had been awhile since she'd gone out with her homegirl Janine, and she couldn't wait to get to the club and shake her ass. She was also hoping to luck up on a baller.

"Girl, I hope there are some ballers up in here tonight. A bitch sure could use a few dollars," she said. Rita noticed that Janine had been quiet ever since she'd picked her up. She started to ask her about her attitude but didn't want to be brought down by her friend's sour mood, so she just kept bouncing to the beat and staring out the window. It took her a few minutes to catch on, but when she did, she noticed that they were headed in a different direction than the club. A few seconds after that, it dawned on her where they were headed.

"Oh, hell no, bitch. I know damn well we ain't stopping over that dog-ass nigga's house."

"Relax, tramp. It's only gonna take a few seconds. I just need to holla at him about something right quick."

"Why the fuck you keep chasing this nigga?" Rita asked, although she already knew.

"Girl, you just don't understand."

"Oh, I understand. Yo' ass is sprung," Rita said, laughing.

"Whatever, bitch. Ain't nobody sprung. I just like getting fucked now and then."

"And ain't nothing wrong with that. But Damon has made it perfectly clear that he'd rather be with that dusty-ass bitch Dani. You need to leave that muthafucka alone."

Janine was only half-listening to her friend. She'd never admit it to Rita but being dumped by Damon hurt her more than she'd let on. One minute, she was enjoying the benefits of being on the arm of a powerful drug pusher, and the next, she was relegated to the role of side bitch. Janine wanted Damon back so badly that she was willing to do anything to make it happen. She once sucked Damon's dick in a crowded movie theater with the hope of having him promote her back to main chick status. Another time, Damon had her dance naked on Facebook Live just to prove to one of his boys that he could get her to do it. While Damon hit her off with bread from time to time, her main goal was to wrest his heart away from Dani. She didn't know what kind of hold Dani had over him, but she was determined to break it.

She pulled up in front of Damon's residence and cut her eyes toward Rita, who just shook her head. Without saying a word, she got out and headed to the front door. She had no idea if Dani was in there, but she just figured that she'd take her chances.

"Don't be in there all night," Rita yelled in her direction.

"Ten minutes," Janine said, looking back over her shoulder. After knocking on the door, she struck her sexiest pose. She planned to give Damon some quick pussy and try to get a few dollars out of him for the club. When Damon opened the door, his dick jumped. The tight outfit Janine had on fit her like a second layer of skin. Still, Damon had to maintain his hard image.

"Janine, what the fuck you doing here? What if my bitch was up in here?"

"Is she?" Janine said, batting her eyes.

"Don't be a smart-ass. Now, what the fuck do you want?"

"Well," she said, walking in uninvited, "me and my girl was on our way to the club, and I just thought that I would come by and see if you had something you needed me to take care of." In one swift motion, Janine turned next to Damon's crotch. She licked her lips as she grabbed his rock-hard member. She was just about to drop to her knees when she sensed the presence of someone else looming. When she peeped around Damon's shoulder, she saw an older man with a lustful look in his eyes. Janine quickly removed her hand.

"Sorry for interrupting, dawg, but I need to take a shower and get this prison funk off me."

"Down the hall and to the right, dawg."

"Who the fuck is that?" Janine asked.

"He's my muthafuckin' uncle. Stop acting like a bitch."

"I'm sorry, babe. I just thought that I could come over and—"

"Yeah, I know what the fuck you were thinking. You're thinking that you were gonna come over here, give me a blow job, and get some bread out of me. Sound about right?"

Janine's voice caught in her throat. Damon had hit the nail on the head. But what neither he nor Rita knew was that Janine had another motive. She had fully intended to try to talk Damon into making her his number one bitch again.

"Yeah, that's what the fuck I thought."

"That ain't the only reason I came by. I really wanted to talk to you about us."

"Us? The fuck you mean *us?* You know I got a bitch, so stop tripping."

"Fuck that dusty bitch. *I'm* the one you should be making your queen."

Tears leaked from the corners of her eyes. She hadn't meant to get so emotional, but standing face-to-face with her former lover had her feeling some kind of way.

"Fuck is wrong with you, ma? You act like we just broke up yesterday."

"It ain't like you gave me a choice in the matter."

"First of all, lower ya' damn voice," Damon said in a low but deadly tone. Her whining was starting to make his dick go soft. "Matter of fact, you need to get the fuck out. I ain't got time for the bullshit." Damon turned to walk away, and Janine fell to her knees and wrapped her arms around his leg.

"Baby, please. I need you back in my life."

"Get the fuck off me."

Damon jerked his leg away from her. In the process, his foot hit her in the chin and snapped her head back. Undeterred, Janine lunged for his leg again. She had finally broke. She'd been hoping that his screwing around with Dani was just a fling. But the reality was finally starting to hit her hard that Dani was his main lady, and there didn't seem to be anything she could do about it.

"Damon, please, I'll do anything."

Damon heard the shower shut off, and a sinister thought popped into his freaky mind. He stared at Janine for a few seconds and then dropped a bomb on her.

"You'll do anything, huh?"

"Anything, baby. I just wanna be yo' number one bitch again."

Janine had utterly forgotten about Rita waiting in the car. From the time she knocked on the door until now, her mission had changed. When Damon knelt to face her, Janine noticed a strange gleam in his eye.

"I tell you what. If you really wanna prove to me that you're willing to do anything to get me back, I have an idea. That dude that just came out here? Well, he's my uncle, and he just got out of prison."

"Oh, okay. I know he probably wants a good home cooked meal."

"Yeah, he does, but that's not exactly what I meant." Damon reached down and grabbed her tit. He gently squeezed her nipple and smiled at her. "You know, if I had to go seven years without getting any pussy, I would go crazy."

"Wait. What the hell are you asking me to do, Damon?"

Janine had a pretty good idea where he was going with his statements, but she had to be sure before she jumped to any conclusions.

"You know what the fuck I'm asking you to do, so stop playing stupid."

Janine's face twisted. Her nose wrinkled up as if she were smelling something rotten.

"Damon, are you telling me that you want me to go back there and fuck your uncle?"

"You said you would do anything," he said, using her own words against her.

"I-I-I know, but this? Damon, I don't know about this. I mean, that's—"

"I knew it! I knew your ass was just talking shit."

"No, baby, it's not like that. It's just that . . . I mean . . . I love you, and—"

"Then prove it! You know what? Never mind. And you wonder why I replaced your ass with Dani. She didn't have a problem doing it when I asked her to," he lied.

Damon had never asked Dani to do anything like that. But, of course, Janine didn't know that. She didn't want to do what Damon was asking, but it might be the only way she could get him back. She took a deep breath and dropped her head.

"Okay," she said softly.

"Okay, what?"

"I'll fuck your uncle. Just let me go tell Rita to take my car and come back and get me in about thirty minutes. Will that be long enough for him to get his nut off?"

"Yeah, that should get it. And don't worry about Rita. I'll go out and tell her. Just go handle ya' business. And don't worry. I got half a stack for you when you come out."

His so-called generosity made her feel worse. Not only was he asking her to have sex with his uncle, but he was also now offering to pay her to do it. Damon watched as Janine walked toward his guest bedroom. As soon as he heard the door close, he walked into his living room, dropped down on the couch, and texted Rita.

The further Rita scrolled down Facebook and Instagram, the more pissed off she became. Although it occupied her attention while Janine was doing God knows what with Damon, she was getting restless. Janine had told her that she would only be gone for a short period, but the time on her cell phone revealed that she'd been gone at least thirty minutes. If she had to guess, she would conclude that her friend was either on her knees swallowing Damon's meat or lying on her back getting pounded by it. She was just about to spark up the blunt she was saving for after they left the club when her cell phone buzzed. After reading the message, Rita got out of the car and headed toward the house. Her three-inch pumps tapped against the cement as she walked up the steps.

Even though she could barely walk in the tight Capri pants she was wearing, she was cute and fly. As soon as she walked through the door, she heard the loud moaning coming from the back. She casually strolled into the living room, where Damon was sitting on the couch, sipping liquor, and kicked off her pumps. She smiled when she glanced down and saw Damon stroking his dick. As fast as she could, Rita pulled off her pants and straddled him.

"Damn, it sounds like he's fucking the shit out of my girl back there. So, uh . . . Why don't you let me show you the attention that your so-called mistress is showing to someone else?"

Rita grabbed Damon's dick and guided it into her juicy hole. The two of them had been carrying on for the last two months. It started when Damon went over to Janine's house drunk one day, trying to get laid. Dani was on her period, so she wasn't an option. When Damon got there, Janine wasn't there, but Rita was. Janine had an errand to run but was expecting a package from the mailman. She didn't want to miss it, so she had Rita come over and stay there until she got back. When Rita answered the door wearing shorts and a tank top, Damon was immediately turned on. After inquiring about Janine's whereabouts, Damon went to the bathroom to relieve himself. After doing so, an idea formed in his head. He wanted to fuck, and he didn't care if it was with Janine or her best friend. Since he was obviously under the influence of alcohol, Damon figured that he had an excuse if he made a pass at Rita, and it went to the left. When he left the bathroom, his pants were unzipped, and his dick was hanging out. As soon as Rita saw him, she covered her eyes.

"Boy, what the hell you think you doing?" she asked. "Cover your damn self."

"Huh? What the hell are you talking about?" he'd asked, playing dumb.

"I'm talking about you bringing your ass out here with your dick . . . hanging out."

Rita's voice trailed off as she uncovered her eyes and saw Damon's semierect penis sticking out. To say that she was amazed at the size was an understatement. Now, she understood why Janine was so in love with him. Damon had a horse's dick attached to a human frame. One thing led to another, and the next thing she knew, Damon had her legs spread and was smashing her out. The two of them had been sneaking around ever since.

After riding Damon's dick until he nutted in her, Rita put her pants back on and headed for the door. It was the first time he'd ever come in her, and he instantly regretted doing it.

"Hey, you *are* on the pill, right?"

Rita simply shrugged. "Maybe. Maybe not," she said, smiling wickedly.

Damon cocked his head to the side and glared at the door.

"I know this bitch ain't trying to be funny," he mumbled to himself. He didn't know why she'd made the snide remark, but she'd better not turn up pregnant. If she did, he would make sure that she turned up dead.

While Rita was walking back to the car, she noticed another vehicle pulling off down the street. She squinted her eyes and immediately burst out laughing when she recognized the car. She continued cracking up until she got in the car and fired up her blunt. While waiting for her friend, she decided to be nosy. She opened the glove compartment and rummaged around in it. She became curious when she saw a box from Amazon labeled "vehicle tracking device."

"The fuck is she doing with this?" she mumbled to herself. "I know she ain't about to try to keep tabs on this nigga."

She quickly put it back in the glove compartment when she saw Janine coming out. As she approached the car, Rita could clearly see tears streaking down her face.

"What's wrong?" Rita asked as she got back into the car.

"Asshole! He's just a fuckin' asshole!" Janine cried. Laying her head on the steering wheel, she sobbed heavily.

"That nigga tricked me into doing something he knew I didn't want to do, and then he reneged on his fuckin' promise."

"Promise? What promise? What did he make you do?" Rita asked, pretending as if she didn't know.

Janine opened her mouth to speak but choked the words back down her throat. What she had allowed Damon to talk her into doing was beyond humiliating and embarrassing.

"You know what? Let's just go to the club. I don't even want to talk about it."

Rita didn't know how Janine would feel if she knew that Dani had been there, so she decided to keep that information to herself.

Dani banged on the steering wheel. Her tears splashed onto the seat as they flowed from her eyes and ran down her cheeks. She was so mad that she could barely see straight. Dani wasn't a fool enough to believe that Damon wasn't sleeping with other women. But seeing it with her own two eyes was just too much. After following his advice and driving over the grass to get around the car that had her blocked in, Dani couldn't wait to surprise her man and give him some of her good pussy. But instead, it was *she* who got surprised. She could have banged on the door after looking in the window and seeing some other bitch riding her man but moving like that on a man such as Damon would have surely gotten her an ass whipping. Because the woman's back was facing the window, Dani had no idea who it was Damon was sexing. She would bet her last dollar that it was that tramp Janine; however, Dani had to weigh her options. Did she want to accept his cheating ways to be the next queen or walk away from him and stick with Sunny and her crew, just in case Damon's plan fell through, and Darnell killed him for his betrayal? She would take her time to decide because her next move would have to be her best move. It was a matter of life and death.

Chapter 27

The long-awaited meeting between Darnell and his capos was finally at hand. The four capos all wondered what it was about, and although sleeping with a member of Sunny's crew had its advantages, Damon was in the dark just like everyone else. Dani still hadn't made her mind up if she would go along with his plan or make her bones with Sunny's crew. When Damon asked her what the meeting was about, she lied and told him that she had no idea. The image of the woman straddling her man was impossible to ignore. It had been two weeks since the incident, and Dani was putting on an incredible acting job. She wanted so badly to confront Damon about fucking another bitch but decided to keep quiet about it until she decided what she wanted to do. She was torn about the situation. She had fallen hard for Damon, which is why his betrayal hurt her so much. But more than that, the way she saw it, Damon had blown her off when she asked him to come and pick her up in favor of another broad. Still, she wanted to be the next queen bitch of the city, so forgiving him for fucking another bitch might be a small price to pay.

Blue fidgeted in his seat. He didn't like meetings, and this one was no exception. He smelled some bullshit coming and didn't want to get caught in a shitstorm.

"Be easy, my dude," his top soldier, Razor, said, patting him on the shoulder.

Never one to miss an opportunity to be an asshole, Damon smirked. "Damn, nigga, why don't you just give him a fucking massage while you're at it," he said, laughing.

"Fuck you say, nigga?"

"You heard me, Mr. Midget."

Blue's face contorted into a mask of anger. Slowly, he rose to his feet and balled up his fists. "You know what, nigga? Every time we have a meeting, you start some bullshit."

"And I'm gonna keep talking shit," Damon said, still laughing.

"Maybe I should just come over there and close that big-ass mouth for you, nigga."

Damon stopped laughing. His nostrils flared as he got out of his seat. "Nigga, I wish yo' ass would."

Razor started to stand up but changed his mind when he looked across the table and saw the murderous look that Moon was giving him. Each lieutenant was allowed to bring one soldier with them.

Trey, who was amused by the entire scene, looked at his lead soldier, Zena, and shook his head. Zena was stunningly beautiful. She had long, flowing hair, but it was natural, not permed. She was six foot even, with a model's smile and figure. But make no mistake, she was as deadly as a venomous pit viper and just as mean.

OG Hann was the only capo who'd declined to bring a soldier with him. He was so well respected by the others that he wasn't worried about anyone wanting the smoke.

Sitting off to the side with an amused look on his face was Duck. He'd been tasked with babysitting them until Darnell and Turiq arrived. He could've spoken up when Damon and Blue looked as if they were going to come to blows, but he wanted to see how it would play out. He would have loved to see Blue beat the brakes off Damon's ass, although he doubted very seriously if he could. After seeing enough, Duck decided to speak up.

"That's enough. Y'all two niggas sit down and shut the fuck up. Damon, leave muthafuckas alone. You always starting some bullshit."

Damon mean mugged Duck as he slowly sat back down. He wanted to pop fly but thought better of it. Instead, he uttered a sarcastic response. "Yes, sir, boss man," he said saluting.

"Nigga, don't get smart with me. I ain't Blue," he said to him.

"What the fuck is that supposed to mean, dawg?" Blue asked, feeling slighted.

"Nothing, my dude. I'm just telling this nigga to fall back."

"Fuck is going on in here?" Darnell yelled as he entered the room.

He had a look on his face that said that he wasn't in the mood for the bullshit. Turiq and Lard flanked him. Walking in behind him was Sunny and Jazmine. Moon took one look at Jazmine and got a hard-on. To him, she was the sexiest thing walking the earth. When he looked at Darnell, however, he had to do a double take.

"Well?" Darnell said, staring at Duck.

"Ain't nothing, my G. Just a little lip service."

"Yeah? Well, I ain't in the mood for that shit today, so y'all knock off whatever the fuck it is."

Darnell walked to the end of the table and took his seat. He focused his gaze on each one of them as he began to speak. "I know that you are all wondering what this meeting is about. Before I go on, I want you all to meet my daughter, Sunny. And this is her friend, Jazmine. She's Turiq's daughter."

Jazmine looked at the stony faces and cringed. Although her father was second in command, this was the first time that she'd ever been around a bunch of drug dealers and killers, and it unnerved her. Sunny, however, had no such qualms. Since being forced to kill her childhood friend, Sunny had changed. Her eyes had grown cold over the last few weeks. The once-alluring smile was now little more than a sneer. She looked around the room and took in all the faces. Her eyes seemed to linger on Moon. He seemed very familiar to her, but she couldn't place him, so she let it go.

"Now, back to the reason you are all here. I've made a decision. It's a decision that some of you won't like, and it's a decision that some of you will downright hate. But it's one that you will have to accept if you plan on continuing to eat off my plate."

The lieutenants all looked toward one another, wondering what could possibly be going on. When Darnell was sure that the gravity of his words had sunk in, he continued.

"I have been in this game a long time, and as far as I know, you all have made hundreds of thousands of dollars by being a part of my operation. We've done well together, but I think that maybe it's time for me to take an extended vacation."

The group of men all looked at one another in total surprise. After the initial shock wore off, Trey was the first one to speak up.

"Wait, hold up. Are you trying to tell us that you're getting out of the game?"

"I didn't say that, Trey. I said vacation."

"So, Turiq is gonna be running shit while out you're outta town?" Blue asked.

"No. I'm gonna have Turiq working on some other shit."

"Then who the fuck we supposed to deal with when we need to drop off some bread or pick up some product?" Damon asked indignantly.

Darnell glared at him. He didn't like his tone and didn't try to hide it.

"First of all, watch how the fuck you talk to me, li'l-ass nigga. And second, I was getting to that shit, so just chill the fuck out."

Darnell's sharp words caused Damon to flinch. He didn't appreciate being talked to like a common street soldier and couldn't wait to end Darnell's reign. He shot a quick but subtle glance at Sunny and decided that as an extra measure of revenge, he may just fuck the shit out of the little cunt before he killed her too.

"Now, like the fuck I was saying, I feel that it's time that I took a much-deserved vacation. If you need to re-up or drop off some bread, see Sunny."

For the second time since the meeting had begun, the lieutenants looked around at each other, this time in total disbelief.

"Anybody got a problem with that?"

Truth be told, they *all* had a problem with it, even OG Hann. He had never questioned Darnell's judgment until today. Leaving a million-dollar drug empire in the hands of a 20-year-old didn't seem like the actions of a rational man. But since

Darnell was the boss, there was nothing that they could do about it.

"Now, I know what you are all thinking, but Duck and Lard will be there if Sunny and her crew should need any assistance. Turiq and I have been training them for the last few months, and we're confident that the business can continue to thrive while we're away."

"How long will you be gone?" OG Hann asked.

"Three months," Darnell lied.

"Where you headed, boss man?"

"Hawaii," Darnell said, a broad smile forming on his face. It was the first time that he'd smiled since the beginning of the meeting. "I leave in four days."

While everyone else seemed to be coming to grips with Darnell's decision, Damon was plotting. His plan was slowly starting to gel. Darnell may have thought he was about to go on vacation, but Damon had no intention of letting him get on that plane.

Chapter 28

The following night, Damon, Moon, Eric, Slab, Paul, and Dani all sat in a smoke-filled hotel suite in downtown Cleveland. Damon smiled as he continued to lay out his master plan. A knock on the door briefly interrupted him, but he didn't mind. He knew exactly who was on the other side of the door. Although they were nearly an hour late, he wasn't going to hold it against them.

"Dani, get the door," he ordered his plaything.

With a slight frown on her face, Dani got up and walked to the door. Damon watched her all the way there. He didn't know what was going on with her, but she'd been acting funny the past few weeks. He decided that enough was enough and was going to make sure that he addressed her attitude after the meeting. He also noticed that Moon's mind seemed to be in a different place. He wondered if Moon was thinking about Turiq's daughter. Damon had seen how he'd gawked at her at Darnell's meeting but didn't think anything of it until now. But Moon was a top-notch soldier. He knew he could count on him.

When Dani opened the door and saw the two imposing figures standing in front of her, she took a cautionary step back. Their entire vibe screamed *goon*. Dani stood there frozen. She didn't know whether to invite them in or slam the door in their faces.

"Jus', Kenne, 'sup up, my niggas?"

"Paper and violence, my dude; paper and violence," the larger of the two men answered. His name was Justin, and if you looked up *thug* in the dictionary, you would see a picture of him holding a gun. He stood around six foot four with a shaved head and heavily tattooed forearms. His full beard was scraggly and nappy. The smile he flashed was highly deceptive. There wasn't a friendly bone in his entire body, and he took great pleasure in hurting people. His cousin Kenne, although not as tall, was quite a physical specimen in his own right. Kenne, standing a shade over six foot one, had the physique of a young Mike Tyson. Cornrow braids sat atop his square head. He had three teeth missing from the top, which made him look like a ghetto vampire. Dani looked back at Damon.

"The fuck you looking at me for? Move the fuck out of the way and let them in," he snapped. He was becoming increasingly more disrespectful toward Dani, and she was getting tired of it. She rolled her eyes and popped her lips as she stepped to the side. While Justin and Kenne were walking in, Damon was quickly making his way over to Dani. By the time she closed the door and turned around, he was practically nose to nose with her.

"Who the fuck you rolling yo' eyes at like that? You know what? I don't know what the fuck has been up with you lately, but you better get yo' shit together. If you wanna be a queen, then stop acting like a royal bitch."

Damon turned to walk away from her but stopped when he heard her sniffles. He turned back to face her and was surprised to see tears roll from the corners of her eyes. Realizing that he may have gone a tad too far, he wiped away her tears.

"Look, baby, I didn't mean to style on you like that. Tell you what," he said, grabbing her hand and placing it on his crotch. "After the meeting, I'll kick these niggas out and bless you with this dick, cool?" he asked as if he were doing her a favor. He didn't bother waiting for an answer, instead, opting to turn and walk away from her. As Dani stared at the back of his head, her lips slowly curled into a sinister grin. Her love for him was quickly waning. Although she loved the orgasmic heights that he took her to, she just didn't know if she could continue to allow herself to be treated like a piece of shit. She walked over and plopped down on a sofa as Damon introduced

Justin and Kenne. When he was done, he made sure that everyone knew the plan. They all smiled and nodded, rubbing their hands together greedily. Everyone was on board . . . except the one person that he needed to be on board.

Chapter 29

Although it was only four o'clock, Kevantae's Lounge was jumping. The live entertainment was scheduled to begin at six, but Dani had taken some of the money that Damon had given her and greased a few palms, ensuring that they started well ahead of when they were supposed to. To Sunny and the rest of her crew, the jazz-style music was not what they would usually listen to, but it was soothing, nonetheless, so they didn't complain. It was nearly ninety degrees outside, but inside the lounge, it was a very comfortable seventy-one. Kevantae's wasn't what you would call an upscale eatery, but it was clean, the drinks were strong, and the food was tasty. Dani, who'd gotten there first, had taken the liberty of ordering enough wings to accommodate everyone's appetite. She had to dig into her memory bank to remember what drinks the rest of them had ordered in Akron, but after thinking long and hard, it came to her.

As Sunny and Butter greedily tore into the wings, Jazmine seemed to take forever finishing her first one. She eyed Dani suspiciously as she sipped on her Long Island Iced Tea. It bothered her that Dani had suddenly suggested that they go out to celebrate Sunny's ascension to the throne. It bothered her even more that she'd volunteered to foot the bill. As far as Jazmine knew, Dani's ass was pretty much broke. Yet, here she was treating the crew like she had an endless supply of cash. Where in the fuck had she gotten all of this bread from? Jazmine also didn't understand how Dani could forgive Sunny so easily after the incident at Sunny's party. Had that been her, she would have been pissed off for months. In a way, Jazmine felt responsible. It was she who had urged Sunny to take it easy on Dani and allow her to remain in their inner circle. But the more attention she paid to Dani, the more she realized that they might have allowed a snake to slither into their garden. Dani noticed the way Jazmine was looking at her, and it made her nervous.

"What's good, J?" she asked.

"You tell me," Jazmine said, shrugging her shoulders. "Seems like you threw this together awfully quick."

"Well, like I said, I just wanted to celebrate boss lady's achievement," she said, motioning toward Sunny.

"Is that right?"

"Of course. I mean, what other reason would I have?"

"I don't know, bitch. You tell me." Jazmine was struggling to try to keep her voice down. Nothing about this so-called celebratory meeting felt right to her.

"Jazmine, stop being so fucking paranoid," Sunny said. "Besides, I know damn well this broad ain't stupid enough to try some slick shit, right, Dani?"

"Of course not, Sunny. I'm not stupid, regardless of what y'all think of me. I'm just glad to be a part of the team."

"The fuck you going?" Jazmine asked as Dani stood up.

"I'm going to take a piss. Is that okay?" she asked, irritated.

Jazmine stared at the back of her head as she walked away.

"What's good with you, J?" Sunny asked when Dani was out of earshot.

"I call bullshit, Sunny. I don't trust that bitch."

"J, *you're* the one who talked me into keeping that bitch around. Now, you say that you don't trust her? Make up your fucking mind."

"I did trust her at first, but over the last few weeks, I've been getting a bad vibe from her."

Sunny thought about it for a second before looking at Butter. For someone who usually had a lot to say, Butter had been pretty quiet.

"What do you think, Butter? You call bullshit too?"

Butter shrugged. "To be honest, I haven't been paying the bitch much attention. But if she is living foul, we'll just have to send her ass to visit Kim."

Sunny and Jazmine looked at each other, shook their heads, and smiled wickedly. Butter was ruthless, and they loved it. Sunny's smile faded, however, when she pulled her vibrating cell phone from her pocket and looked at the screen.

"What the fuck?" she yelled, causing other patrons to stare in her direction.

"What's wrong?" Butter asked.

"Go get Dani now! We have to go."

Without asking why, Butter got up and sprinted toward the bathroom. When Sunny showed Jazmine the photo that had been texted to her, Jazmine gasped.

"Oh my God," she said, covering her mouth. Ten seconds later, Butter came out of the bathroom pulling Dani by the arm. The four women then proceeded to head for the exit.

"What's going on?" Dani asked . . . as if she didn't know.

After slamming his suitcase shut, Darnell walked into his living room and grabbed a bottle of Hennessy off the bar. He poured a generous amount into a glass and took a sip. He looked at Joy, who was sitting on the arm of the couch with her arms folded. Darnell knew that she was upset, but she would just have to get over it. He then glanced at Turiq, who was sitting in a chair, trying hard to hide a smirk.

"Joy, why are you sitting there looking like somebody kicked your damn dog?" Darnell asked, although he already knew the answer to his question.

"Stop acting as if you don't know why I'm pissed, Darnell. I asked you to wait a couple of weeks so that I can fly to Hawaii with you."

"Joy, we've already talked about this shit. How would it look if you just up and left when your coworker was just found dead under suspicious circumstances? And before you say it, I know that they don't have anything to tie you to the scene, but I'd rather not take any chances. It won't kill you to wait two more weeks."

Darnell walked over to her, cupped her face in his hands, and gave her a gentle kiss. After releasing her, he dug into his pocket and pulled out a huge knot of one-hundred-dollar bills. He counted out thirty of them and handed them to her. A grateful smile crossed her face.

"You sure I can't take you to the airport?"

"Come on, Joy, you know damn well that's not a good idea. A cop riding to the airport with a suspected drug lord? You trying to get yourself in trouble?"

"No," she said dejectedly.

"Okay, then. Just keep up appearances, and I'll see you in two weeks, okay?"

"Yeah, all right. I'd better get going. I'm already late for work. Call me the minute you land," she said, punctuating her message by stabbing her finger into his chest.

"Cross my heart and hope to die," he said.

"If you don't call me, you just might," she said. After giving him a long hug and an even longer kiss, Joy headed for the door.

"I don't see shit funny, nigga," she said to Turiq as she walked past him. As soon as she was out the door, Turiq turned to Darnell and shook his head.

"What the fuck are you shaking your head at?"

"Your lying ass. Nigga, the only reason you don't want her to go out there with you now is that you wanna get out there and sample some of that Hawaiian pussy," Turiq said, laughing.

All Darnell could do was shrug and laugh. "Well, she doesn't have to know that."

"You got that right," Turiq said. "We need to get going if you're going to make your flight, though," Turiq said, glancing at his watch.

Chapter 30

At the end of the street, Damon, Eric, and Moon all sat in a pitch-black SUV waiting for Darnell and Turiq to exit Darnell's house. Sitting across the street from it, posing as electricians in a white van, were Justin and Kenne. The two hoodlums couldn't wait for it to go down. They'd both heard of Darnell and knew that he was the unquestioned kingpin of Cleveland, but their desire for the almighty dollar overruled any respect they may have had for the drug lord. The plan was simple. When Darnell and Turiq came out of the house, Justin and Kenne would ambush the unsuspecting pair. Since at least one of them would be transporting luggage to the car, it would give the two thugs an advantage that, along with the element of surprise, should be enough to get the job done.

All five of the men's dicks got hard when they saw the sexy, brown-skinned young woman walk out of Darnell's house. The passenger door to the van opened briefly but closed just as fast as it opened. Immediately, Damon took out his cell phone and called Justin.

"Hey, what the fuck is going on up there?" he asked.

"Man, this pussy-thirsty muthafucka was about to get out of the van and try to holla at that bitch."

"What? Man, fuck that bitch. She ain't part of this equation. Tell that nigga to stay the fuck on point."

Damon hung up without saying another word. "Silly muthafucka," he mumbled.

"What's up, Nephew?" Eric asked.

"Man, that nigga Kenne was about to get out and try to shoot game to the bitch."

Eric chuckled slightly. Since he'd just smashed his first piece of pussy in seven years, he was in no position to tell another man he couldn't crack on a piece of ass.

"Shiiiit, man, you can't blame a nigga for trying to get his dick wet, Nephew."

"I can when the shit is interfering with my plans. He's just gonna have to do that shit on his own time. We got business to attend to."

Damon looked at Moon and noticed a peculiar look on his face.

"You good, dawg?" he asked.

"Yeah, man, I'm straight."

What Moon didn't tell him was that he recognized the woman coming out of Darnell's house. Six months before Moon had joined Damon's team, Joy and another cop had rolled up on him as he sat on a bench at Gordon Park smoking a blunt. The other cop wanted to take him to jail, but Joy convinced him that the paperwork wasn't worth it. Moon didn't know why there was a cop coming out of Darnell's house, and until he found out, he decided that he would just keep that information to himself.

"Yo, Nephew, let me run something by you right quick," Eric began. "I know that you're planning to take over the dope game, but why stop there? We can get a stable of hoes and put the bitches to work."

"You mean pimp them bitches out? Man, I don't know shit about that."

"Well, lucky for you, I do, and we can start with that bad bitch that came over the other night."

Damon rubbed his chin as if he were contemplating the idea, which, indeed, he was. He opened his mouth to speak, but a huge grin replaced his future words.

"Showtime," he said as he eyed Darnell and Turiq coming out of the house. He watched in anticipation as they made their way to the trunk of Darnell's whip. He continued to watch as his two hired goons crept up behind them and put pistols to the back of their heads. He became downright ecstatic when he saw Justin bring the butt of his gun down on the back of Darnell's neck, rendering him unconscious. Seeing how he was outmanned, Turiq quickly surrendered.

"Time for phase two," Damon said, taking out his cell phone. "Good work," he said when Justin answered. "Now, put your gun in his mouth, take a picture of that, and send it to me."

As soon as he received the photo, Damon forwarded the image to Sunny's cell phone with a message attached.

Meet me at Gordon Park in two hours, or this muthafucka is dead.

Chapter 31

The sound of silence was deafening as Sunny and the other three members of her crew sat in Jazmine's living room. Every few minutes, Sunny would check the time. It had been roughly an hour since she'd received the photo and text, and she had yet to utter a word to anyone. Sunny knew that she didn't have much time. She knew that she had to come up with a plan that would not only rescue her father but one that would also keep them both alive. Finally, after an hour of silence, she stood up and spoke.

"Jazmine, have you been able to get in touch with your father?"

Jazmine shook her head slowly. "Not yet. I've called him five times, and it's gone to voicemail every time."

Sunny cursed and headed to the kitchen. She quickly made herself a drink and took a large gulp. Although she was a proud person, Sunny knew that to save her father's life, she would need a little help. After looking at the address that she'd been given, she called Duck and Lard and informed them of the situation. At first, they were upset because she hadn't told them earlier, but that emotion would have to take a backseat to what was going on. By sheer dumb luck and coincidence, Duck was very familiar with the address Sunny was being called to. It was an abandoned building that sat on the corner of Eighty-Sixth and Wade Park. Long before hooking up with Darnell, he used to hustle out of it every night, so he knew the ins and outs of the place. Sunny, Duck, and Lard devised a plan that would even the odds. After that, she went back into the living room to gather her troops. Her face was hard and determined as she looked at them. She took turns glaring at each one of them, commanding their attention.

"All right, you all know the situation here, and you all know how dangerous this is, so I won't blame you if you wanted to stay out of this. But if you're gonna ride and be down with me, then fucking *be down with me.*"

"Sunny, I can't speak for these other two bitches, but you can always count on me," Jazmine stated.

"I'm a fucking soldier, boss lady. I'll be there 'til the casket drops," Butter proclaimed.

All eyes then turned to Dani.

"Well, Dani? You in or out?" Sunny asked.

Dani's mind flashed back to how Damon had been treating her over the last few weeks, so with a crooked grin, she slowly nodded her head.

"I'm in. Fuck Damon's bitch ass! It's time he gets what he deserves."

"Good. J, do you know where your father keeps his guns?"

"Hell yeah."

"Cool. Get a few of them. And hurry. We only have forty-five minutes left to get there and save my dad."

It took Jazmine less than a minute to come back with three handguns and an Uzi. As the four young ladies walked toward the door, Sunny took out her cell phone and quickly sent a critical text. The unique vibration sequence alerted the recipient that it was Sunny sending the text. The four young ladies then made their way to the garage.

"Let's put the guns in the trunk for now," Sunny ordered. "That way, if we get stopped, we don't have to worry about being caught dirty."

Sunny popped the lock on the trunk and opened it. Butter was about to toss her gun inside when Jazmine subtly grabbed her hand. When Butter looked at her, Jazmine slowly shook her head. As soon as Dani put the gun she was given in the trunk, Sunny blew off the back of her head. Blood and brain fragments coated the inside of the trunk. As Dani's body fell into it, a wide-eyed Butter looked from Sunny to Jazmine.

"Trifling-ass bitch," Jazmine spat.

"Okay, should I be worried?" a shocked and confused Butter asked.

"Not unless you're playing both sides of the fence too," Sunny said. "This scandalous bitch knew all along what was going on. Remember what she said back at the house? About how it was time that Damon got what he deserved? Well, how in the hell did she know that it was Damon who'd sent me that message? I never mentioned who texted me that message. The only way this slimy ho could have known was if she was in on it in the first place."

"Then you made the right call by killing that bitch. As a matter of fact," Butter said, before aiming her gun at Dani's corpse.

"Don't," Sunny said, stopping her. "Before the night is over, you may need those bullets. Let's roll."

With disgust, Sunny slammed the trunk shut. She had no way of knowing that Dani had planned to double-cross Damon and shoot him as soon as she got the chance. Now, she never would.

Slab and Paul stood behind the Glendale Building, sharing a blunt and sipping on cups of liquor. Neither of them was particularly thrilled with their assignments, but Slab seemed to be extra pissed.

"Man, this is some bullshit! How in the fuck is Damon gonna have us doing this sucka shit, while his uncle and Moon do the glamourous shit?" Slab asked.

"Man, look, I know how you feel, but look at it this way. We're making easy fucking money just for keeping our eyes open," Paul reasoned.

Slab's eyebrows shot up. "So, you content with just being a lookout boy now?" he asked his partner.

"Lookout boy? Man, what the fuck are you talking about?"

"Nigga, what the fuck you mean, what am I talking about?" Slab replied, answering Paul's question with one of his own. "We ain't nothing but well-paid lookout boys today. You cool with that shit?"

"Yo, man, I ain't saying all that, but shit, man, we're basically making bread without doing shit."

Slab smirked and shook his head as he snatched the blunt out of Paul's hand. "Nigga, yo' ass is blind as fuck." Slab took a quick hit from the blunt and a small sip from his cup before holding up his finger, indicating that he was about to try to make a point. "All right, what about this bullshit then? When Darnell had that meeting, where the fuck was we? Exactly," Slab yelled before Paul even had a chance to answer. "We were circling the hood, keeping an eye on the soldiers pitching on the block."

"So?"

"So? Nigga, is you high? Why the fuck should we have to do that shit when we've been down with Damon longer than Moon?"

"Slab, you need to calm the fuck down. Maybe Damon didn't trust Moon enough to keep an eye on things while he was busy. Did you ever think of it that way?"

"Hell nah, and you shouldn't either. I'm telling you, man, that nigga Moon is up to some bullshit. I don't trust that nigga."

"Man, why you got such a hard-on for . . . You know what? Never mind," Paul said, smiling.

"The fuck so funny?" Slab asked.

As soon as the question left his mouth, he wished like hell he could take it back. He'd opened the door to a running joke between the two of them, and Paul was about to walk right through it.

"I forgot. That nigga did put the paws on you back in the day," Paul reminded him. The smile he had a few seconds ago had been replaced by a chuckle.

"Man, fuck you," Slab spat. He'd never gotten over Moon's beat-down and got pissed whenever Paul teased him about it.

"Nigga, don't get mad at me because that nigga beat the brakes off yo' ass."

"Whatever, nigga. I just pray that nigga is ready when I decide to execute some payback on his ass."

"What? Man, you can't be serious. That shit was years ago."

"It don't matter. I owe that muthafucka, and I aim to collect. And the way Damon is shitting on us, I got a good mind to call Duck or Lard and tell them what the fuck he's doing."

"Dude, you need some fucking counseling. I'm going to take a piss."

Paul walked around the corner of the building, shaking his head. When he got around the corner, he smiled deviously. He had been waiting for a chance to get even with Slab ever since he walked in on him fucking the mother of his child. Even though he'd told Slab during a drunken rant that he didn't care if he fucked her or not, he did. Paul didn't understand that instead of pretending that he didn't care about her by looking hard in front Slab and his boys, he should have treated her like a queen instead of a pauper. To this day, Slab had no idea that Paul had witnessed them screwing, but his mouth had just given Paul the ammunition that he needed to get even. Paul took out his cell phone and pressed *stop* on the recording function. He'd recorded every word that Slab had said. When Damon heard the recording, all Paul had to do was sit back and wait for his revenge to be complete. Unfortunately, he would never get to expose his partner.

The two goons were so invested in their petty argument that they never noticed that a black SUV had pulled into a driveway across the street.

Lard grinned wickedly as he screwed the custom-made silencer onto the end of a high-powered rifle. After that, he aimed at Slab, who was leaned back against the wall rolling another blunt. Moving the rifle to the left, he let the crosshairs come to rest in the middle of Paul's forehead. The only decision to make was who to kill first. Lard rolled down the window and pointed the rifle out of it. His lips curled into a sick smile as he closed his right eye and peered through the scope with his left. Then, just as Slab was inhaling the blunt he had rolled up, Lard pulled the trigger. The bullet split the blunt in half just before entering Slab's mouth, exiting out the back of his skull and becoming embedded in the brick wall. Slab slowly slumped to the pavement. He never had a chance.

Meanwhile, Paul was just finishing up polluting the ground with his urine. He stuffed his dick back in his pants and made his way back around the building. He stepped around the corner of the building, and his jaw dropped. There was his long-time partner lying on the ground in a puddle of his blood. Paul quickly looked around and scanned the area. He was at a supreme disadvantage. Not only did he not know where the shot had come from, but he also had no idea who had fired it. But one thing was for sure. Paul had no intention of sticking around and being the second victim. He was just about to take off running when his right knee exploded in pain.

"Ah, shit," he screamed as he fell to the ground. Ignoring the pain as much as he could, Paul pulled himself up and began hopping on one leg. He knew that his chances of getting away were slim, but he also knew that his chances of surviving were zero if he stayed there. He had just reached for the vehicle's door when another bullet ripped through the back of his neck. And just like that, the Grim Reaper had claimed another victim. Lard then pulled out his cell phone and called Sunny.

"Yeah, that situation is taken care of. What do you want me to do now?"

"Nothing. Things just got a whole lot better for us," she said, just before hanging up.

Chapter 32

Damon, Moon, and Eric pulled into the parking lot in front of the building. Pulling up beside them in the white van were Justin and Kenne. Although the building was abandoned, Damon had scouted the place and found an unusual feature about it. It had an underground basement, and if everything went according to his plan, it would not only be the final resting place for Darnell but also for his daughter and anyone else who stood in the way of his ultimate goal of being Cleveland's next kingpin. To be on the safe side, Eric suggested that he and Moon, along with Justin and Kenne, do a perimeter sweep. Damon thought about it but decided that time was of the essence, so he concluded that it wasn't necessary. The three of them got out of the car and walked toward the van. When they got there, Justin had opened the back door and was pulling a still unconscious Darnell out of it. Damon looked at Turiq, who was tied up and gagged, then smirked.

"Sit tight, nigga," Damon laughed as he slammed the doors shut. "Follow me," he told the rest of them. With relative ease, Justin slung Darnell over his shoulder. Damon led them down a flight of stairs and into a large concrete room. The room was pretty much empty except for the four chairs sitting in the middle of it. In front of one of the chairs was a digital clock. But what caught everyone's attention were the four bricks of C-4 placed in the corners. Damon smiled evilly as the rest of them looked at each other in shock. All except Moon, that is. He was the only one that Damon had shared his plan with. For all the rest of them knew, they were going to get Darnell, his daughter, and her friends in the basement and shoot them, but now, it was evident that Damon had something more sinister in store.

"Put that bitch-ass nigga in the chair and tie his ass up," he told Justin. While Justin was following his orders, Damon's cell phone went off for what seemed like the hundredth time that day. He didn't even have to look at the screen to know who it was.

"Bitch, what the fuck do you want?"

"Nigga, you know what the fuck I want. I wanna know why you did that foul shit to me. You promised me half a stack if I fucked your uncle, and then you reneged on that shit."

"Bitch, be cool on that shit. I told you I got you, but you're gonna have to set that pussy out more than that if you think I'm gonna give your ass half a G. We'll talk about the shit later. I'm busy, so don't call me again today." Damon hung up and was about to speak until his phone buzzed again. He started not to answer it but changed his mind when he saw that it was Rita. As soon as he answered the phone, she started talking.

"Damon, we need to talk. I don't know what you did to Janine, but you need to make that shit right. Her ass is losing it."

"I just got off the phone with her. It was just a little misunderstanding, that's all. I had her do something for me, and she was under the impression that she only had to do it one time. For five hundred dollars, she's gonna have to perform that act a few more times."

"Half a stack? Shit, baby, you shoulda called me for that."

"Next time, maybe I will. But look, I have to go. Swing by my pad later, around nine."

"Okay, but wait. There's something else you should know about—"

Damon hung up before Rita finished her sentence. In his mind, getting Dani, Rita, and Janine to become his whores was good for his introduction into the pimp game. After hanging up, he turned off his phone.

"I'm gonna run outside and check on that other asshole. Kenne, wake this muthafucka up before I get back. Moon, come with me."

When they got to the top of the steps, Moon was instructed to wait there. He watched as Damon walked over to the van and opened the back doors. Damon appeared to yell at Turiq just seconds before drawing back and punching him in the face. He then slammed the door and walked back over to where Moon was standing.

"I've wanted to do that shit for a year now," he said, rubbing his knuckles. "Darnell's slut daughter and her friends should be here shortly. When they get here, bring them down in the basement. I'm gonna send Justin and Kenne up here to make sure those hoes ain't strapped when they come down. In a few short hours, this city is gonna belong to us. And just so you know, I want you to be my second in command. Slab and Paul won't like it. Neither will my uncle, but I don't give a fuck. *I'm* running this show," Damon said before trotting back down the steps and leaving Moon standing there, speechless.

When Sunny pulled into the parking lot of the building, her heart sank. She was hoping that they would be able to somehow surprise and ambush Damon and his crew, but the three large men with automatic weapons standing guard nixed that idea.

"Fuck," she screamed as she came to a stop.

"Get the fuck outta the car and keep ya' hands where I can see 'em," Justin screamed at them. He and Kenne both had their weapons pointed inside the vehicle, while Moon's pistol remained tucked inside his waistband. Sunny, Jazmine, and Butter got out of the car. Moon looked at them and frowned.

"Ain't it supposed to be four of y'all? Where's the other bitch at?" he asked.

"Probably looking at your baby pictures," Sunny said smartly.

"Oh, I see you one of them smart-mouthed bitches, huh?" Kenne said. He drew back his hand to slap Sunny, but Moon grabbed it.

"Man, this bitch needs to be put in her fucking place," he spat.

"I'll take care of her," Moon said. "As a matter of fact, take these other two hoes down in the basement while I have a little word with her," Moon said, cracking his knuckles.

Justin smiled as he and Kenne ushered Jazmine and Butter down the steps. Moon was trying his best not to look at Jazmine. Despite the situation, he still found her extremely attractive. When they were gone, he turned his attention back to Sunny.

"So, I guess that was your way of calling my mother a bitch, huh? Bring your smart-mouthed ass on!" he yelled. Thirty seconds later, Moon was walking behind Sunny, forcing her down the steps.

Kenne laughed out loud when he saw the bruise
on Sunny's cheek. It was apparent that Moon had
hit her. Sunny looked at her father and her friends,
who were all tied up and gagged. She sprinted toward her father and threw her arms around him.

"Daddy! Are you okay?"

"About as well as a dead man can be," Damon
cracked. Sunny whirled around and shot daggers
at him.

"Nigga, what the fuck do you want from us?"

"First of all, li'l bitch, I don't want shit from you,
'cause you ain't got shit to give. You see, that's the
fucking problem right there. I've been out here
on these streets busting my ass for this nigga, and
he wants to just give the entire kingdom to you?
Someone who don't know shit about the drug
game? Nah, that's some bullshit right there. Moon,
take the tape off that nigga's mouth. I wanna hear
what he has to say about that shit."

To keep anyone else from beating him to the
punch, Justin rushed over and ripped the tape
off Darnell's mouth. He loved inflicting pain on
another human being. With a knot on the back of
his head, Darnell glared at Damon.

"Nigga, you know you dead for this, right? The
other capos—"

"Fuck them lame-ass niggas. Once your ass is
in the ground, they won't have a choice but to
fall in line or join your ass in the afterlife. Moon,
tie that bitch up," he said, nodding toward Sunny.

"My father is gonna kill all of y'all for this betrayal," Jazmine told them. For the first time since they'd been captured, it occurred to Sunny that Turiq wasn't there.

"Is that right? Well, I don't know how the fuck he's gonna do that. Your punk-ass daddy is probably in hell sucking the devil's dick right about now," he said, making it seem like he'd killed Turiq.

Jazmine's heart caught in her throat. It hadn't occurred to her that her father could have been a casualty in Damon's hostile takeover. Tears flooded her eyes.

"Aaaah, ain't that a shame. Her daddy gone bye-bye," Justin said, snickering. Damon and his men all laughed out loud. He then made his way over to Darnell and leaned down to face him.

"Did you *really* think that you were just gonna hand an entire empire over to your daughter and ride off into the sunset, and I was gonna be okay with that? Are you fucking crazy?"

Damon then slapped Darnell in the mouth so hard that blood flew from it.

"It's time to end this shit," he said, taking out his cell phone. A sudden thought occurred to him as he was setting the timer for the C-4. "Hey, where the fuck is Dani?"

"How the fuck should we know? Ain't she *your* bitch?" Sunny said.

Damon smirked. The fact that Sunny knew about him and Dani told him that she was probably dead. Since it wasn't a great loss to him, Damon simply chose to shrug his shoulders and keep it moving.

"Whatever," he said, setting the timer. "Since I did make a lot of money with you, I'm gonna allow you to have twenty more minutes with your daughter before y'all go *boom*. Let's go, boys."

With that, Damon led his crew up the steps. He instructed Justin to put Turiq in the trunk of his car. After it was done, Damon reached into his pocket and took out cash to pay Justin and Kenne for their services and sent them on their way. Normally, he wouldn't want to be anywhere around a crime scene, but this one, he couldn't resist. He was going to watch Darnell go up in flames, and he was going to enjoy it.

He looked at his cell phone and saw that Darnell had only three minutes left to live. With a satisfactory smile, he pulled out a cigar and lit it. Then he pulled out two more and passed them to Eric and Moon. Five minutes earlier, he'd texted Slab and Paul and told them to come around the front so they could celebrate the takeover, but so far, they hadn't arrived. When there was only one minute remaining, they all jumped in the car and moved to a safer distance. They had just parked and got back out of the car when a loud boom echoed through the air. A fiery glow filled the sky. Damon smiled triumphantly. He only had one more piece of business to take care of, and then his takeover would be complete. He opened the doors to the van and had Eric pull Turiq out. After standing him up, Damon took the tape off his mouth.

"Man, what the fuck?" Turiq asked. "This shit wasn't part of the plan."

Damon shrugged. "Sometimes, you have to improvise, my nigga."

"Yeah, whatever. Is it done? Is that nigga *and* his daughter dead?"

"Dead as a fucking doorknob."

Turiq smiled and nodded his head. Moon and Eric looked at each other, confused. They had no idea what was going on. From the second Darnell approached Turiq with the idea of Sunny taking over his drug business, Turiq began plotting. Despite appearances, Turiq had always had designs on being the next king. If Darnell wanted to step down and ride off into the sunset, Turiq was fine with it. But there was no way that he was going to put in all that work for all those years and play second fiddle to the man just to have to do the same thing with his spoiled-ass daughter. And to top it off, he wanted his own daughter to be second to him. It turned his stomach to even think about it. So, during a routine money drop by Damon, Turiq sold him on the idea that if they got rid of Darnell, they could both run the city as equal partners. The one thing he hadn't counted on, though, was that a snake, by any other name, was still a snake.

"Good shit."

An awkward silence filled the air as Damon and Turiq stared at each other.

"Well? The fuck you waiting on? Untie me, nigga," Turiq said.

Damon just smiled. "Well, you see, there's a little problem with that."

"What? Nigga, what the fuck are you trying to pull?"

"Nothing. I just think it's time to renegotiate."

"Renegotiate? The fuck are you talking about? Nigga, if you don't fuckin' take this rope off of me, I'll——"

"What? Nigga, what the fuck you gon' do?"

Turiq glared at Damon.

"That's what the fuck I thought. Now, like I said, we need to change the terms of this little agreement. I think that I should be the——"

Turiq's loud laughter drowned out the remainder of Damon's sentence.

"You hear something funny, nigga?"

"Nah, I hear something hilarious, nigga. If you think I'm gonna let you pull some shit like this, you may as well shoot me now."

A sinister grin appeared on Damon's face as he slowly nodded his head. "So be it then, nigga."

Damon reached into his waistband and pulled out his gun. "And don't worry about ya' daughter. You'll see her soon enough."

"What? Muthafucka, you killed my daughter?"

Forgetting that he was tied up, Turiq tried to make a move toward Damon and fell flat on his face. Damon and Eric nearly split their sides laughing. Moon merely shook his head. He reached, grabbed Turiq by the back of his collar, and snatched him to his knees. Tears were streaming down his face. He'd made the cardinal sin of trusting a snake, and now it was going to cost him everything he held dear.

"Any last words, nigga?"

"Yeah, fuck you!"

"Nah, nigga, fuck *you*," Damon said, cocking the hammer on his pistol. A satisfied sneer creased his lips as he pointed his gun. Before he could pull the trigger, however, Moon intervened.

"Hold up, man. You need to let me handle this shit. If you were serious about the position you want me to play, you need to let me prove it by putting a couple of hot ones in this piece of shit."

Damon thought about it for a second. As bad as he wanted to blow Turiq's brains out, he told himself that Moon had a point.

"Okay, my nigga. I'm gonna let you push this nigga's shit back. Do ya' thug thizzle," Damon said, tucking his gun back into his waist.

Turiq closed his eyes as he felt the cold steel press against the back of his skull. A few seconds later, he felt a hot breath touch his ear.

"This ain't personal, dawg. It's just business," Moon said.

Turiq braced himself when he heard the hammer on Moon's gun cock. Three shots echoed through the air, and once again . . . The Reaper had come calling.

Chapter 33

Rita looked at her watch and saw that it was now almost 9:45. She was going to give Damon another fifteen minutes before she left. She didn't want to appear thirsty, so she made the decision not to call him. Of course, she would rather have her legs in the air with Damon pounding her sweet spot, but there was only so long she was going to sit there and wait. She'd spoken to Janine earlier and told her that she was coming by later, so not to leave the house. That way, she could wait on Damon without having to worry about Janine showing up. It wasn't that Rita didn't feel like shit for betraying her friend like she was doing. It's just that getting a piece of that good dick, combined with Damon telling her about the half a grand he was willing to give to Janine, had her feeling scandalous. Rita had no idea what Damon had asked Janine to do, and she didn't give a damn. In her mind, half a grand was a good chunk of change, and she might not come across this opportunity again. She was about to bite the bullet and call him anyway when her cell phone buzzed in her hand.

"Hello?"

"Girl, where the hell are you? I thought you said that you had something to talk to me about," Janine stated.

"Yeah, I do. I'm on my way now."

"Cool. Have you left the house yet?"

"Yeah."

"Cool. You know what, though? I really don't feel like sitting in this house. Meet me at the bar. I'll be waiting in the parking lot."

"Uh . . . okay. I'll see you there."

Rita sighed and started her car. As bad as she wanted to wait on Damon, she didn't want to run the risk of Janine finding out that she was sleeping with him. Ten minutes later, Rita was pulling into the bar's parking lot. She cut her engine, but before she could get out, Janine had got out of her vehicle and was making her way to the passenger's side. She was carrying a bottle of wine in one hand and a couple of glasses in the other. After Rita unlocked the door, Janine climbed into the seat.

"What's up, girl?"

"Uh . . . not much. Why the hell are we sitting in this car?"

"I just thought we could drink a few glasses before we go in and get broke. Plus, I need someone to vent to for a minute."

"What's wrong?"

"Girl, I think I'm gonna stop fucking with Damon."

"For real?" Rita asked. She was already making plans to slide into Janine's time slot.

"Yeah, girl. I'm just tired of that nigga fucking me over. He and that bitch Dani can have each other."

After handing a glass to Rita, Janine reached into her pocket and pulled out a corkscrew. She quickly opened the bottle and poured them both half a glass.

"Here's to friendship," Janine said, raising her glass for a toast. Rita instantly felt like shit. In a moment of extreme guilt, she wondered if she should tell Janine about her and Damon.

"To friendship," Rita said with a quivering voice. After tapping glasses, the two women lifted their glass and took a sip. For the next ten minutes, they shot the shit and downed half the bottle. Rita was just about to take another sip when Janine took it there.

"Rita, why were you sitting in front of Damon's house tonight?"

The question damn near caused Rita to spit out her wine. "Huh? What the hell are you talking about?"

"You know what the fuck I'm talking about."

"Janine, your ass is tripping. I wasn't over at Damon's house."

Janine's eyes narrowed into slits. She was crushed that her friend would play her like that.

Even though she and Damon were no longer a couple, the fact that they were at one time should have made him off-limits to Rita. Shaking her head, she reached underneath the passenger's seat and removed the device that she'd placed there when they were together earlier in the week. Janine was hoping that she was wrong. She was hoping that it was just a figment of her imagination. But the starry look in Rita's eyes whenever Damon was even mentioned told a different story. So instead of keeping tabs on Damon, she decided to keep tabs on Rita.

"What's this?" Rita asked when Janine placed the tracker in her hand.

"What the fuck do you think it is?"

Rita's stomach tightened up. When she first saw it in Janine's glove compartment, she assumed that Janine purchased it to keep tabs on Damon, but she was wrong—dead wrong. Janine looked past Rita and out of the driver's side window.

"I guess my former man is checking up on us, huh?"

When Rita turned and looked out of the window, all she saw were the other cars parked in the lot. Only then did she realize that she'd been duped. Before she could turn back around, Janine plunged the corkscrew she had used to open the wine bottle deep into Rita's neck. Blood spurted out of her neck and onto the seat. Rita gurgled and choked as she reached for her throat. It took less than fifteen seconds for her to bleed out and her head to fall forward onto the steering wheel. A single tear ran down Janine's cheek as she stared at Rita. Rita's lack of loyalty hurt her ten times more than Damon's did. Damon was a dog, so she pretty much expected him to behave like one. But Rita was her girl. In her mind, they were close enough to be sisters. In the end, however, she was the only one of them who thought that way.

Epilogue

It was barely seven o'clock in the morning when Moon walked down the stairs and headed for the kitchen. Without hesitation, he reached on top of the refrigerator for the bottle of Cîroc. After taking it down, Moon walked to the first unoccupied seat and plopped down in it. He unscrewed the cap and took a swig. The last twenty-four hours had been quite traumatic for him, so the eyes that were now staring upon him would just have to forgive him for partaking of the devil's juice so early in the morning. Moon had been hit with a barrage of questions, but all he wanted to do was rest, with the promise that he would reveal all the next morning. Now, the following day was here. It was time for him to spill the tea on what had really transpired. Moon went to take another swig, but someone snatched the bottle from his hand before he could complete the task.

"Enough stalling, young man. I think it's time that you told us what the fuck is going on," Darnell bellowed.

Moon looked around at the faces who would have been considered enemies just twenty-four short hours ago. Darnell was seated next to him. Although he was grateful that Moon had saved him, his daughter, and her friends' lives, he still wanted to know what the hell was going on. Sunny was seated next to her father, while Lard and Duck were sitting directly across from him. Jazmine had asked to be dropped off at home so she could wait for her father. Butter also had been dropped off at home.

Moon took a deep breath and began. He started from when Damon had first started talking about overthrowing Darnell and his regime. He quickly moved to the part where Damon had hired a couple of goons to help him with his plan. He told them about how he'd slipped a knife into Sunny's back pocket, which enabled her to cut the ropes and free everyone else. That part they already knew because Sunny had told them. However, Darnell was stunned when Moon revealed to him that Damon and Turiq had plotted to kill him and become equal partners. He and Turiq had been partners for years, and it hurt him deeply that his friend could betray him that way.

"Continue," he told Moon after the shock wore off.

"Well, after I put one in Damon's head, I shot the nigga that was with him. I think his name was Eric, and I think it was his uncle. After that, I had to take care of that snake-ass nigga Turiq."

"So, you killed my friend?"

"Friend? You call that nigga a friend?" Moon asked, his face twisted.

Darnell rubbed his chin. Taking a deep breath, he simply shook his head. Moon had a point. There was no way a friend would plot on him the way Turiq did.

"Daddy, does Jazmine have to know what kind of traitor her father was?" Sunny asked.

"No, she doesn't. She also doesn't have to know who killed him."

After a brief hesitation, Sunny brought up the thing that had been on everyone's mind for the last twelve hours.

"I still don't understand why you helped us," Sunny said.

"Yes, young man, the one thing that you haven't told me is why. Why in the hell would you help us? I have to assume that since you were one of Damon's top soldiers, he was paying you well. So, help me understand this shit. What's *your* angle?"

"I don't have an angle."

"Don't bullshit me. No one puts their life on the line for nothing. No one takes money out of their own pocket."

"True, but some things are more important than money."

"Oh yeah? Like what?"

Moon stared at Darnell for a few seconds before reaching into his back pocket and taking out an old, wrinkled photograph. After handing it to Darnell, Moon crossed his arms and waited for a reaction. Darnell's mouth dropped open as he slowly raised his head and stared at Moon.

"Where the hell did you get this picture?"

"My mother gave it to me."

"What's going on here, Dad?" Sunny asked.

"Be quiet, Sunny. Young man, I'm going to ask you one more time, and I want the fucking truth. Who gave you this picture?"

"Like I told you the first time, my mother gave it to me."

The two men glared at each other for what seemed like forever before Darnell broke the silence.

"What's your mother's name?"

"Debra."

Upon hearing his ex's name, Darnell fell back down in his seat. He looked at the picture again and then back up at Moon.

"Look, young man. You do realize that I'm *not* your father, right?"

"My mother told me that you never gave her a chance to tell you that you were going to be a father. Hell, she just now revealed to me that the man I grew up around wasn't my real father, so I guess both of us have been deceived."

"So, let me get this straight. I'm just supposed to take your word for this?"

"We can get a DNA test if you want to. But I saw the look in my mom's eyes when she told me, and there wasn't a hint of deceit in them. Look, I was just as shocked when I heard it as you are now, but it is what it is. And if the last twenty-four hours have shown me anything, it's that you can't trust anybody *except* family."

"What the hell is that supposed to mean?" Sunny asked.

Moon smiled as he looked at his sister. He felt bad for putting that bruise on her face, but he had to make it look like he was Damon's accomplice. "That means, sister, that if *our* father still wants to get out of the game, his business will be well in hand with his daughter *and* son running the show together. So, what do you say, Pop? How about it, sis? Let's do this shit."

Darnell slowly walked up to Moon and pulled him into a tight hug. After releasing him, Darnell looked directly into his eyes. "Look, this is a lot to process, and I hope this doesn't offend you, but I'm going to have to verify this information. If what you say turns out to be true, then I would be proud to include you in the family business, provided Sunny doesn't have a problem with it."

All eyes turned to Sunny. After thinking about it for a few seconds, she walked up to Moon and looked him in the eye.

"As long as you remember one thing . . . *I* run the show. Welcome to the family, bro," she said, wrapping one arm around Moon and the other around her father.

Coming Soon . . .

RICO 2: Sunny's Reign!